JEWELS

DEAL WITH THE DEVIL

SAVANNAH BLAIZE

www.savannahblaize.com

Cover Design by Jay Aheer

www.simplydefineart.com

I would like to thank the Melbourne Romance Writers Guild, my friends and family, who have been a constant support on my writing journey. Either with encouraging words, proof reading, technical assistance, and/or enduring faith in my ability to tell a story.

DEAL WITH THE DEVIL

PROLOGUE

YEAR 1990

My name is Harper Cole. I'm an adrenaline junky, I'm a bit of a loner and I'm a reformed gambler. Tonight, I am also a thief.

1
HARPER

I live my life on the razor's edge of danger. There is nothing like the thrill of dodging a bullet, jumping off a building or hurling through the ocean in a speedboat. But the buzz I wanted to experience tonight was of a different kind. I wanted to see how the other half lived. Being a body double and personal shopper for actress Mindy Michaels had its advantages. The gold embossed invitation I had "borrowed" to the private club, tucked securely in my black patent leather clutch purse was one of them. Not to mention the designer gown I had decided to test out before I gave Mindy my seal of approval. The fact that Mindy wasn't aware or missing either of these items, was a bonus. She had taken advantage of her co-stars' availability and had jetted off to Paris for the evening, leaving me in Monaco with time on my hands. Leaving me wondering what it would be like to be surrounded by the kind of wealth that actresses and highflyers are used to every day. Leaving me no choice but to risk my job and raid her newly delivered shopping packages for the thrill of pretending to be Mindy.

I paid the cab driver, passed a few others waiting in line and sashayed up to the man mountain bouncer at the door of the club. I was tall at five foot ten inches in my stocking feet, but he was so much taller, and built line a line-backer. No one would mess with him and get away with it. I flashed my . . . sorry, Mindy's . . . invitation, slid the fake fur wrap from my shoulder, hung it over my arm and looked him in the eye. With a sardonic twist of my lips, I dared him to deny me entry. I'd watched Mindy with the same expression on her face so often, that it came almost naturally. He pushed open the door and stood aside to allow me to pass. My intuition and tiny hairs standing up on the back of my neck told me he was checking out my ass. I glanced back and he quickly turned back to the line up outside the door. There was a cloakroom off to the left. I checked my wrap then kept walking down the passageway toward the sounds of the music. The small tables dotted around the dimly lit room were fully occupied, so I made my way to the bar at the far end of the room. The blue neon lighting behind the bar gave everyone's skin a strange hue and accentuated anything white. Teeth, dresses, bra straps, tiny thongs on unsuspecting women who chose to wear gold mesh dresses. Or maybe not so unsuspecting, given the way they were parading around the room.

The backless black sheath adorning my body, thanks again to Mindy's great fashion sense, clung in all the right places. I had pinned up my long blonde hair in a French roll to allow the dress to shine. The satin cowl neckline shimmered over my breasts and skimmed my hips before opening up on one side with a split from thigh to toe. Underwear was not an option. No one wants a VPL in a designer gown. I carefully hitched up the skirt a little and slid my bottom onto a bar stool. I was aware that I was showing a lot more skin than I had originally intended. I crossed my legs to hold the skirt in place. I signalled to the bartender.

"Dirty Martini, si vous plait."

"Coming right up." said the bartender. He prepared the cocktail, placed the glass in front of me, speared an olive with a cocktail stick and dropped it into my drink.

I held out some bills. He took the cash, winked and moved off to serve someone else. He was very handsome. If he'd made an exceptional martini, I would leave him a tip.

I swirled the olive around the glass, popped it into my mouth, and disposed of the cocktail stick in the ashtray. I took a sip of my drink then closed my eyes to better enjoy the taste.

"Is it dirty enough for you?" Warm, minty breath imbued my olfactory senses and caressed my cheek and ear.

"I've had dirtier." I opened my eyes and turned to the man on my right, who had moved onto the adjacent stool and had the audacity to invade my personal space. If I said he was gorgeous, I would be grossly understating how handsome this man was. I had to remember to keep my mouth closed and not gape at him, although I had the impression he was used to being admired. He had black wavy hair, fashionably cut, high cheekbones, and his dark eyes of indescribable color assessed me beneath perfectly arched thick black eyebrows. His full generous lips were smiling, showing off his whiter than white perfect teeth in this eerie light. He had a perfectly sculpted five o'clock shadow on his tanned chiseled jaw, and last but not least, I could detect a little cleft in his chin. Kirk Douglas eat your heart out.

"You were saying?"

"It's . . . really good." I felt lost for words. Tongue-tied. Very unlike me. My lips seemed incapable of forming a sentence. Who was this Adonis?

"Luc."

"Sorry, look at what?"

"You were wondering about my name. It's Luc Nightingale. And yours?"

"Harper." *Damn. I should have said Mindy.*

"Unusual. I like it."

"My mother loved To Kill A Mockingbird, by Harper Lee. She named me after her." *What am I doing? Too much information!*

"Can I buy you another Dirty Martini, Harper?"

"Yes." I made the mistake of turning back toward Luc. His eyes bored into mine, and I couldn't think straight now, let alone speak. Time stood still. The room around me lost importance as I stared into those fathomless depths. I opened my mouth, but nothing came out. I turned away from his penetrating gaze so that I could focus. "Sorry, you seem to have a bad effect on me. I'm not usually lost for words."

"It happens a lot around me. Don't worry." Luc signaled to the Bartender.

The Bartender placed another drink in front of me.

"Aren't you going to have one?" I stirred my drink with the olive and took a sip. Then another to quench my thirst. I wondered if they had raised the temperature of the room.

"Not at the moment. Would you like to dance?"

"Dance?"

"Yes. You know. Move on the floor, my arms around you, to the music. The band's over there. They're rather good."

I turned to look where he was pointing. I hadn't noticed a small four-piece band had started paying in the corner. The saxophone hit some high notes and I shivered. The thought of being so close to Luc, thigh to thigh, bodies touching had lots of appeal. I finished my drink.

"Sure. Oh, my purse." I slid off the seat with as much decorum and I could muster.

Luc signaled to the bartender and he took my purse and placed it under the bar.

"Shall we?" He held out his right hand for me and gestured with his left toward the few couples already swaying gently on the small dance floor circled by tables. I took a good look at his expensive suit, his crisp white shirt, his expertly placed bow tie. He was well over six feet of perfection.

I don't know what I'd expected, but as we moved on the dance-floor, I was extremely aware of his body. Luc's hand on my bare lower back burned into my flesh, warming me through to my bones. Sparks were going off in erogenous zones, I had long forgotten about. Separation from my husband had come at a price, and my libido had taken a hit. Sex had been off the table for me for a long time. We had been arguing so much, due in part to the time I spent working on location far away from home, and his insistence on starting a family. Which if I was completely honest, I had no intention of having. We had both decided that we needed a few weeks break from seeing each other and being in each other's company. That was why this overseas stint with Mindy to Europe had its appeal. Up to this point I hadn't missed him. What did that tell me?

"You move rather well, have you taken dance lessons?" Luc asked.

"My drama teacher insisted I learn the popular dances from the forties, fifties and sixties. I must admit it has come in handy."

"Dancing is a great way to get to know someone. It reveals more about a person that has good rhythm." Luc leaned in and inhaled my perfume, also borrowed from Mindy's extensive supply. He brushed his lips over my earlobe. "It's fascinating."

"How so?" A delicious tingle ran down my spine.

"For or a start. You like to be in control. You're trying to lead, instead of allowing me to do so. There is a lack of trust showing right there. You're gripping my hand quite tightly, which indicates you're nervous. Your body temperature has risen quite considerably since we started to dance and I have to wonder if it is because our bodies are so close, or because you're afraid of being exposed."

"I don't know what you mean."

"Oh I think you do. But if you want to play coy, I'll indulge you."

The band stopped playing. Luc did not let me go. I had no problem with staying exactly where I was within his arms. A trickle of sweat worked its way down from beneath my breast and over my stomach. He was right, I was getting hotter by the minute. A female singer in a shimmering red sequined dress, moved to the microphone. Luc lowered his hand and slid his arm around my waist pulling me up against him and the band began a slow sexy number. Flush against Luc meant I could feel every muscle in his chest, his hard stomach, his thigh and other parts of his anatomy that had decided to step up and join in the conversation. Yes, this part of his anatomy was talking a language I could understand, and my body had already begun to react. My nipples rubbed against his chest, and tightened, painfully. I had already imagined his lips on mine, and now I was imagining his mouth on my breast, nuzzling, sucking, . . .

"Do you want to play roulette?" Luc whispered in my ear.

His question drew me right out of my fantasy.

"What? Roulette? Here?"

"Yes, upstairs. A private game."

My heartbeat had quickened at hearing the word. I loved roulette. A game of chance, a throw of the dice, lady luck. My Achilles heel. I took a step back and searched Luc's face. He was smiling down at me as if he had guessed all my secrets. This is the part where my common sense and months of training with Gamblers Anonymous should come into play. I should say no and return to the bar.

"Yes. I would like to play roulette." *Well that didn't go as planned.*

Luc took my elbow and steered me toward the bar to collect my purse. He guided me through a door set into the paneling that I hadn't noticed before. A staircase led to another door with a spy hole. He knocked and the spyhole opened up. He held up a card. The door slid open and we were led inside a private gambling club. My heart raced, and my throat became dry. I ached to sit at the tables, to place a bet, to hear the croupier call the shots.

"Roulette? Over here." Luc led the way to a table and pulled out a seat for me. I opened my purse to find some cash.

"My treat." Luc pushed some chips into my hand.

I didn't even glance at the chips, and placed them all on Red. It won. I placed another bet. It won. And another. It won. I pushed the pile of chips I had collected onto black number three and held my breath. The ball took forever to fall into the slot. Number three. Red. I won again.

I gathered up my growing stacks of chips with shaking hands. We had to go. All of the work I had gone through to fight my addiction was going down the toilet in one night. I wanted to gamble, I longed to gamble so badly that I was desperate enough to risk it all. This was bad, so very bad.

I tried to stand, but Luc bent down to whisper in my ear.

"I know you want to, so do it. Go on. Put it all on number six. Your fingers are itching to do it, your heart is beating so fast every time you win, the thrill this is giving you is better than sex. I know it, and you know it. Number six."

I turned my head, took his face in my hands and kissed him. Time stood still. I was sucked into a heatwave unlike anything else I had ever experienced. Flashes of crimson and orange and gold exploded behind my closed eyelids. Pleasure radiated from his lips, suffused my senses and rippled along my skin. Tingling from head to toe, I held on tight. The smell of his cologne and his warm male skin intensified, the sounds in the room became fainter, every nerve ending suddenly sensitive even to the air around me. He pulled away from my grasp and I immediately felt the loss. I drew in a huge shuddering breath. What the hell was that? I had never experienced a kiss that intense in my life, and I had kissed some pretty swoon worthy actors over the years. I pressed the back of my hand to my throbbing lips, aware they were swollen.

With trembling hands, I pushed the chips onto number six, and nodded at the croupier. Luc took my hand, and I squeezed his tight. Number six won. I stared at the piles of chips being pushed in front of me by the croupier. I was sure there was more money on this table that I had ever won before. Maybe several thousands.

"We have to go. I'm afraid I might lose this if I stay. This money can make a big difference in my life. We have to go." I begged him to get me out of there. "Please Luc. Save me from myself."

Luc motioned to the pit boss standing near the wall. The croupier removed the chips. The pit boss had a whispered conversation with Luc and came back with a banker's cheque., which he handed to Luc. I had a few minutes to collect my thoughts, and I wanted to clear the air.

"I am sorry. I had no business kissing you. I'm married, and I shouldn't have done that. I don't want to give you the wrong idea."

"Don't be sorry. I rather enjoyed it. I believe you did too."

"Nothing else is going to happen. I just want to make sure you know that. You are a very handsome man and I'm sure you can have any woman you want. But I'm married, and I'm saying no."

"Duly noted. But I didn't ask you Harper. And if you're happily married why did you feel the need to kiss me?"

"Actually, I'm not so happy, but I'm trying to work it out." I stood, suddenly desperate to get away before I placed another bet. I retrieved my purse from the table. "I really have to go. Thanks for a lovely evening."

"You're forgetting something."

Luc handed me the cheque. I glanced at it, then did a double take. There were lots and lots of zeros on that cheque. "There has to be a mistake. This is huge. Millions? This can't be right."

"Yes, it's correct. You were playing at a high rollers table."

❧

When I came to, I was laying on a red velvet couch in a small office, and Luc was holding a damp white linen napkin to my brow. I tried to get up.

"Woah. Don't sit up too quickly. You passed out."

"Low blood sugar, I think. I haven't eaten all day. And shock probably had something to do with it."

"Take it easy. I've called my driver; I'll take you home."

"I'll call a cab."

"I don't think that's a good idea. I'll make sure you get home in one piece."

"I'm staying at the Hyatt. Thank you."

"My pleasure. I'm really good with damsels in distress. That's a nice hotel."

"My boss is paying for it. She has the penthouse I have a tiny broom closet room."

"Your boss?"

"I work for Mindy Michaels, the actress. I used her invitation to get into the club."

"I see. The resemblance is striking, now you mention it."

"I'm her body double in her last three movies. I'm a stunt artist. I take all the falls.

"Let's make sure there are no more falls tonight."

Luc picked me up as if I weighed nothing at all. Pressed against his chest, cradled in his arms, inhaling his woody cologne and listening to the steady beat of his heart, I was aware of just how much I wanted to be held and cared for by a strong man. Dean had been distant for about a year now, and I wasn't sure if we were ever going to get back what we once had. His constant reminders about having kids soon was getting on my nerves. I had always tried to be upfront with him, but I knew I was putting it off. Having kids was a bad option with the kind of work I did. Although I loved the adrenalin rush, I knew I couldn't work as a stunt double for long. The body could only take so much. But maybe this money could make a difference, and I could do something else. Not that the idea of having kids had anything to do with that decision.

Luc walked through the rear staff entrance of the club and placed me on the back seat of the waiting limousine. He slid in beside me. Someone handed him my wrap, they had retrieved from the cloakroom. I was acutely aware of the magnetic pull of his long, toned body. I folded my hands in my lap, tried to slow my racing pulse, and turned my head to the window. The driver eased into the traffic and I watched the neon street signs flash by in silence until we covered the short distance to my hotel. The driver got out and opened the door on my side of the car. I leant over and kissed Luc's cheek. My lips tingled again with the brief contact.

"Don't get out. I'm fine, really, I am. The doorman is right there. I can't thank you enough for tonight. You have no idea how this money will change my life." I clutched the purse and the wrap to my chest and took the hand of the driver as I climbed out of the car. He closed the door, and the window slid down soundlessly.

"Take care Harper Cole. I'm sure we'll meet again soon." The window slid up and the car pulled away into the traffic. I turned to walk inside, the doorman welcomed me . . . and I stopped in my tracks.

"Hang on. I don't remember telling you my last name!" I yelled at the limousine. But he was too far away to hear me.

2

HARPER

Mindy had returned to the hotel in a foul mood. I had managed to stay out of her way, but had been summoned to her room, and stepped into the same elevator as her room-service breakfast delivery. Her bodyguard was a good friend of mine and had spilled the beans earlier over coffee and an almond croissant in the coffee shop. It seemed her co-star had drunk to excess, had side-stepped her advances, and had groped another woman in a Parisian Club, who ironically had also been the owner's girlfriend. They had been unceremoniously thrown out.

Mindy opened the door of her suite, dressed in a belted white hotel robe. She motioned me to come inside and dismissed the waiter. I wheeled the trolley over to the table by the window. She returned to her bedroom but left the door ajar. From what I could hear, she was on the phone to her lawyer, discussing the incident and stating her intention to sue the establishment if mere mention of their ejection appeared in any of the trash magazines. I don't know if she was more upset that her co-star groped someone else or that he seemed disinterested in what she had to offer. Mindy was beautiful, and quite a talented actress, but she was a royal bitch with a capital B. She knew how to twist men around her little finger, but she had little regard for their feelings once they were infatuated with her, and she was tired of them. She kicked them to the curb quicker than you could say "self-centered". Not many of them complained, as I was usually sent on a mission to buy a watch from Cartier or a bauble from Tiffany as a gesture, accompanied by an autographed card which simply said, "I will treasure our time together. No hard feelings." I had the embossed cards always at the ready. Mario on the other hand, was not getting that kind of parting gift.

"I'll make sure that man never works again on any of my pictures. It's just as well we're nearly finished filming. Thank God I don't have any more love scenes with that excuse for a man." She slammed down the hotel phone receiver and returned to the sitting room.

"There's something I need to discuss with you." I wanted to hand in my resignation pronto, while she was concentrating on being a bitch to someone else.

'What's on the agenda for today?" Mindy ignored me, sat down by the table and helped herself to breakfast from the covered dishes in front of her. She selected eggs and bacon and mushrooms and began to eat.

"I'm going back home to the States. I've booked a flight later today. My contract is up now that all my scenes have been shot for the movie. The risky stunts and constant travel have been taking their toll on my body lately. I've decided to look for something I can do near home for now. I'll get back into movies later"

"What?" Mindy put down her fork, laden with eggs and mushrooms, and sat back in her chair. "You *have* to be kidding me. You're going to quit now? Today? You love this life. You love the adrenaline rush."

"You said it yourself the filming is nearly over. I have no more action scenes to film. All those are in the can already. There's just the wrap up."

"This is typical. I've given you a great start in your career, and now you want to leave me. Just when things were going so well. Just when I've trained you, I've taught you everything you need to know to be my double. . . "

"Hang on! Let me stop you there. You haven't trained me. I had a stunt career before you left a fledgling singing career and broke into acting and I became your body double. The resemblance to you was a lucky break, for you and for me. But I can do other films. They don't all have to be Mindy Michaels "International Spy" movies."

"No one will hire you when I'm finished." Mindy's mouth settled in a thin mean line.

"I had a feeling you would say that. Lucky for me I don't have to rely on your recommendation." Anger rose in me, twisting and turning in my stomach. The rush of adrenalin I normally experienced when I was performing a stunt flooded my body, and I threw caution to the wind. "Oh, and for what it is worth. Mario is gay, and he only agreed to go with you to Paris as his beard. He would never have given you what you wanted. What he does with you on film is called "acting". I would wager he deliberately caused the problem at the nightclub to get away from your grabby little hands. He'll be thanking his lucky stars he doesn't have to work with you again."

"Get out! *Get out!*" Mindy picked up her plate and threw it in my direction. I ducked. Food splattered over the tiled floor, and the plate smashed against the wall. I left the room as she let out a string of expletives that would have made a sailor proud.

I didn't take long to pack my bags, and after a clear run on the freeway I was sitting in the airport bar sipping champagne and thinking about the look on Mindy's face when I told her Mario was gay, and that he was using her to keep his sexuality a secret. I had no idea where that bitchiness came from, it was as if a little devil had taken over, hell bent on doing the most damage to our working relationship. I watched the people move about in the lounge around me and thought about their story. Some were happy, their eyes bright with the excitement of travel. Some were sad and I wondered what had happened to bring them to the airport today. Everyone has a story to tell. Mine was complicated. I was thirty, I had a husband of five years I had grown apart from, and a job I had now left behind for an unknown future. How I had arrived at this point in my life? I had hoped that I could have left Mindy's employ without drama, but I should have guessed she wouldn't have been happy to see me go. I had lots of secrets I could leak to the media. Although I had signed a confidentiality clause, and it wasn't in my nature to do so. I nibbled on some nuts and ordered another glass of bubbles. It was going to be a long flight home to the States, but I was hoping I could sleep through it if I drank enough alcohol.

The airline had mistaken me and upgraded me to business class, helped along by my resemblance to Mindy Michaels. Maybe they thought she was flying incognito under an alias. I wasn't going to complain. At least I could stretch out and enjoy the trip this one last time.

I opened my front door and placed my suitcases on the cream tiled floor of the entrance hall. *Home at last!* It didn't have the same ring to it that it once had. I wasn't sure what I was going to say to my husband about quitting my job, and how I was going to explain the money I had won. I had promised I was through with gambling, and I had gone against that promise. Maybe he would forgive me when he realized how much we could do with the money. I slipped off my shoes enjoying the cool tiles beneath my bare feet, and that was when I noticed scattered clothing on the floor in the living room through the archway. I heard the faint sound of a woman's laughter and glanced up the staircase to see a red lace bra hanging on the bannister. Taking each step very slowly and making sure to avoid any contact with the walls I crept to the top and inched my way around the corner. The master bedroom door was wide open. The mirror on the wall opposite the bed allowed me to get a good look at the woman my husband was groping while she straddled his hips. Angela Bennett, the woman I had introduced him to only one year ago at my Pilates class appeared to be enjoying everything my husband had to offer, judging by the squeals and moans of pleasure assaulting my ears. As she bounced up and down on top of his erection, she cupped her large silicone filled breasts, tweaking the nipples between her fingers, while Dean thrust up into her from below. She watched herself in the mirror opposite the foot of bed. Neither of them could have stopped if a plane had appeared crashing through the ceiling, they were so intent on the final few seconds of release.

I backed away quietly, their loud moans following me down the stairs. My stomach was in knots. I returned to the entrance hall, slipped on my shoes and picked up my suitcase. No one heard me leave or heard my heart breaking. No one heard my silent wish that they would both die a horrible death when that imaginary plane did indeed crash through the ceiling, consuming them in a ball of fire. Lucky for me the taxi was sitting at the end of the street while the driver had a cigarette break. If he was surprised by a weeping woman banging on the window demanding to return to the airport, he did not show it.

❧

I had always wanted to go to Hawai'i. I hadn't expected to be going there depressed and alone, but it was the first flight leaving the airport, and I needed to be far, far away as quickly as possible. I did not miss the irony that I had been in a hurry to get home yesterday, and in a hurry to leave home today.

The pink and purple sunset did little to lift my mood as I made my way past the pool to the bar of the five-star hotel. Dressed in a dark blue halter-neck cocktail dress which sat just above my knees, silver heels and purse, and made up to the best of my ability, I walked with a confidence I did not have. I tried to hide the swollen puffy eyes and red nose with bangs. I was already tipsy and intent on getting very drunk. I was even considering picking up a stranger to fuck as my way of revenge. Hell, make that two strangers. I was pretty limber. I could manage two.

I slid onto a barstool, waved at the bartender, ordered a Mai Tai, and told him to keep them coming. He placed a bowl of nuts and pretzels in front of me. I waved them away. I had almost finished the third drink when a large male hand descended on mine and removed the glass.

"Hey. Give that back."

"I think you've had enough."

"Nope I've only just begun. I am going to get drunk enough to pick someone up. . . hey. . . I know you. . . Luc, what are you doing here?" He had his arm around my waist and was sliding me off the barstool.

"Come on. Let's get you out of here."

"Ah, yes, let's go back to your room. Mine is far, far away from the bar."

"Let's take a walk by the pool. Sober you up."

"I don't wanna get sober. I wanna get laid. Or as they say in Hawaii "Get Lei'd. Did you see what I did there?"

"The fresh air will do you good."

"You're ignoring my good jokes. You're no fun."

Luc supported me as we walked around the pool, and I tried not to topple out of my high heels. I gave up and slipped them off before I twisted an ankle. I pushed him away and flopped down on a sun lounge by the water's edge. My purse slipped off my shoulder onto the sun lounge. My head was spinning. I should have eaten those pretzels.

"Did I tell you my husband is having an affair. With my Pilates instructor?"

"No you didn't."

"He's a bastard. He should pay for this. I'm going to make him pay."

"I'm sure you will."

"What are you doing here anyway? Are you following me or something? Did Mindy send you? Are you a private detective? Oh . . . that's funny . . . a private dick. And I wanted to jump into bed with a stranger. What luck I have my own private dick to jump into bed with. You see what I did there? I'm on fire tonight. You're not laughing. Why're you not laughing? Let's go to your room and I can show you some of my moves. I have moves you know. I'm very bendy."

Luc compressed his lips together and shook his head. "We're not going to my room, we're going to your room, and you aren't going to show me any moves. You're going to sleep it off." He picked up my shoes, looped my purse over my shoulder, pulled me to my feet, threw me over his shoulder and headed to the hotel.

"Hey put me down. Everyone can see my underwear."

"Yes they can. And very nice underwear it is. Now stop wriggling." Luc slapped me on the bottom. His large warm hand stung my flesh. But it also had the effect of sending a bolt of lust to my core. I wiggled some more. *Do it again. Oh please, do it again.*

Luckily the elevator was empty. My embarrassment level was rising, and cheeks at both ends of my body were red. When we reached my room, he found my key in my purse and unceremoniously dumped me on the bed. He selected a large bottle of water from the mini fridge, unscrewed the top, sat on the edge of the bed, and held it out to me. "Drink. Please."

I drank some of the water to keep him happy and put the bottle on the bedside table. I grabbed Luc's arm and pulled him down on top of me. His eyes bore into mine; his beautiful mouth was inches from my lips and then I was kissing him . . . without holding anything back this time. Once again, I was swept into a tornado of emotions and sensations as heat coursed through my body shooting bolts of intense pleasure to all of my female anatomy. Oh my god the man was only kissing me. . . or rather I was kissing him. . . and I was nearing coming on the spot. What would it be like to actually fuck him? I wriggled my body closer in an attempt to find out. But Luc was having none of it. He sat up pulling me with him and sharply broke the kiss. He appeared to be perfectly composed, his crisp white open neck shirt uncrushed under his back jacket and tucked neatly into black slacks. Not a hair out of place, not a bead of sweat. On the other hand, I was a heaving mess of swollen lips, sweat soaked hair, heavy breathing and rabid hormones.

He grabbed the bottle again. "Drink it all. I'll get you another." He rose from the bed, slipped off his jacket and I got another good look at his firm butt cheeks. They were clenched. I knew it. He was holding himself in check. He didn't want to show me he was affected by that kiss, but how could he feel nothing when it rocked my world. I pulled my dress up over my head, reached around and unclipped my bra and slipped off my underwear. When he turned around, I was perched on the side of the bed naked and willing.

"Put your clothes back on. We are not doing this."

"I can tell you want me, and I want you so what's stopping us?" I cupped my breasts in my hands, offering them to him. "Come on Luc."

"I am not going to be your revenge fuck."

"But why. It would be mind-blowing. I know it."

Luc picked up his jacket from the chair and draped it around my shoulders, covering up my naked breasts. He sat down beside me, put his arm around my shoulders and kissed my forehead. "I am certain that sex with you would be sensational, but I am not going to be part of the sex orgy you are cooking up in your brain to get back at your husband."

"I want him to suffer. I wish I could go back a year. I wouldn't introduce him to Angela. Actually, I wish I could go back a year and end it before the affair even began. We haven't been good for a while now. I would divorce him before I won the money. If I divorce him now, he'll get half and he doesn't deserve it."

"I can help you with that."

"How?"

"It's simple. I'm the Devil, so I can help you go back a year so you can divorce him."

"Yeah, sure you are."

Luc smiled, looking self-assured and calm. I swiveled out of his reach to face him.

"Oh my god, you're serious. You think you *are* the Devil."

"I *am* the Devil, and I *can* help you, but I want something from you. I want your firstborn son. I want to teach him my devilish ways. I'm not getting any younger and I need to pass on some of my knowledge. I'd like to see what it's like to have a child to follow in my footsteps."

I had finally admitted to myself that I had no intention of ever having children. That was one of the biggest bones of contention between Dean and me. So, I had no problem in giving in to Luc's demand. That, and of course Luc believed he had powers, and perhaps if I told him what he wanted to hear we could get back to kissing and actually end up in bed together. I could hear that magnificent orgasm calling my name. Hell, the way he kissed I was hoping he would be up for an all-nighter.

"Okay. You can have my firstborn son. But don't hold your breath. It isn't going to happen."

"Just to be clear, Harper, you have just made a deal with the Devil. There is no turning back once you shake my hand and repeat the words, "it's a deal."

I held out my hand, and Luc took it firmly in his. What did I have to lose? This guy was clearly delusional.

"It's a deal." I said. There was a flash of light. Then complete darkness.

3
HARPER

ONE YEAR EARLIER - 1989

I opened my eyes, lay still and tried to process what had happened. I was laying on my side, naked between white cotton sheets and facing the window of my bedroom in California. I recognized my earrings on the bedside table, my shoes on the floor by the chair, the blinds pulled down to block out the early morning sun. It was indeed my home. How did I get here? Did I have a stroke, a bad dream? Did I imagine the whole scene with Luc? I lifted my head and glanced at the bedside digital clock, with the time and the date. It was a year earlier. He did it. I don't know how he did it, but I had gone back twelve months exactly. The bed moved and Dean mumbled good morning, rolled his naked body in behind mine and cupped my breast. This morning routine was as familiar to me as breathing. His morning erection prodded me in the back, and he nuzzled my neck and rubbed my erect nipple between thumb and forefinger with what he considered to be foreplay. His fingers worked their way inside my clamped thighs and found what he was looking for as he eased himself inside me from behind. I knew his morning glory was something he was very proud of. My body responded as it had many times before and I rocked back on him and enjoyed the sensation of fullness, the building pleasure, the race to orgasm before Dean finished, slapped me on the butt cheek, kissed my shoulder and slid out of bed to shower for the day ahead.

Our sex life had become a habit, a ritual, there was nothing new or exciting about our coupling after four years of married life together. I knew the routine when I was at home and not on location. When he would be in the mood, when he would demand rough mattress pounding sex after a bad day at work, or when he would be gentle and coaxing after I had been punched and pounded all day for a movie scene. Or when he would be passionate and loving and desperate to make love to me when I had returned from weeks on location. Those were the times I enjoyed best. And of course, he couldn't waste his God given morning erection. I imagined he took care of that very well by himself when I was on location.

My heart continued to race, even after the orgasm faded because I had come to realize, I was getting my wish. My deal with the Devil was already in play. It didn't surprise me that Dean hadn't tried to kiss me or turn me over to look at me. I had become like the expensive coffee machine he used in the kitchen, or the massage shower head he had installed in the bathroom. I had become functional, a pleasant start to his day, something to put him in a good mood for the onslaught at work.

Dean charged out of the bathroom, dripping wet and with a towel draped over his hips. He came to stand at the bottom of the bed, waving a packet of contraceptives at me.

"Why do you still have these? I thought we discussed this, and you were going off the pill?"

"No, you told me you wanted me to get off the pill. I told you that I wasn't going to do that. No one will hire a pregnant stunt girl."

"If I get this promotion, I'll get a raise. I'm making good money. When you get pregnant you can quit your job. Do something else later when the kids get older. Maybe when all the kids go to school. My mother stayed home when we were kids. Dad took care of the family. As it should be."

"Your folks immigrated to America from a small town in Italy where women traditionally stayed at home to bring up a family. Life is different in America. Women want to work now. They contribute and make decisions about the life they lead."

"I want to have kids and enjoy them when I'm young enough to play with them. Shoot some hoops and go skating and play baseball with them."

The arguments had returned back to this old chestnut again, and suddenly it became clear to me that this was my "get out of jail free" card. I took a deep breath before the nerves got the better of me.

"I don't *want* kids now Dean! I never really wanted kids if I am to be honest about it. I had hoped that would change, but it hasn't. So. If you want kids, then you had better go and find a wife who does. Someone who is happy to be at home and play the happy, dutiful, docile little housewife."

"What are you saying?"

"I want a divorce!"

"Just like that? No discussion?"

"You've been laying down the law to me long enough, and I've been fighting to keep a piece of myself intact. I've given in on so many things. Your fascination with electronic gizmos, your obsession with sports, your wardrobe of designer clothes, and this expensive house we live in to keep up appearances with your work colleagues. Although I love the house too. But I will not give up my job . . . or my body. . . to service your need for offspring. This has to end. For your sake and for mine."

"I don't believe this. It's typical of you. If you can't get your own way, it's all or nothing."

"Maybe you should go and find a nice compliant woman who will allow you to make all her decisions for her, and who will fill your house with children. That's not me."

"No, you were always all about yourself. I should never have married you. My mother was right about you. She told me you didn't have child-bearing hips. Too skinny she said. She'll never have children she said."

"You can call her and tell her she was right after all. Then you can both be happy."

Dean looked at me with disgust, threw the birth control pills on the bed and marched back into the bathroom. I pulled the covers up over my head and stayed then until I heard him leave the room. He didn't waste time in the kitchen. I heard the faint buzz from the electronic garage door as it rolled up. I jumped up and peeped out the corner of the window to make sure he left. He backed the car out of the garage into the street, and with the tires squealing, took off faster than he should have. I pitied anyone who got in his way today.

❧

Sourcing a lawyer wasn't easy considering I wanted someone with a good track record for getting the job done quickly. Johnathon Spencer, of Spencer and Son, was recommended and although his exorbitant fee meant I'd probably be eating packet mac and cheese for the next few months, so be it. I made a list of all the things I was ready to give up, for a quickie divorce. Basically, Dean could have the expensive luxury car the check for my last movie had paid for, and all the electronic gizmos he loved to play with, and half the money in our joint account if he signed on the dotted line. I wanted the house. I had loved it on sight, and we had moved in only a few months before. He fought me of course, on principle, but he eventually relented when I agreed to give him three quarters of the money in the bank. I think he knew it was pointless to argue, and our marriage wasn't one to fight for.

Dean hardly came home. When he did, he was either sullen and ignored me or angry. I wasn't sure which I preferred. I suspected he wasn't staying with his parents, but I didn't ask him. I stayed well away from Pilates class, knowing that I did not want to bring Angela Bennett into my life, or specifically Dean's. I ran around the park, drank less and monitored my intake of carbs to keep fit. My body began to react to the new regime, and my muscles thanked me by becoming more toned.

When I got the contract for Mindy Michael's new movie being filmed on the other side of the country, I think he was relieved he did not have to see me for a couple of months. It was strange knowing that I had already lived this part of my life, already done the stunts, already thrown myself off buildings and out of cars. I had to be extra careful not to jump ahead in the movie script, which was very familiar to me, and keep my own council when the rushed job resulted in one of the actors almost being injured before the last scenes were filmed. The director was very happy with me when I suggested a work around, which was only possible because it had occurred the previous year with great results.

I thought about Luc all the time. I searched for him on set, expecting him to pop up and reassure me I wasn't going mad, and this was not some weird déjà vu. I sensed his presence around me especially if the stunts were especially dangerous. I could smell the strong sandalwood cologne with his own masculine twist.

The day the papers came through to confirm my Divorce was one I shall never forget. I had returned home to pack for Europe when the courier arrived with an official looking envelope. I closed the front door and read the contents. We had both agreed to waive the Decree Nisi, so this was the final paperwork. I closed my eyes and let the tears fall. Although I knew it was the best solution, divorce is never easy. The aroma of sandalwood and vanilla, of exotic spices, filled the air. I did not need to open my eyes to know Luc stood beside me. The soft pad of his thumb stroked a tear from my cheek, and he tipped up my chin. I opened my eyes to look into his and all I saw was kindness and caring and a touch of knowing, as if he could also feel my loss. Although I had been determined in my action to rid myself of the man I knew did not really love me, the fact that I was not enough for Dean, could never be enough, that he would easily find someone to replace me and have an affair, did hurt. It seemed that everyone I had ever cared about, did not love me enough to stay. My parents both died when I was young, my aunt and uncle who took care of me had moved to Australia as soon as I got married. And now Dean. I had no one I could call my own.

Luc leant forward and placed his lips on mine. My eyes fluttered closed again. His kiss was gentle, lips on lips, not a deep passionate kiss. No intense heat this time. My body stilled. I could hear my heartbeat echoing through my head. *Thud. Thud. Thud.* Warmth rose from my diaphragm, rushed up my neck and flushed my cheeks. I felt the tug of my heart, and in my mind's eye, I saw the gloom of sadness transferring from me to Luc. He absorbed it all and replaced the grey clouds with a kaleidoscope of colors and happiness unlike anything I had ever experienced. Peace washed over me. I opened my eyes and Luc was gone.

However, everything had changed. I was standing in the same spot, wearing the same clothes as when I had returned from giving Mindy my resignation, and a suitcase with international baggage tags sat at my feet. I walked round the house to check. All of the expensive kitchen gadgets, state of the art stereo sound system, TV's and electronic gizmos were gone. I opened the door to check in the garage. My Jeep was the only occupant of the space. Dean's expensive toy was gone. I opened my purse and the banker's check was safely tucked inside.

Luc had done it. He had brought me back to ground zero. Now all I had to decide was how I could change my future with this windfall.

4

HARPER

AUGUST 1990

The phone call summoning me to headquarters meant only one thing. Mindy had been on the warpath and had called my boss, Nancy Davis. In response, I took the time and dressed to impress. I walked into The Stunt Agency building with my head held high and a spring in my step. The heads turning as I passed by confirmed the effort I had taken and helped to bolster my confidence. If I was going to get "the talk", I was going to be prepared and ready for combat.

Nancy was in the open office space talking to her secretary but paused when I approached. "Would you look who's back early."

"I need to talk to you. In private please." Nancy's right eyebrow arched up, but she didn't argue.

Nancy beckoned me into her office and returned to her chair behind the desk. I closed the door behind me. Not that it mattered, as the glass wall provided very little soundproofing and meant everyone in the open office had a bird's eye view. I settled my long body into the low-to-the-floor "inquisition" chair. Nancy's chair was positioned much higher to give her the advantage.

"Oh, don't worry. I know about your stupid decision to leave the shoot. Mindy called me before you had even left the hotel. She's determined to make your life miserable. What the Hell did you do to tick her off so badly?

"I told her the truth. She didn't want to hear it."

"She wants me to find another stunt double for her next movie. Newsflash! She also wants me to drop you from the agency."

"Doesn't surprise me. I think she's going to cause trouble for Mario."

"Why? Did you and Mario get up to no good?"

"No, Mario is gay. Totally in the closet, but definitely gay."

"No way. Testosterone oozes from the man. Mario is dating a model and has a huge female fan club. He's featured in every woman's magazine with models and actresses draped all over him." Nancy sat back in her chair and folded her arms over her chest. She obviously didn't believe me.

I sat forward to make my point. "He's as gay as they come. Testosterone counts for nothing. He still prefers guys. I inadvertently caught him with someone. You don't have to be effeminate to be gay. But he's worried it will hurt his career if he comes out."

"True. He won't get as many of the leading roles." Nancy unfolded her arms, pulled a cigarette out of a case and held it between her fingers.

"I thought you'd given up smoking?"

"I have. But I still like to hold one. Old habits die hard." Nancy sniffed the tobacco, replaced the cigarette in the case and pushed it away. "Mindy said you were rude and insulting to her."

"I told her that Mario wouldn't want what she had to offer. That he probably set up the scene to get thrown out of the club. Did she tell you Mario had groped the owner's girlfriend? Now she's probably demanding that the producers and directors blackball him in future projects. I guess telling her the truth is insulting, cos everyone tiptoes around her in case they get in her bad books. She is a real

Diva on set, with a celebrity rider as long as your arm, and a nasty, mean streak."

"So, if Mario wants to keep his sexuality a secret why did you tell Mindy? She'll blab it to anyone who will listen."

"I saw red. I suppose I had a bit of the Devil in me that day. I wanted to see that smug look wiped off her face."

"Right then, down to business. There are a couple of assignments I think you might be interested in, but they're not for a few weeks. I'd rather let it appear that I am bowing to Mindy's wishes. She'll soon have someone else to boss around and forget about you. There will be some long-term travel involved, but that's never bothered you before. I'll print off the details."

"Actually, that's what I wanted to talk to you about. I'm thinking of stepping away from the stunts for the moment. I'm seriously looking at getting into something closer to home, and not as hard on my body. I'm thinking of buying a business."

"Wow, I thought the divorce had cleaned you out. Did a relative die and leave you money?"

"Yes. Exactly. That was why I came home early."

"Lucky you." Nancy looked impressed. "Maybe you'd like to buy the Agency. I hear the owners are looking to offload it."

"I didn't know that. I'll have my financial advisor look into that for me." I didn't have a financial advisor, but I had better get one. Pronto.

"You *are* serious?" Nancy's wide-eyed expression made me smile.

"I sure am. At least it's a business I know. Apart from the day to day running, and the office stuff."

"A good office manager can take care of all that for you." Nancy sat up straighter and put on her best fake reassuring smile.

"I'll take it all under consideration. I'd better go. I have an appointment with the lawyer for my uncle's estate." Wow. Lying was becoming easier.

I left the building and headed to the bank with a plan forming in my brain. I stepped off the sidewalk and a cab came screeching to a halt, horn blaring. I jumped in fright, and my right hand flew to my throat.

"You're going to get yourself killed if you don't look both ways before stepping into traffic." Luc had appeared by my side between me and the taxi, with his hand on the hood of the cab. The taxi driver yelled out of the open window.

"Oh my god. That was close." Luc took my elbow and we both took a step back onto the sidewalk. The sizzle of contact worked its way up and around my arm like a snake, until he let me go.

"My point exactly. Focus Harper. What were you thinking stepping off the sidewalk into the traffic? Didn't anyone teach you about looking left then right, then left again?" Luc had on his usual dark suit, but today he looked a bit ruffled. Not as perfectly put together as usual.

"You look like you dressed in a hurry" I took a step closer and turned down the collar of his jacket and straightened his lapels. I reached up to touch his check. His skin was very warm, but he did not look flushed in the face. The warmth spread through me, sending flutters of pleasure to my core. I gasped and removed my hand.

"I did dress in a hurry, due to the fact that you were about to be splattered over the hood of that cab. Where were you going in such a hurry?" Luc tilted his head to the side and narrowed his eyes. "Ah yes. The bank. I'll join you."

"You can do that? Read my mind?"

"Yes."

"How? Why?"

"Being the Devil has lots of advantages. Because you interest me. Because we have a deal."

"Surely the deal is not to follow me around. Or is it? Are you going to be my shadow until I give you what you want?"

"Precisely." Luc's smug expression made me smile.

"You might be waiting forever."

"Forever is overrated. Mark my words."

I fell into step as Luc took command of the sidewalk and everyone more or less moved aside to let him pass. He flowed through the pedestrians like a salmon swimming upstream, hardy causing a ripple in their stride but leaving his mark on everyone he passed. Some women wore an appreciative smile as they openly checked him out, but they ignored me. Some men looked guilty when they glanced at me and then withered under Luc's stare. It clearly wasn't often they saw someone in broad daylight, whom they perhaps thought was Mindy Michaels, walking down the street with such an imposing man.

"After you." Luc held open the door to the Bank and I walked ahead. We took our seats outside the manager's office.

"Do you really have to be here?"

"Of course, I do. I want to make sure you get the best advice."

"What are you going to do? Torture the poor man if he doesn't help me?"

"I don't know what books you've been reading but I don't torture people on earth. Correction, not often anyway. I wait until I can take them home."

"And then you torture them? When they're in Hell?"

"Precisely."

"Is that something you enjoy?"

"Let's get something clear. Most people who end up in Hell are not nice people Harper. They've caused a lot of damage to their fellow men. . . and women. My job is to make them see the error of their ways."

"Not that it matters because they can't change things."

"Ah that's where you're wrong. You're not the only one who's gone back to change the past. But some people don't want to pay my price."

"I still don't know why you want my yet-to-be-born son. What are you going to do with him when you go back to Hell?"

"I want to teach him my devilish ways. Pass on all the knowledge I've gained over the centuries. Teach him the tricks of the Hellish Trade. That sort of thing. I thought I might leave him with you, when I go back to Hell, so you can teach him about all the human stuff. I'll just pop in and out of his life, like a joint custody sort of arrangement."

"So, you get to be the "good" parent, show him an exciting life, and

I get all the mundane things and I get to be the "bad" parent with all the rules. It doesn't seem fair."

"I think it will work out perfectly. Now all you have to do is fulfill your part of the deal. You owe me one son. Good looking of course, he will have your looks, smart of course, he will have your street savvy... tall and perfectly proportioned... let me think . . . we will just have to find you someone tall, over six feet with good genes. Maybe Nordic, yes strong and good looking."

"Anything else on the list of traits you require?"

"I'll let you know." Luc was looking pleased with himself. Which was a dangerous sign.

The secretary called my name and invited me to follow her to see one of the Financial Advisors. Luc stood. It was obvious I wasn't going to be allowed to do this by myself, so I may as well embrace it. The Financial Advisor was a woman, a very attractive blonde who appeared to be in her mid-thirties, by the name of Pamela Hampton. She stood behind her desk and motioned for us to take a seat. Luc did most of the talking and Pamela only had eyes for him. Within a few minutes she had walked around from behind the desk and sat perched on the edge near to Luc's chair. She played with her hair, leant forward to listen to his pitch, licked her lips. I tried very hard to hide my amusement at this obvious flirting. It wouldn't have mattered what I said, she would have granted me any wish to see him smile. She took my cheque to deposit in the bank. I left with the assurance that I could go ahead and buy the Agency, and the bank's secretary would take care of all the initial paperwork and call me when it was ready. Perhaps it had been a good idea for Luc to tag along. I hated paperwork.

5

HARPER

SEPTEMBER 1990

Bumper to bumper traffic was never a good thing, but today my stress level had hit an all-time high in peak hour. I thankfully slid my car into the allocated space in the underground parking lot, purchased a coffee to-go from the café on the ground floor and headed to the elevator. I had thirty minutes before the last candidate for the operations manager's position was due to arrive for an interview.

"Come on, come on!" I jabbed at the button, while trying to balance the coffee cup and my briefcase, and files. The cup wobbled precariously. A hand shot out and grabbed the cup before it toppled over.

"You look like you could use some help." A very tall attractive man in a well-cut grey business suit, who appeared to be in his mid-forties, held my coffee cup. His blond hair shot with silver was styled a little longer than was fashionable, and strands curled around his ears, but it suited him. His build and broad shoulders suggested strength and he had a quiet confidence about him. The pale blue tie he wore was the same color as his eyes, and little laugh lines fanned out around them onto tanned cheeks. I surmised he was a fan of the outdoors. He watched me giving him the once over and smiled at me. I smiled back. My heart did a little tango. He reminded me of a handsome Viking. The doors slid open and we stepped inside the empty elevator.

"Thanks. My white shirt is grateful. Would you press the button for number thirteen, please?"

"Unlucky for some."

"But not for me." We moved to the back to let others enter. The elevator filled up.

"Do you work at the Agency?" he asked, in a lowered voice.

"You could say that." I whispered back.

"Is it a good place to work?"

"I think so, but I'm biased." The doors slid open on the thirteen floor "Thanks for your help. I'll take that now." I juggled my packages, stuck out my foot as much as my navy pencil skirt would allow me to stretch, to stop the elevator closing and I held out my hand.

Mr tall, blond and helpful handed over the cup. I headed for my office and didn't look back. As I passed the front desk, Audrey handed me some envelopes and messages.

Ruby, my secretary, glanced up as I approached her desk. "Can you take care of these? I have an interview this morning. I handed over the messages.

"Sure. I've cleared your calendar till lunch. Do you want to grab a bite downstairs?" Ruby took the envelopes.

"It will be a short break, but sure."

Although Ruby was now my secretary, she had worked in the agency office and we had been good friends before I took over the business. I was grateful for her help setting up my office, and her invaluable intel about the staff loyalty. She took on the role of my gatekeeper and jumped up to guard the door when someone had an issue and demanded to see the manager. The funny thing about that was she was five foot two inches tall, and petite with fiery red curls, and didn't look at all threatening. I relied on her, and we worked well together. I knew she didn't begrudge my new status as her boss. I didn't have many close girlfriends, but I counted her as one.

I had always been a bit of a loner and preferred my own company. It was one way to protect myself. It was apparent women felt threatened by me, and I couldn't quite work out why. Perhaps because having no parents had taught me to keep my own council and take care of my own problems. I wasn't into socializing or sharing details about your private life with women who would talk behind your back at the drop of a hat. Or perhaps it was because many of their husbands had attempted to make a pass over the years. That gets tiring pretty quickly.

❧

I logged on to my computer to check my workload, and prepared some questions in readiness for the interview. This candidate had already gone through interviews with the recruitment agency and been selected as the front runner, but I wanted to get a feel for the man myself.

Ruby buzzed the intercom on my desk. "Mr Erickson is here to see you." She sounded pleased. He must be good looking. I opened my door and was surprised to see the man from the elevator.

"Mr Ericson?" I held out my hand. He shook it firmly. "Harper Cole. Come in and take a seat Mr Ericson."

"Thank you. When you said you were biased, I can see why." He waited until I sat behind my desk, to sit down. "A lovely view and a corner office."

"Yes, the view is a bonus. Let's get down to business, shall we. I've read your résumé. Quite impressive. I need someone who knows the stunt business and someone who also knows how to run a busy office going through transition. I see you worked in movies in Europe."

"Yes, when I was a lot younger. And fitter. In my late twenties and thirties. I already had my business degree and decided I might be better suited on the other side of the camera, directing the stunt action, mending my broken bones and letting the younger guys take all the falls. I really prefer the organized side of things, the nuts and bolts of running a business, and sourcing the talent for the new action movies being made."

"I also see you are not an American citizen. I detect an accent."

"I've been traveling to and from the states for many years and living here about twenty years. I'm Norwegian. I was married to an American citizen, so I can work legitimately."

"Was married?"

"Divorced. Five years now."

"Kids?"

"No."

"Why did you leave your last job?" Mr Ericson

"Please feel free to call me Richard. I thought I would try my luck at working for myself. But the money wasn't coming in as fast as I would like. So, when I saw the advertisement for an Operations Manager, in a business I am very familiar with, it seemed like the right thing to do. To at least apply."

"The business is going through changes, least of all the name change to Devil Dares Stunt Agency. You would be responsible for keeping the business running smoothly, and making sure that filming was on track, and the contracts were being fulfilled. If you were to be successful, that is."

"I understand. I have worked through changes in the past. And I have been trained in resolution and conflict management. In business marketing and change management."

"As I said, it's quite impressive." I tapped the résumé with my pen and tucked it into the file containing all of the information on the candidates who had applied. "Are there any questions you would like to ask me?"

"I am presuming this is not a nine to five position. Will there be flexibility in hours. I like to keep up with my fitness training in the morning. I want to be able perform the stunts, so I know what's required of my team. The expectations run high with this new technology and I don't want to lag behind. I am happy to work later evenings to make up the time."

"There would be an expectation to work longer hours, especially in the beginning. I'm sure your training could be slotted in."

"Where would I be based? Is there a vehicle with the job? I don't currently own one. Who would I be reporting to?"

"You would be based here, at HQ. Your office would be next to mine. Yes, a vehicle is provided. You would be reporting to me. Do you have a problem reporting to a woman Richard?"

"No. I have no problem reporting to a woman."

"Excellent. I have no problem bossing a man around. So, we have a win/win solution here, don't we?"

He sat perfectly relaxed, legs together, hands resting on his thighs. His body language gave no indication that he had any problem with a woman being in charge. Good.

After a few more questions, and some details about salary and benefits, and healthcare, I walked Richard out to reception and shook his hand. I noticed those laugh lines deepened around his eyes when he smiled at me. *He's honest and kind.* I don't know why I knew this, but I did. Though we had only met a short time ago, I felt comfortable and comforted in his presence. Protected almost. I watched him walk down the corridor to the elevator, and nod to Ruby and then Audrey the receptionist. He stood aside to let others enter the elevator, moved to the back and turned around. Our eyes met again over the heads of the other occupants, and my heart beat a little faster. As the doors closed, he held the connection, and I had an image of him in command on the bow of a Viking ship, bare chested, with longer straggly hair flowing back from his bearded face as he braved the fierce weather at sea, wielding an axe with a long shaft. I blinked, the doors closed, and the image disappeared. What the heck was that?

I returned to my office and poured a glass of water. What just happened? Was that my imagination working overtime, or am I tired, or is the problem my low blood sugar? There were no other applicants to see, so I pulled out his résumé and sat back in my chair to read it through once more. By the time I had read the last page, I was convinced he was the right man for the job. I mulled it over through the morning and discussed all the pros and cons with Ruby at lunch.

At the end of the day, after considering all the applicants, and what they had to offer, I buzzed through to Ruby and asked her to type up a contract for Richard Ericson. I could tell she was smiling when she hung up the phone.

The alarm sounded minutes before dawn peeped over the horizon. The day I had declared I wanted a divorce I'd moved my things to the bedroom at the back of the house. I had decided I liked this bedroom better. I had a view over the tops of the houses around me, it was nearly as big, and the bathroom was right next door. I had planned to change the drapes, paint the walls, and burn the bed in the master suite. But common sense prevailed. I gave the bed frame away to charity, sent the mattress to the dump, left the room empty and remained in the room without the bad memories.

I had a shower, wrapped the soft fluffy pink bath sheet around me and secured it under my arm while I brushed my teeth. I looked up into the mirror and swore loudly, spraying toothpaste over the shiny surface. Luc was leaning against the door frame, casually elegant in a crisp white shirt with the top button undone, deep red velvet smoking jacket, and black trousers. He held a cup of steaming coffee in his hand. There is something about the smell of coffee first thing in the morning that makes your mouth water. Or was it Luc, who also smelled delicious.

"You really should knock or give me some warning when you do that."

"I like to surprise you. I like to think it puts a little pep in your step."

"No, it puts a few more grey hairs on my head."

"What did you think of Richard?"

"Richard who?"

"Your new Operations Manager. Richard Ericson"

'I haven't given him the job yet. Or at least he hasn't accepted."

"Oh, he will. And you're welcome."

"I'm welcome? Did *you* have some hand in this? Why?"

"I knew you needed someone who could guide you and not have any problem working for a woman. A much *younger* woman. I made sure he saw your advertisement. Also, he is very good at what he does. He's also a dare devil like you."

"Am I going to have any input into this agency, or are you going to make all my decisions for me, and I won't know it until later?"

"I have every faith in how you will run the agency. Oh . . and I do like the name change. . .But . . ."

"There's always a but, isn't there."

"If you need some help you know who to call."

"A bit like batman?"

"Exactly. There's no light you need to shine up into the heavens for me to see. You just have to think of me, and I'll be here."

"Well . . . that isn't exactly true is it. Because here you are. . .and I wasn't thinking of you."

"Really? Are you sure?"

I bent down to rinse my mouth, and to cover the fact that my cheeks had gone red. A short while ago when I awoke with my hand between my thighs, I was thinking of Luc. I was thinking of his soft lips pressed against mine, I was thinking of his broad shoulders and strong chest. And I was thinking of how I would like to peel off that elegant exterior to seduce the Devil beneath.

I looked up and he was gone. I thought I heard a faint chuckle in the distance. He'd left me the cup of coffee on the vanity counter, and it was still steaming hot. The steam had misted the mirror above it. The words "Kissed by the Devil. You're welcome." were written in the mist. I blew cold air on the coffee and sipped from the cup and tasted Luc's lips. And I wanted more. Much more.

6
HARPER

24th DECEMBER 1990

There was no denying Richard has been a godsend. Or in my case a devil-send. In the three months since he started working at Devil Dares Stunt Agency, he has known exactly what to do, exactly who to talk to in the film industry to get more work for the agency, charmed and wormed his way into everyone's good books, and has people walking away from meetings with a smile on their faces. We had been working long hours in the office to accomplish the change-over in management, and now I vowed I would take full advantage of the chance to relax. Christmas was not a favorite holiday for me, since both my parents died in a car accident when I was twelve, and my Aunt and Uncle brought me up. They tried hard to give me a good life, but they were used to living without children, and I caused them a lot of grief during my rebellious teenage years. Which is probably why I accepted as many jobs on location that I could, moved to the other side of the country and finally married at twenty-five, to get away from them and find a place I could call my own. Dean had tried to involve me with his family to make Thanksgiving and Christmas special over the years, but I couldn't get into the spirit, and I preferred to work through the holiday if I could. This year it would be even more lonely by myself.

The late afternoon staff meeting had gone on longer than I'd intended, but I'd wanted everyone to know how much I appreciated their hard work and commitment. I also wanted to give everyone a personal Christmas card with their bonus check As staff left the agency on Christmas Eve for the start of their holiday break, there was a lot of good cheer and hugs and yells of "Merry Christmas" on the way to the elevator. Ruby had left earlier for a family holiday interstate. Richard and I were the only ones left on the thirteenth floor. He passed by my door and I motioned for him to come in.

"Good work today. Everyone was happy with your speech and the bonus check." I rolled my chair back from the desk.

"They've gone above and beyond in the last couple of months."

"Agreed." I pushed my fists into my lower back and rotated my shoulders. My neck muscles tightened.

"How about a drink in the bar downstairs? I could really use one, and I can tell by the look on your face that you could use one too."

"Actually, that sounds like a great idea. I didn't drive to work today, so it's a perfect end to a very busy week. My neck is really killing me, and a couple of shots of alcohol would probably help." I rubbed my neck muscles.

Richard walked toward me and rubbed his hands together. He held them up, palms facing me.

"May I?" He asked.

I nodded, a little unsure if this was appropriate office behavior. He stood behind me, placed his large warm hands on my neck and shoulders, the pad of his thumbs against the base of my skull, working in small circular motions against the knotted muscles. It was soothing and painful at the same time, and I gave in to the pleasure and pain combination, enjoying the skin on skin contact, which I had been missing for a long time. Regardless of the fact this was a therapeutic massage, the pure bliss of tense muscles relaxing had a strange effect on me. My nipples tingled, tightened and protruded like two small bullets, pushing out the flimsy lace bra and the silk shirt I was wearing. From his vantage point, there would have been no doubt of my aroused state. My nipples had declared, without my consent I may add, that they were ready for action. His hands worked down the column of my spine and more heat, more arousal overcame my body. My breathing changed and my head slumped forward. I heard a soft moan and realized it came from me. I stood up quickly and his hands fell away.

"That was . . . wonderful thank you. I'm good now." I rubbed my tingling, warm neck, walked around the desk to collect my belongings from the chair in the corner, and tried to return to some semblance of the boss lady I was supposed to be. Yes, damn it, I wanted to sit back down and enjoy his hands some more. I had to get out of this office and his close proximity before desire overcame discretion. The man worked for me. I wasn't going to go there.

"After you." He held open the door.

I chanced a glance up at him as I passed by. He was smiling. He had been fully aware of what he was doing, damn him. We walked side by side to the elevator. Even in my highest heels, he was so much taller than me. I had always been attracted to tall men, they made me feel feminine. The rough and tumble nature of my job, the muscles I had toned and the fact that I had martial arts training, made me less appealing to most men who wanted a princess for a girlfriend. I was no one's fragile princess. I was a warrior.

The bar on the ground floor was jumping with Christmas Eve revelers. The bar staff wore Santa hats and red vests. We found a table in the corner, and I ordered the first round of drinks from a passing waitress. Two glasses of scotch and soda were placed in front of us with a complimentary dish of pretzels. They went down very quickly. Richard ordered two more. We both clinked glasses and wished each other well for the holiday season. We really should've eaten the pretzels. After a lot more business talk and another round of scotch I got up to go to the restroom, found myself a little unsteady, bumping into Richard's chair.

"Are you alright? Perhaps I should walk there with you?"

Richard gathered up our belongings, took my elbow and steered me through the crowd. He waited patiently outside in the hallway, and we made it back to our table to find it was already occupied.

"That might be my cue to head home. I think I've had enough alcohol. I need something in my stomach."

"Let's go. I'll hail you a cab." He helped me with my coat and fastened his. He wound a red cashmere scarf around his neck. He noticed I did not have a scarf, took his off and wound it around my neck. "You can give it back to me after the holidays." As he secured it, his hands brushed my jaw. I saw a look in his eyes that I recognized.

We walked to the sidewalk but there were no cabs in sight, other than occupied ones. "It's a busy time of the year. We might have better luck if we walk to the hotel down the block. There are usually cabs out front."

"Good idea. Let's go." I pulled my coat tighter around me.

"Take my arm. I don't want to risk you falling down in those heels." Richard pulled me in close. "I love seeing all the lights in the store windows at Christmas."

I was totally aware of his warm body cocooned inside his long wool coat, snug up against mine, his long legs slowing their stride in time with mine. We could hear carols on someone's radio. A doorman helped a man carry Christmas gifts from his taxi.

"There's something about Christmas that brings out the best in a lot of people. There is a feeling of happiness and goodwill that doesn't appear at any other time of the year." He said.

"And the kids are being good in case Santa Claus finds out, and they don't get any gifts. What are you doing for Christmas this year? Are you going back home to visit family in Norway?"

"No. I'll be staying in town and having Christmas on my own again. I quite like it here during the holidays when everyone leaves. It is quiet and I can run around the streets or through the park early in the morning and you feel as if you are the only one on earth."

"Oh yes I forgot you live in town"

"Yes over there. That building with the Italian café on the ground floor. They make a great pizza. What do you say we grab a bite to eat?"

"I'd like that." I turned, stood on something on the sidewalk, and my foot went from under me. I was swept up in Richards arms before I could react. He held me as if I weighed nothing at all. I put my arms around his neck. His face was very close to mine. I watched his lips.

"You're safer up here I think."

"Yes I think I am." My heart skipped several beats. We crossed the road. Then I kissed him. Because he had saved me from falling. Because he had saved me from going insane in the last three months running a business that I had no real idea how to run. Because he was kind, and thoughtful and my heart was beating faster and I wanted to taste a man's lips, feel a man's hands on me, experience the joy in another man's embrace. And hallelujah, this man could kiss.

He didn't break the kiss, he walked past the restaurant, into the building and up to the waiting elevator. He broke away for seconds to punch in the floor, then returned to my lips. As soon as the elevator doors slid open, he strode down the hall to his apartment and stood me on my feet while he searched for his key. He closed the door but didn't turn on the lights, took my hand and led me into his apartment to where the floor to ceiling window showcased the twinkling lights of the city around us.

"Oh, she is so beautiful at night." I placed the palm of my hand against the unadorned glass, admiring the city.

"Yes, she is. Beautiful day and night." Richard wasn't looking out the window. He was looking down at me. "Tell me. Do you believe in love at first sight? Because I do. I have loved you from the moment I saw you struggling with the papers and the briefcase and the coffee. I have wanted to kiss you, to taste your lips, to feel your breath mix with mine, to hear your soft moan in my ear since that moment."

"This is crazy. You don't know me. How can you be in love with me? You've never shown even the slightest interest . . . "

"Haven't I? How many times did you have a fresh croissant on your desk in the morning when you had arrived early without breakfast? How many times did you miss ordering lunch, and by chance I had an extra sandwich in my order? How many cabs have I shared with my thigh pressed up against yours? How many meetings have I taken over for you or late nights I've worked when I didn't need to, very aware you and I were the only ones in the building?

"And I never…"

"Noticed? Yes. I figured as much."

"I thought Ruby had left me the croissants. I often pick her up a coffee on the way in the morning. I presumed you didn't have enough room in the cab, you're a big guy. Yes, I knew you worked late, but I thought you had work to catch up on . . . like me." The reality of the situation was only just beginning to sink in. My heart rate picked up. Happiness sizzled a little inside me. "I'm sorry Richard. I've been totally unaware of how you felt." I raised my hand and cupped his cheek. He turned his head and kissed my palm. Butterflies skittered through my stomach. "I feel a little foolish." I lowered my eyes.

"Are you unhappy knowing how I feel about you?"

"No not at all. I'm surprised. Flattered even."

"Do you find me attractive?"

"Yes, you are a very attractive man."

Richard's large capable hands were resting on my shoulders. He untied the scarf from around my neck and used it to pull me toward him. His lips were soft, teasing, and coaxing on mine. His tongue swept over the seam of my lips, tentatively, requesting entry. He pulled back to look at me, and smile. I gave him permission with a small nod of my head. His hands swept up the sides of my neck into my hair, one hand cupped the back of my head while the other gently supported the base of my skull. His deep, commanding kiss came out of left field, swept me up into a tornado of liquid heat and fire and passion. This was no amateur kiss. This was an expert in his craft. His tongue danced over mine, then delved deeper, pulling me further into him. I saw red and orange and flashes of bright blue behind my eyelids. Every cautionary thought I'd had, disappeared as soon as his tongue entered my mouth. I wanted him, and I wanted him now. On the floor, on the couch, or on the kitchen table. A bed was not required.

Coats were discarded, clothing hastily peeled away. I rushed the job, intently aware that I wanted to disappear inside his kiss once more. In the few seconds that we were separated, Richard had returned with a condom. He peeled open the packet with his teeth and sheathed himself. It was then I took a good look at what I had signed up for and began to have second thoughts. Sensing I was anxious, Richard placed his hands under my arms and picked me up. I wrapped my legs around his waist enjoying the warmth of his chest and the security of his large powerful frame and buried my head into his neck. His arms enclosed me. He kissed my shoulder, then my neck, and my ear and coaxed me back to his waiting lips. As soon as I tasted his desire, I knew I would be able to take whatever he wanted to give me. We did not make it to the couch or the kitchen table. Richard took me standing exactly where we were, with a backdrop of the twinkling lights of the city.

In the stillness of the early hours I awoke and became aware of the covers pulled down to my waist and Richard's presence beside me. His breath on my shoulder, his hand moving gently down the slope of my breast and skimming the areola around my nipple. Tiny electric particles sparkled along my skin, and arousal brought my nipple to life. Watching the slow deliberate descent of his mouth, the way his tongue flicked out to wet the tip of my nipple, how he pursed his lips and blew cold air across the surface was so fascinating and titillating at the same time. The sudden whoosh of sensual desire when he sucked the erect nipple into his warm, wet mouth drove a shudder of pleasure through me and spiked between my thighs. The scene played out in slow motion. I wanted to be taken deliciously slowly. And as he towered above me, I gave in to the fact that at that moment I was a princess in his eyes, and I enjoyed every tiny nuance of body movement, every slight variation in depth and tempo, until the conclusion could no longer be held back.

I never imagined that I would be showering with a handsome six-foot, five-inch male on Christmas morning, but here I was, enjoying Richard's soapy hands on my back and sharing warm wet kisses under the warm spray.

"I think this calls for pancakes, with maple syrup and crispy bacon."

"Are we going out to eat? Is the restaurant downstairs open?"

"No, but my kitchen is open for business."

"You're cooking?"

"Yes, I'm starving. Aren't you? The leftovers we had last night didn't last long."

"I didn't know you could cook."

"There are a lot of things you don't know about me."

"I'm looking forward to finding out."

"Let's get dried and dressed and I'll take you on a culinary discovery tour."

"But before we go, can you show me that weightlifting trick again."

"Weightlifting?"

"Yes I think I weigh about 150lbs."

Richard smiled, shut off the water, and demonstrated his skill.

7
HARPER

APRIL 1991

Days flew by, and turned into weeks, then a month, then three months and I realized I had not spent one night alone. I was either in Richards bed or he was in mine. I had been worried that working together would cause problems but in actual fact we were getting on better than ever before, and the office appeared to be running very smoothly. I was happy. I was content and strangely enough I was thinking of myself as one half of a couple. Richard had not talked about a future, and I presumed this was because we both had been divorced. I still had not used the L word, even although I had been tempted in the last few days. Richard told me he loved me at every opportunity. My heart did a little happy dance whenever he was near me. That sure had to be a sign. Right? Maybe I was just being overly cautious because of Dean. Why rush into things.

I left the office on time for a change. Richard had not been back to the agency after his meeting but had asked me to meet him at his apartment for a home cooked meal. He opened the door with a flourish and swept me into his arms. The smell of garlic and aromatic spices made my mouth water.

"Something smells delicious." I spun away and inhaled deeply. "A curry?" I unbuttoned my coat and dropped it on the chair.

"I've made a special dinner for us tonight. Come have some champagne."

"Champagne? A special dinner? What's the occasion?"

"Our three-month anniversary."

"You sure don't act like any other man I have ever known. You cook, you clean, you treat me like a princess, you remember anniversaries. What did I do to deserve you?"

"I guess you bring out the best in me. Which is why I want to ask you a question?"

"Okay."

"Will you marry me?"

"Whoa! What? Marry you. We've only been going out for a few months."

"The heart knows what the heart wants. When you're with me, I feel the happiest I have ever been. Don't you feel it too?"

"Yes, I feel happy. But marriage."

"Are you worried about the business. I'm happy to sign a prenuptial agreement, if that is what you're worried about."

"What's the rush Richard?"

"I'm not getting any younger, and I want to spend as much time with you as I possibly can."

"You're forty-five not seventy-five. There's plenty of time."

"Is there? You told me when your parents died in that car crash, your father was forty-two and your mother was thirty-eight. My parents both died within a year of each other in their late sixties. I always thought my father died of grief. He loved my mother so much."

He pulled me into his arms and brought both my hands to his lips. "I love you, I want to be with you, to wake up with you, and go to sleep with you in my arms. I cannot envisage my life without you in it. From the day I met you, I have become a better man. *You* have made me a better man. I promise to continue to treat you like a princess. I love you with all my heart Harper."

Richard brought his lips to mine and kissed me softly. There was a question in the way he looked at me, head slightly tilted, sincere expression on his face, and he needed an honest answer.

"I have wanted to tell you how I feel for a while now. You do make me happy, and content. I find it hard to remember what it was like before you came charging into my life on your white horse to save my coffee from tipping all over me. And then to save my business. You said it was love at first sight for you, but for me it has taken a little time."

"Taking time to make up your mind is a good thing. . . does that mean?"

"I do love you Richard."

"So now I can show you this." Richard took a small black velvet box from his pocket and dropped to one knee. He opened the box. The beautiful diamond solitaire set in platinum sparkled in the light. "Harper Cole. Will you do me the honor of becoming my wife. I promised to show you just how much you mean to me every day, in every way I can."

"There is something I need to tell you first. I don't want children Richard."

"I don't think we have to worry about that. I was married before for many years and we were never able to have a child although my wife desperately wanted one. It's not important. What is important to me is you. You are all I want. You are all I need."

"Then yes, I will marry you." My heart beat faster, and suddenly I felt sincerely happy. Richard rose and kissed me.

"You have made me a very happy man. Let's have some champagne to celebrate."

We toasted to our future life together. Richard served up the fragrant curry while I switched on the radio. The first song that played was "Love and Marriage", sung by Frank Sinatra. I had no proof, but I had the definite feeling that Luc was somewhere close by and had a hand in all this.

8

HARPER

JUNE 1991

We got married on a beautiful Friday afternoon in Vegas. An intimate service with all the glitz and glamour that Caesars Palace had to offer. Ruby was my bridesmaid, and Richard asked his friend Oliver, whom I had never met, to be his best man. Ruby also thought he was the best man, because by the time the small reception dinner party of four was over, Ruby and Oliver were exchanging phone numbers and Ruby looked mighty pleased with herself.

"I think it's time we said goodnight." Richard whispered in my ear as we two-stepped slowly on the small dancefloor. He slipped his arm tighter around my waist and nuzzled my earlobe.

"We can't just leave Ruby here on her own." I said quietly.

"Of course we can. And she's not on her own. Oliver will take good care of her. Look at how well they're getting on."

They did appear to be happy, and by the look on Ruby's face,

Oliver was indeed charming. We left the dancefloor and headed back to our table.

"Hey guys. My husband and I are going to call it a night." Richard took my hand. "Oliver, I'm trusting you to take good care of Ruby, okay?"

"I'm fine. We're going to go play a little blackjack. I might even win some money, and I can move into the Penthouse for the weekend." Ruby stood and took Oliver's arm. "Lead the way. I'll see you two lovebirds in the morning."

"Goodnight." Richard called over his shoulder and steered me to the elevator. "I want to have you all to myself." he whispered.

The elevator was busy, and there were people walking down the corridor outside of our suite, but as soon as the door closed behind us, Richard pulled me into his arms and hugged me tight. "I can't believe it has taken so long to get you alone. I've been wanting to do this all day." He traced my eyebrow with his fingertip, then tucked a stray lock of hair behind my ear. He bent down and placed his lips against mine. Richard's kiss was gentle and loving and tender. He took a step back to look at me. "My wife. My beautiful wife."

I reached around my back to unzip my long ivory dress. It slithered over my hips and puddled at my feet. I stepped out of it. I was wearing a cream colored corset, sheer lace top stockings, no panties, and the highest cream leather stiletto heels I could find to bring me nearer to my new husband's height. I began to slip off the shoes.

"No please keep them on. I love this look. I want to make love to you just as you are." Richard bent down, slid an arm under my knees, lifted me up, walked through the suite and placed me on the end of the bed. The bedside lamp was turned down low. I watched as he kicked off his shoes and removed his suit, his formal shirt and his underwear. His upper body was strong and powerful. He had a trim waist and narrow hips, and his manhood stood proud and ready for action. He had muscular thighs and very shapely legs for a man. I thought myself very lucky to have married such an attractive specimen. He knelt on the bed between my open legs, lifted one stiletto encased foot and placed the heel on his shoulder. He cupped my bottom, lifted me off the bed a little and edged inside me. I watched his face as pleasure took over and softened his features. My own pleasure was building, and he held on until he was sure he wasn't going to leave me behind. The orgasm rolled over me and wave after wave of pleasure had me gasping for air and clawing at the sheets. When Richard collapsed on to the bed, I knew that it had taken a mighty effort on his part to make sure we would climax together. I heard the word "perfect" whispered in the air and caught a whiff of sandalwood and spices. Luc? Was Luc here. I lifted my head and searched the room, but there was no sign of him.

❧

I managed to stay away from the roulette table for the entire weekend. The trick was to keep busy. Richard rented a car, and the four of us enjoyed seeing the sights. Richard and Oliver took turns driving out into the desert and marveled at how dry it was and how much money must be required to keep the city pumping with entertainment day and night. We ate in the numerous fancy restaurants along the Strip, and enjoyed the live shows at the Colosseum at Caesars Palace. We flew back on Monday morning, dropped off Ruby and Oliver first, and directed the taxi to take us to my house. The silence was golden after the action-packed weekend. I could never imagine living somewhere so noisy and flashy and bright twenty-four-seven.

I made coffee and carried it to the living room. Richard was sprawled on the couch, with his eyes closed. "I know we've discussed keeping both the apartment in the City and this house, but I've been thinking about it. How do you feel about selling the apartment now that we're married?" I asked

"I've been thinking about it too. I was hoping we might keep the apartment, sell this house and buy something together. Something where we can make new memories." He sat up to take the coffee.

"Do you have anything in mind?" I asked.

"How about the Hollywood Hills"

"Isn't that a bit far out?"

"It's a bit out of the city, sure, but think of the advantages. We could have a place to entertain, and a view and maybe even a swimming pool."

"I guess it's worth taking a look. I guess a pool would be good for us to keep fit." I said.

"We could keep the apartment if we needed to be close to the office, since it's only a short walk away."

"I thought you liked this house."

"You moved to the guest bedroom because the master suite has ghosts you said. Why stay in a house that has ghosts?" Richard took my hand in his. "It would be a house we picked together. We could have a home gym and exercise together. We could do laps of the pool. We could get a dog."

"I've never considered having a dog before because I've always travelled a lot. It does sound appealing. What kind of dog would you like?"

"Something big, something that could protect you when I'm not here. A guard-dog."

"I thought it was going to be a pet?"

"A pet can still be a guard-dog, if it's trained well enough."

"Okay, I guess we should start looking for a house, before we look for a dog."

"Deal?" Richard held out his hand "Why are you laughing?"

"Deal" I shook his hand. I had a strange sense of Déjà vu. I remembered the last time I shook hands on a deal. But this time nothing changed. No flash of light, no time skip, just Richard's warm hand in mine.

9
HARPER

AUGUST 1991

The temperature had soared over last few days, and sleep had been broken and uncomfortable. At least for me anyway. Richard seemed to sleep through anything and awoke full of beans and raring to tackle the day. I dragged myself out of bed and into the shower, aware we had an appointment with a realtor Richard had found, to view a house in the Hollywood Hills.

The roads approaching the house were exceptionally steep, but once at the peak, the road flattened out, and we turned a corner into a dead-end street. The house sat at the end of a small crescent of attractive homes.

Barbara James, the realtor, met us at the door to show us around.

"Welcome to the Hollywood Hills, Mr and Mrs Erickson. Please come in and see what this location has to offer." Barbara held out her hand, and Richard shook it.

"The house does have street appeal, and I like the wide entrance." I shook Barbara's hand, noted her sharp, firm grip, and took a good look at the woman in front of me. Her smart navy designer suit, cropped blonde hair and Italian leather purse, indicated she had expensive taste. I surmised she made a good living selling houses. I didn't get any negative vibes from her. She had the air of someone who was confident, competent and straight forward. All good points to note.

"I take pride in matching the home to the clients. I hope I can find what you're looking for. This offering has only just come on the market. The family is moving overseas and needs a quick sale. Having said that, the property is not cheap, but the price is reasonable, and the house has a lot going for it. Let's begin in the study here at the front. All the main rooms are at the rear, because of the view. This study has space for two desks, as per your discussion with me on the phone, Mr Erickson."

"It's a lovely big room, and quiet. I like the large window overlooking the garden and the street, it's light and bright, the trees are pretty in the front yard. Different to what I've been used to, living in the city." Richard said.

"You won't get through traffic either, being at the end of a cul-de-sac." Barbara said.

"It's quieter here than in our home on the other side of the city." I said.

"You'll find this area is pretty exclusive. I've sold houses to some pretty influential people. It's a good neighborhood. Having Warner Brothers Studio nearby is a draw for actors."

"It's one of the reasons we're looking to buy in this area." Richard said.

"Let's move on. There are four bedrooms. These two here off the entrance hall, and two on the other side of the living room, but we'll look at them shortly." Barbara said.

"I don't know that we'll need four bedrooms Richard." I glanced at the walls and noted the many family portraits lining the hallway.

"Let's continue down to the living area. The kitchen has recently been renovated. And you need to see this view." Barbara walked ahead and then turned to the right, where the kitchen was positioned in this large, bright family room combination. A long breakfast bar, with oak bar stools underneath, separated the kitchen from the family room. The walls and kitchen cabinets were painted a warm vanilla color. Gleaming appliances, and glass fronted cabinets sparkled in the sunlight. An American oak dining table sat in the recess of a bay window with a padded window seat. This would be the perfect spot to have morning coffee, looking out over a pretty flower garden. On the opposite side of the room, to the left, two butterscotch leather couches and two armchairs faced the television console against one wall of the family room. Although there were several items of furniture in the space, it did not appear overcrowded. A bowl of seasonal fruit on the kitchen counter, bright flower arrangements on tables, and artwork on the walls made the rooms welcoming. I walked over to the window. There was a pool in the rear garden. But the view of the sky was what drew me to the floor to ceiling windows and beyond. I opened the sliding doors, walked out into the sunshine, to the far edge of the paving surrounding the pool, and looked down on the homes below and the city spread out in the distance.

"Magnificent!" The view took my breath away. It was as if we were on top of the world.

The tiered garden below had wide stone steps cut into the hillside, descending to the fence of the neighboring property. This garden was beautifully maintained, with some areas of lawn, colorful plants and succulents.

Richard appeared beside me and let out a low whistle. "A million-dollar view."

"I can imagine the view would be spectacular at night too." I said.

"Come take a look inside. If you can tear yourself away." Richard took my hand, and we walked back to the house to view the bedrooms and bathrooms. All of the rooms were a good size, the master bedroom was light filled and spacious and had the view of the valley below. I couldn't fault the house, every part of it was appealing.

. . .

Barbara returned to her car for some paperwork and left us alone in the family room to discuss the house.

"Well what do you think. I'm sold" Richard said.

"It's too big for us. Four bedrooms plus a study? A three bedroom is more than enough. We don't need all this space."

"The price is appealing, they want a quick sale, and didn't I hear you say the view was magnificent"

"Yes, the view is magnificent, but... "

"Let me set the scene for you. We get up in the morning, take a swim in the pool, or work out in the gym we are going to set up in one of the bedrooms, have fresh fruit and juice, and eggs sunny side up, which I have lovingly prepared, on the terrace. Get some work done in our home office and make our way downtown after the rush hour has passed."

"Not practical. What if I need to go to a meeting? Or you need your car."

"Okay we take 2 cars. You're not seeing the big picture here. Imagine hosting a client cocktail party out by the pool in the summer. You must admit it's very impressive."

Barbara appeared and Richard joined her to look at the brochures she brought from the car. I took another walk by the pool, admired the aqua blue tiles and the crystal-clear water, and climbed down the stone steps to the semi-circular garden seat below, set into the hill-side. It was a warm day. I slipped off my shoes and dug my bare toes into the soft grass. It was so peaceful in the garden. Butterflies flitted about and bees buzzed nearby. I closed my eyes and lifted my face to the warm sun.

Sandalwood and spices filled the air. I opened my eyes and Luc was sitting on the seat beside me. The top two buttons of his white linen shirt were undone, showing a smooth tanned chest, the shirt sleeves rolled back to his elbows. His corded forearms rested on his thighs. This was his only concession to the warm day. His shirt was tucked into perfectly pressed charcoal trousers. Which, in conjunction with black socks and shiny black leather shoes, were at odds with his more casual upper body appearance. His beautiful face was also tilted up to the sun. He slipped off his sunglasses and bestowed on me his most persuasive smile.

"You must admit it is a beautiful house." Luc bent down, picked a pretty pink flower from the garden and held it out to me. "This would be a lovely place to come home to each night. A fresh start for you and Richard. No ghosts."

"It's too big for the two of us."

"Not for long."

"I told you, don't hold your breath." I sighed.

"How are you feeling Harper? A little tired"

"Yes I'm a little tired. But I haven't been sleeping."

"Really. How about a coffee to perk you up?"

"Yuk. The thought of coffee is . . . hang on."

"You usually love coffee Harper."

"What are you doing?"

"Me? I'm not doing anything." Luc was smiling. Happy. Beaming actually. Suddenly it clicked.

"No. No way. I'm not."

"Oh yes you are."

"Pregnant. No, Nope. Not pregnant."

Luc was laughing at me. He looked super pleased with himself.

"You're just a little bit pregnant. No bigger than a poppy seed right now."

"You did this didn't you?"

"Me? No. You and Richard did this. That's how it works. When the man puts his . . . "

"Okay I get it. Oh God."

"No point calling on him now. You made a deal. Now you're going to deliver. Literally." Luc beamed.

I felt sick. I couldn't quite believe it. But I had been tired, and I had been feeling a bit off lately.

"You really do want this house. It will be perfect for you and Richard and Domenic."

"Domenic?"

"Yes. Your son is going to be called Domenic."

"That wasn't part of the deal."

"I've been looking at baby names, and I rather like that one."

"What if it's a girl?"

"Of course, you'll have to try again. But don't worry, it's a boy."

I put my head in my hands. It all made sense, and I hadn't put two and two together on my own.

"I'm not ready for this. I've only just got used to being married to Richard and now . . ." I looked up and Luc was nowhere to be seen. Richard called my name. I sighed and got up.

I shouldn't fight it, because my fate has already been sealed. I'll go and tell my husband that I thought about what he said, and he's right. A new husband, a baby on the way, and now it looks like I'm buying a house in the Hollywood Hills.

I headed up the steps to tell Richard he was going to be a proud papa.

I could hear Luc laughing in the distance.

10

HARPER

MARCH 1992

I could hardly move without feeling exhausted. My once fit body was no longer toned, no longer trim and no longer attractive. I looked like I'd swallowed a beach ball. A very large beach ball. I had to wear slip on shoes. Nothing fitted me anymore. I resorted to wearing Richards shirts at home, and loose maternity dresses when I left the house, which reminded me of a Hawaiian Muumuu. And to add to the embarrassment, the elastic broke on my underwear while I was in the supermarket the other day. I was forced to abandon my shopping cart and I only just made it to the bathroom stall before they slithered to my feet. I had to stuff them in my handbag and go commando.

Everyone said I was glowing, but I knew I was sweating from the extra weight I was carrying around. I wanted this baby out of me. I wanted my old body back, to run around the block, and the ability to tie up my own shoelaces again. My breasts had their own ZIP code. Richard made a big fuss of them and I knew he would be sorry to see them go. The thought of breastfeeding filled me with terror, my nipples were already so sensitive.

"Get this baby out of me." I begged the doctor at my weekly examination.

"It's not far away Harper. Any day now. You're doing great." Dr Patel patted me on the arm. "You can get dressed. Make an appointment with my nurse for next week. But I might see you before then."

"I can't go another week. Can't you do something?"

"Let nature take its course. Your body will know when it is time." He gave me his arm to sit up, then left the room. I struggled into my clothes and bent down to pick up my handbag. I felt a pop and water ran down my legs. I pressed the buzzer for the nurse. It had begun.

❧

"I want an epidural." I panted between contractions.

"It's too late for that. You said you wanted a drug-free labor. It's better for the baby." Dr Patel lifted his head to look at me over the drape of the sheet. "You're well on your way. This baby will be here soon. You are doing swell."

"Arrrgggghhhh." I groaned, I pushed, then panted as I had been instructed between contractions.

Richard squeezed my hand. "You're doing great."

"You have to say that. Men have no idea."

Richard held the straw next to my lips and offered me some water. "You're amazing. Just breathe. Hold my hand."

"Oh God!" I squeezed his hand tighter as a strong contraction gripped me. I caught the fragrance of sandalwood and spices in the air. "Luc?"

"Look at what?" Richard asked.

"He's here." I said

"No, but another big push, okay?" Dr Patel disappeared under the drape of the sheet between my knees. "That's it. Now stop pushing and pant, the head is crowning.

I panted as I was told, concentrated on my breathing. I glanced up and saw Luc standing in the corner of the delivery room, dressed in scrubs like the nursing staff, bearing witness to the moment Domenic entered the world.

He slid out and into the sure grip of Dr Patel, and cried out as they cleaned his face, clamped the chord, before placing him on my breast. My heart lurched in my chest. The surge of emotion that swept through me was like a physical blow. This tiny infant who had given me so much grief over the past few months, was the most beautiful thing I had ever seen. He had a cap of dark hair, and his big eyes started at me with such concentration, I could not look away. Tears ran down my cheeks. So, this was true love. Nothing compared to this. No one could have convinced me that my heart would be changed forever by having a child. Until now.

Richard stroked the baby's soft cheek, then gently kissed me on the lips. I could see the pride in his eyes.

"My son." Richard put his arms around us both and spoke softly to the baby. "We've waited a long time to meet you."

"What are you going to name him?" Dr Patel asked.

"Domenic." I said. I looked at his little face and realized it suited him perfectly. I glanced in the corner and thought I saw tears glisten in Luc's eyes. He mouthed "Well done. He's perfect."

The doctor took him from me, checked him out, wrapped him up to keep him warm, then and placed him in Richard's arms. When I checked again Luc had gone.

❧

I couldn't sleep in the hospital unless Domenic was in the same private room, I did not want to let him out of my sight. I had images of Luc appearing and claiming Domenic, and I had my argument all ready. Luc could have something else. He could have his money back. Well maybe not all the money, but I could work out a payment plan.

Domenic was such a good baby, he nursed and slept and hardly ever cried. Richard was over the moon and so proud of his "little man" as he called him. He brought gifts for the baby every time he visited. The hospital room looked like a toy store.

It was day two in the hospital, nearly time to go home. I fed Dominic, put him in the bassinet and went into the adjacent bathroom to wash my hands. When I came back into the room Luc was standing by the crib, dressed completely in black, holding Dominic in his arms. The baby held his finger and looked up at him with the same concentrated look he gave me when I held him. I rushed to take my baby back.

"Give me my baby." My heart nearly lept from my chest.

"Woah. We had a deal" He lifted him high, and held him above his head, like a sacrifice to the Gods.

"Give me my baby Luc!" I yelled. I tried to reach for him, but Luc was too tall. My blood pressure was going through the roof.

Domenic burped and a stream of milk vomit dripped down onto the front of Luc's black shirt and black tie. He glanced down with a disgusted look on his face.

"I think it's best that you keep him, at least until he's house-trained." Luc lowered the infant into my arms.

I clutched him to my chest protectively.

"Don't ever do that again. You frightened me." My heart only slowed down when Domenic was placed back in my arms.

"We have a deal Harper. You shook on it, remember? One day he will be mine." He scrunched up his nose, pulled tissues from a box and wiped his shirt and tie.

"Not if I can help it."

There was a knock on the door and a nurse popped her head in. I turned around and stood between the door and Luc. "Dr Patel says you can go home tomorrow. That's good news, isn't it?" I waited for her to ask about my visitor. Women always noticed Luc. She closed the door.

I turned around and Luc had disappeared again.

The maternity ward was busy, and the nurse in charge of reception was on the phone when I approached. She finished her call and looked at me expectantly.

"I'm being signed out today. Do you have any idea what time the doctor will be making rounds?"

"He should be here shortly Mrs Erickson. I'll get him to come directly to your room when he arrives on the floor."

I turned around and bumped into Luc's chest. He was impeccably dressed in a dark blue Armani suit, white shirt, red tie and matching kerchief in his breast pocket. He looked like an English gentleman.

"Do you need transport? I'll get my driver to collect us at the front door." Luc said.

"No Richard is coming to collect us, but I cannot leave until the doctor checks Domenic and signs us out."

The elevator doors opened and Richard appeared. "Hello darling." Richard kissed my cheek and turned to be introduced to Luc.

"Richard this is Luc, an old friend, from out of town. He heard about our new addition to the family."

"Luc Nightingale." Luc held out his hand.

"Richard Erickson" Richard shook Luc's hand and stared intently at him. "Have we met before?"

"No. I don't think so."

"Are you sure. You look familiar to me. Have you been in any movies?"

"No."

"Maybe you should consider a career change. You would be a great English villain."

"Richard!" I exclaimed.

"Darling you must admit he has the perfect look. Suave, sophisticated, handsome. A friend of mine is looking for someone to play the lead in a new movie he's producing. You have the look they want. Yes even that quirky eyebrow lift you're doing now. Fantastic. The strong silent type I see. They need a millionaire businessman with a devil may care approach to life. Have you done any acting?"

"All the time. I play many parts . . . in amateur productions of course. Nothing permanent, always a short run."

"You're stretching the truth a bit there." I mumbled under my breath. Luc grinned at me.

"Excellent." Richard extracted a business card from his pocket. "Here's my card. Come and see me at the office. We'll talk to him. I would be happy to sign you up to our talent agency and represent you if you're interested."

Luc tucked the card into his breast pocket, behind his red kerchief. Dr Patel approached, and we were ushered back to the private room where Domenic lay sleeping in his crib. Luc had taken the opportunity to disappear again.

I wondered if Luc would visit Richard and take him up on his offer. Although it pained me to admit it, I had read that script and Richard was right. Luc was perfect for the part.

11

LUC

YEAR 1970

My sensitive hearing picked up raised voices in the alley behind the restaurant.

A tall emaciated man in ripped jeans and filthy sweatshirt, brandishing a dangerous looking hunting knife, had a young couple backed up against the wall at the end of the alley in an attempt to rob them. The thief was demanding money, their watches and their jewelry. I could tell by the way the tall young man tilted his head and narrowed his eyes that he was not going to give this thief what he wanted. I surmised he was assessing the best way to disarm this whacked out junkie, who twitched, couldn't keep still and waved the knife about. The tall man moved to shield the woman with his body. The thief waved the knife near his chest, threatening to open him up.

The thief didn't hear me approach from behind. "You really should put that weapon away before someone gets hurt." I stood a foot behind the man with the knife. He turned quickly, raised his arm and lunged at me. I stepped back, and to the side with lightning speed and the knife sliced the air inches from my neck. He tried again to stab me, and I easily dodged out of his reach. It was like playing with a toddler. The blond man jumped on the thief's back and tackled him to the ground. There was a brief struggle. I reached down to separate them and put a stop to this, and the thief got up, staggered back, and attempted to run down the alley. I grabbed him by the neck with one hand, lifted him off his feet, and gave his neck a tiny little squeeze. He fell to the ground, unconscious. It was then I turned around and saw the blond man lying on the ground with the knife wedged under his ribcage. The woman was sobbing and trying to stop the flow of blood.

"Oh no. Very gallant young man, but unnecessary." I pulled the hysterical woman to her feet and gave her a nudge down the alley. "Go and get help. I'll look after him." She ran screaming for help.

This man had been courageous enough to try and stop me from being harmed. It was a stupid move, but he didn't know that at the time. This was the first time this had happened to me. The first time someone had stood up on my behalf to save me from harm. Usually humans run the other way when I'm around. It was my turn to help him. I swiftly pulled out the knife and he passed out. His body was going into shock, and he had lost a lot of blood. I laid examined his wound to get a better idea of the damage. I estimated the long-bladed knife had penetrated his liver and damaged some arteries. I had to fix the tear and stop the bleeding. My blood would heal a wound on my body within minutes if I was cut. Perhaps it would help a human too. It was worth a try. He would die soon if I didn't help him. I used the knife to cut the vein on my wrist and allowed my blood to drip into the wound on the man's chest. The slice in my skin got smaller and smaller until it disappeared altogether. I had to trust that there had been enough blood transferred to make a difference.

A siren rang out in the air and the woman came running back up the alley with a uniformed office. Paramedics followed closely behind with a stretcher. I stood aside to let them lift the wounded man onto the stretcher, carry him down the alley and load him into the ambulance. The assailant I had placed my foot on to stay still, woke up and was hauled to his feet and handcuffed before being marched to a waiting police car. The officer had asked me to come to the station, but I made sure he, and all the other participants of this interesting interlude, had forgotten all about me by the time they had reached the end of the alley. I checked up on him, to make sure he recovered. The ER deemed his injuries were minimal, but they admitted him for observation. They allowed him to leave the next day.

Over the years I kept an eye on the Blond Knight, as I fondly called him, who had tried to come to my aid. I found out his name was Richard Erickson.. My experiment with a human had worked. Within months he swapped his safe secure office job, for a life of thrills and spills in the movies. Richard became a stunt actor. He turned into a bit of a dare devil. I had an inkling he got that from me. I felt a little bit like a proud father.

So this was what God felt like when he dabbled in people's lives.

12

HARPER

APRIL 1992

I opened the door to find Luc, partially hidden behind a luge bouquet of flowers and holding a pale blue teddy bear.

"What are you doing here?" I asked, baring the door.

"It's lovely to see you too. Yes of course I'd like to come in and see the new addition to the family?"

"I didn't invite you in. Does that mean you can't cross the threshold?"

"No. I'm not a vampire Harper. I don't require an invitation. I can go anywhere I please. And tonight, it pleases me to be here, with you."

"Who's at the door darling?" Richard yelled from the living room. I took a step back. He approached us, holding the baby on his shoulder. "Don't keep the man waiting on the doorstep. Come in Luc. Meet my son."

I accepted the flowers and teddy bear and followed the men back to the kitchen. Luc stared down at the child, now held low in the crook of Richard's arm. Domenic was perfectly calm and content.

"Would you like to hold him." Richard placed the baby in Luc stiff arms. Domenic looked up at Luc and smiled.

"He's smiling at me. Hello there. I'm Uncle Luc."

"That's only gas I'm afraid. Babies of that age don't smile." Richard voiced what I was thinking but didn't have the heart to tell Luc.

"I think you're wrong. Let's try a little experiment. Would you like a million dollars in your Trust fund for college?" Luc asked. Domenic smiled again. "See, he knows what I'm talking about. Smart kid."

"Do you even have a million dollars to give him for a college fund?" I asked.

"Of course I do. I'm rich Uncle Luc. I'm going to play a millionaire businessman in the new movie your husband's friend is producing." Luc grinned at me. "It's only the start. I'm sure I'll get more offers."

"You took the part?" I asked. It seemed astonishing to me that Luc would even consider this.

"Of course. Richard thinks it would be perfect for me."

"He auditioned and nailed it." Richard said.

"You're going to be seeing a lot of me. I've decided to stay in California for a while. I'm looking for a place to live." Luc winked at me, like this was the best news I could possibly have all year. I was skeptical.

"I'll give you our realtor's details. Barbara found this house for us. She got us a sweet deal. It's a great location. You might find something this side of the city. Near the studio." Richard went in search of Barbara's phone number

"Exactly what I was thinking." Luc said.

"Heaven help us." I mumbled

"What was that?" Luc asked. He was grinning at me.

I knew he'd heard me, there was nothing wrong with his hearing. I could whisper at fifty paces and he would hear me. I just had to think of Luc, and he would hear me. And as much as I tried to not think of him, he kept popping up in my dreams, and the memory of his kisses were always the same. A passionate inferno of emotions. I loved my husband, but Luc had charisma in spades, and you would have to be dead not to be affected by his sensuality whenever he was around.

Living nearby to Luc was going to be claustrophobic.

A week later Luc arrived on my doorstep, holding a pink box from my favorite bakery. As he waved it under my nose my lips watered. I could smell the sugar and cinnamon. I heard the thud of calories whooping and yahooing as they walloped onto my thighs in anticipation. Oh yes, he knew how to get to me through all of my weak spots. I ushered him into the kitchen to see what delicious treats he had brought.

He was also full of praise for a house Barbara had shown him.

"The house is fabulous. And the best part is that It's just around the corner from you." Luc helped himself to a slice of angel food cake.

"Really. I'm surprised." I wasn't surprised at all. He'd visited four nights out of seven in the last week. It seemed as if Luc was entrenched in our lives, whether we liked it or not. At least he's arriving at the front door, and acting like a normal visitor, bringing wine, or delicious desserts, or a gift for Domenic, and always the gentleman. Richard obviously likes him, so what can I say. I helped myself to a piece of cinnamon coffee cake and licked the fragrant sugar off my fingers.

"Are you going to make a habit of this?"

"Of what?"

"Being here. Dropping in all the time. Aren't you bored? Don't you have other things you have to do? People to make deals with and bring out their wicked past? Villains to torture? Hobbies?"

"I've decided to give myself every second night off to spend with the Erickson family at the moment. A bit of rest and recreation makes me work harder on the job. I give it my all."

"What are you trying to achieve?"

"I want to get to know you better. And Richard, and especially Domenic."

"He's a baby Luc. He just wants fed and changed and a comfy crib to sleep in."

"Domenic is not like any other child. He's picking up on everything around him. Believe me, he is more aware of his environment than you realize."

"Oh, should I expect him to start talking soon? Then walking?"

"I wouldn't be at all surprised."

Domenic woke up and let me know he was hungry. He didn't cry exactly. It was more like a mental nudge which caused "let down', and suddenly my milk bar was open for business. I left Luc eating the cake he brought, went into the nursery to feed the baby, and closed the door. Richard had bought me a rocking chair, and I made myself comfortable and settled Domenic onto my breast. It took a few seconds, but I was getting pretty good at this routine by now, and it wasn't as painful anymore. As I fed him, he laid his tiny hand possessively on my breast.

"He looks content, but I haven't met a male yet who doesn't like breasts." Luc stood inside the door, arms folded, head cocked to one side.

I jumped. I know I should be used to Luc popping in and out, but he still had the ability to surprise me.

"Some privacy would be appreciated."

"Why? I've seen all of you, in every possible position, in every possible scenario. No need to be shy with me."

"Let's change the subject, shall we. This house you're thinking of buying. Where is it exactly?"

"If you stand on your front step facing the road and look to your left. It's above yours. The main road winds up and around the hillside. It has a better view actually."

"You're going to be above us? Great. There goes any privacy we have."

"Did you miss the part about me being able to see all of you. I don't need an invitation, remember? I can come and go wherever and whenever I like. The Devil, remember? I have a platinum back-stage pass. Sometimes you see me, sometimes you don't."

"I'm going to try and forget you said that."

"Just go about your business. Don't stress the small stuff. Now about that college fund I started in Domenic's name. What college would you like him to attend? Stanford? Berkley?"

"We have to wait until the child shows some interest in subjects."

"We'll get his name on the list and then he can choose his subjects."

"What if he's not academic?

"Oh, please." Luc shook his head at me. "He's exceptional, I told you."

I lifted Domenic to burp him.

"Can I try?"

"He might mess up your shirt."

"I'm getting better at avoiding that." Luc picked up a swaddle wrap and placed it over his shoulder. I handed him over. Domenic settled on Luc shoulder, Luc patted his back, and hummed a little tune. Domenic burped loudly.

"You *are* getting better at this. I'm impressed. I also think you're starting to enjoy it."

"This tiny human was not what I had expected."

"Don't tell me you're feeling real emotions Luc. Like affection?"

"He is rather cute. He looks a bit like me, don't you think? He has my dark hair. And eyes."

"Don't say that around Richard. He's sure that Domenic looks exactly like him when he was young. Except he was blond."

Richard arrived home. He was pleased to see Luc, who had made himself comfortable and didn't appear to be going anywhere soon. They did a lot of that hand-shaking-back-slapping ritual that never ceased to amuse me. If it was two women, they would have hugged affectionately and kissed each other on the cheek and been done with it.

I made tuna pasta for dinner, and Richard invited Luc to join us. They talked about the movie, and Luc's part in the production, and the other cast members. Luc started to talk about funding and helping to find locations. I began to nod off. I took myself to bed and left the men to discuss the ins and outs of life behind and in front of the camera.

An hour or so later Richard brought Domenic in to be fed and climbed in beside me.

"Has Luc gone?"

"Yes he left after Domenic woke up. He's really good with him. I like Luc. I've been thinking about the future. What if something happened to us? Our son will need someone to look after him. What do you think? We could ask Luc to be Domenic's Godfather."

"Where did this idea come from. Did Luc say something?"

"No. I get a really good feeling whenever he's around. He's *your* friend. And I trust him near our son. He has his interest at heart. I know he does. Have you seen the way he looks at him? He is fascinated. Are you aware he's set up a substantial college fund for Domenic?"

"Yes. He told me. It's very generous, I know."

"It's a formality, a safeguard in the event . . . not that I'm saying . . . I just want to make sure he will be taken care of. There are no grandparents or aunts and uncles."

"I get it. Okay Richard. If that is what you want."

There was no point in fighting this. Although the irony of the title was not lost on me, I had to be honest. The idea of Luc as the Godfather, getting to know Domenic, spending time with all of us was better than Luc deciding that he wanted to collect on his deal. Because there was no way I was willingly handing over my first-born son to the Devil. He would take that child from me over my dead body. I was becoming more aware however that Luc had softened up a little since a certain small infant had held his hand and looked up into his eyes with solemn interest. Whether he likes it or not, Luc has shown that he has heart after all.

It was no surprise that Luc was thrilled with his new title of Godfather and two months later he still took his role very seriously. He spent more time with Domenic than ever before. It appeared as if I had two husbands to cook for, two husbands who doted over Domenic, but only one husband that I took to bed. Although I did often dream about Luc, and the dreams were very real. I had the strangest sensation when I woke up. It was as if I had moved into another dimension, and I actually was with Luc, and I actually was kissing Luc. My body responded to these kisses, and for a brief time I fought against the reality that I was being unfaithful to my husband. But can one be unfaithful in a dream? My lips felt swollen when I awoke, and my body responded very quickly to any foreplay my husband initiated. I tried to push the lustful episodes deep into my subconscious, compress the memories in between the pages of the teenage crushes I had experienced. But these were unlike any other infatuation I'd ever had. They lingered in my waking hours, making me restless and wanting. Richard accepted the benefit of these lustful thoughts gratefully and without question.

I tried to talk to Luc about the dreams but chickened out every time. I was embarrassed to actually talk about it, even although I knew he could read my mind. I wanted to see Luc yet was ashamed of my body's reaction to him. I blamed the hormones coursing through my system after giving birth.

For all our sakes I have to get over this and stop behaving like a horny teenager. I can't afford to get pregnant again. One child and two men is enough to look after.

13
LUC

Being the Devil has not been an easy road for me to travel. The constant bad press, mixing with the scum of the earth on a day to day basis. Obviously, it would have an everlasting effect on me! I was once the chosen one, I was beautiful and beloved. Then all that changed, and I was cast out of that heavenly place to find my own way in life and given a role no one wants to take on. But I gallantly made the job my own, I stepped up, as the Tormentor of Hell, I owned the title of the Devil, in all its gruesome, grisly, garish, ghastly glory. I was filled with fury, and anger and in a very dark place. Literally. But now I feel the need to reinvent myself. On Earth I have returned to my once angelic appearance to cloak my devilish guise, and if I do say so myself, I am rather a handsome Devil. Humans find me charismatic, and sexually appealing, which has its benefits, let me tell you. Although, I can change my appearance to any form I wish, and occasionally do so to tempt humans or for my own amusement.

I can pass from this world to the Underworld through what I describe as The Veil. Only a few demons with superior powers can do so. We cannot have the general population of Hell popping back and forth at will. I can open The Veil anywhere. I equate it to parting a curtain between reality on Earth and reality down below.

In recent years, much to my amazement, I have found a tiny bit of enjoyment in helping a few people on Earth, not only in torturing the inmates of perdition. However now I need to find a worthy replacement to guard the gates of Hell and torture all the evil souls while I work on the Devil mark ll edition. Someone to take over the business, so to speak. A family business would usually be handed over to a son. I had planned on teaching Domenic the business. But I fear at the moment he has too much of his mother and father in him, too much humanity to be a really good fit. I will have to spend a great deal of time with the boy, make sure he understands all the intricacies of the job, the nuances of what separates just bad from really evil. In the meantime, I guess it's all down to me to make sure I meet my KPIs and rid the world of those bad guys. Harper did mention I reminded her of Batman. Maybe I can make Domenic my Robyn, my wingman, and he can step into the big man's shoes and give me some downtime, when that day comes.

Hell knows I need a break.

14
HARPER

FIVE YEARS LATER - SEPTEMBER 1997

I'm nervous but excited for Domenic's on his first day at school. Domenic on the other hand is quiet and composed, holding my hand and walking into the school grounds by my side. Not like the other children on the playground who are running around or talking and laughing in small groups.

Luc drove up, parked the car by the side of the road and got out. Domenic turned and saw him before I did and ran to him.

Luc shook his hand. "Congratulations. This is a big day for you. Are you excited?"

"No."

"Nervous?"

"No."

"Good man. You'll be fine." Luc bent down and whispered in his ear. "Remember what I said, and you'll be fine."

"What was that all about?" I asked Luc.

"I gave him some advice about his first day at school. That's all."

"Advice? Did you ever go to elementary school?"

"Well no, but I have observed so I do feel qualified to give advice. After all I am the child's Godfather."

"We had better go inside. Are you planning on joining us?"

"No. I just wanted to be here for his first day. Give him some moral support. I'll call by tonight. How about I bring over pizza? Domenic's favorite."

I watched as Luke drove off, and Domenic tugged at my hand to go inside.

❧

Domenic knelt on the floor beside the toy box and selected all the blue blocks of Lego, then all the red, then all the yellow. He carried them over to the child sized table, sat down and began to construct a building, which was quite detailed, considering he was only five. It was strange watching him, playing like a child of five in one minute, answering questions like a teenager in the next.

He had been assessed and offered a place at Riverside, a school for gifted children. We were waiting on his teacher to arrive for a formal introduction. I'll admit nerves had set in and I'm jumpy. Today will be the first time Domenic has been away from my side for a full day, from the time he was born. He had been my little shadow, interested in everything the world had to offer. He walked and talked very early, and managed complicated tasks like no other child I had ever encountered. Richard thought I was biased when I told him Domenic was gifted, but when Domenic took an interest in the daily newspapers, and then read them aloud to Richard when he was two years old, he could no longer deny it. I have done my best to teach him at home. I have borrowed books from the library, rented DVD's and purchased anything educational I could find to help him to learn and absorb the world around him. I just couldn't keep up at the rate with which he was learning. He was used to spending time with adults. Children his age couldn't relate. . . or rather Domenic couldn't reduce his intellect sufficiently to fool them. Kids picked up on his differences and were wary. I had no choice but to enroll him in a school where they would allow him to mix with other children of a similar level and become more socialized.

I left him in the capable hands of the teaching staff, had a little cry in the car, and drove downtown to the agency office. Devil Dares Agency was growing rapidly. We had taken on extra clients. Richard had joined forces with his friend Ralph Donnelly and they were now making movies together. Luc had invested in Richards movies, and was a silent partner. Life had taken on a comfortable rhythm.

"Welcome back to full time, boss." Ruby jumped up and gave me a hug. "I've tidied your desk and printed out a list of new staff members for you to meet."

"You really are wonderful Ruby. I've really missed being away from the office. It will take a bit of getting used to, so be prepared for a million questions."

"I'm up to the challenge. What's first on the agenda today?"

"Let's start with some coffee and a meeting in my office, so that you can bring me up to speed with the current contracts. Then I'd like to meet the new staff this afternoon, straight after lunch. I have to leave to pick up Domenic after school."

"I'll make the coffee and be right back."

Ruby rushed off and I sat down behind my desk to get reacquainted with my surroundings. I had enjoyed being a full-time mother and part time worker in my home office. Domenic was a child who benefited from my attention and constant care. Gifted children are not the easiest to keep amused and engaged. They need to be encouraged to reach their full potential. But now I had to get used to being at work and letting someone else take the reins with his education.

The school called me at twelve noon. Domenic had gone to the bathroom on his own and had not returned. He had disappeared and they were searching the school and the grounds.

My first thought was that Luc had taken him. My heart pounded in my chest. I sent a furious mental message to him. *Bring back my son. Now!*

"Ruby where's Richard?" I called out to Ruby at her desk.

"He's in his office having a meeting with the production team." Ruby answered.

Luc rushed up the corridor, past Ruby, and into my office. He closed the door. He looked disheveled and concerned. "What do you mean bring him back? I don't have Domenic."

"Well where is he Luc? Richard's here in the office." Now I was not just furious but suddenly afraid.

"I'll be back. Don't worry." Luc turned around, wrenched open the door and headed for the elevator. I knew that when the elevator doors opened on the ground floor, he would not be aboard.

15

LUC

I sent a telepathic message to Domenic to try to pinpoint his location.

"Do you know where you are Domenic?"

"No. I'm in a house, but I've never been here before. The man said Mom had asked him to pick me up early from school."

"I'm on my way to pick you up. Just keep thinking of me."

"Mom didn't ask them to pick me up, did she?"

"No, but don't say anything to the man. I'm coming. Okay."

I silently entered the house through the kitchen door. One man was sitting at the kitchen table reading the newspaper. Another man was sitting with his back to me in the next room watching a kid's cartoon show on television with Domenic. The volume was up loud. Domenic stayed perfectly still although he knew I was there. The joker at the kitchen table turned and tried to stand up. I gave his neck a little squeeze and I quietly placed his head down on the table for a nap. I stood at the archway and addressed the other joker.

"We haven't been properly introduced. Your name is?" The man rose up, saw his friend unconscious on the table and came rushing at me, attempting to throw a punch. I moved out of the way and grabbed his shirt.

"Now, is that anyway to introduce yourself? I turned him around, twisted his arm right up high behind his back and pulled him in close to my chest. I asked him again, my lips pressed against his ear. "Who are you, and what are you doing with this boy?" I pushed a little harder on his arm. Another couple of inches and the arm would pop out of its socket.

"Joe Spicer. I'm just doin' a job for a guy. He asked us to pick up the kid, keep him here for a while. No harm done to the boy. He's fine. See."

"He looks fine. Are you fine, Domenic? Do you mind taking the keys for this man's van, over there on the table, and waiting on the front porch for me? We're going to get you back to school."

As soon as Domenic left the room, I shoved Joe's arm up a little harder and took great pleasure in hearing a pop, as the shoulder socket gave way and his arm popped out. He started to scream, and I put my hand over his mouth and squeezed his lips together rather hard. Blood oozed onto my fingers.

"Shhhhhhh. I presume you are doing this for money. Who asked you to bring the boy here?" I removed my hand from his mouth. He was shaking and in a great deal of pain. I wiped my bloody fingers on his shirt.

"A guy I met in a bar. Dean Natoli." He sobbed

"Why would Dean Natoli want this boy?"

"He says his ex wife has hidden him, kept him from him, and he's his son."

"I'm going to let go of you now. Let me assure you that if you or that idiot asleep on the kitchen table ever come near this boy again, I will come after you and personally pull off both your arms, and stuff them down your throat. If I were you, I wouldn't attempt to contact Dean, if you know what I mean, I'm already mad, and it could get nasty. I would leave town for a while. But first I want Dean's address."

"I don't want no trouble." He whined.

"Where does he hang out? I can find him myself, but it will take precious time." I shoved him down onto his knees and brought his other arm up his back. His injured arm hung loose. "I'll give you to five, and then both arms will be useless. One, two… "

"The bar on the corner of Cherokee Avenue and Hollywood Boulevard."

"Okay. Say goodnight." I squeezed his neck. He passed out on the floor. The man on the kitchen table began to move. I lifted his head by his hair and gave his forehead another little tap on the table. They would both be out for a while.

I yanked the phone off the wall and shattered it with the heel of my shoe. I drove Domenic back to school in the van, and he didn't say a word. He didn't need to. We had an understanding. He knew I had his best interest at heart. I was very proud of him for being so brave, and I told him so. When I arrived at the school, I parked around the corner and left the keys in the ignition. Not my problem if someone took the van, or the cops impounded it. Once Domenic was back in class I called Harper from the school office, and told her he was fine. I handed over the telephone handset to the school secretary and left her to deal with Harper and their lack of security.

I had other urgent business to attend to with Dean Natoli, Harper's ex-husband.

❧

My human costume of choice for the meeting was a tall blonde and buxom female, wearing spiked heels, a short red dress, and very little coverage over my prominent assets. The snake tattoo on my wrist was a nice touch. I thought the red lipstick was very becoming on my full lips. I flicked my long wavy hair over my shoulder and sashayed into the bar like a hundred-dollar-an-hour hooker.

Dean was drinking tequila shots. He turned and watched me slide on to a stool at the other end of the bar. The bartender poured me a wine. Dean finished his drink and swaggered over.

"Hey, baby, what's a good lookin' woman like you doing in a dive like this?" Dean asked, sliding onto the stool next to mine.

"Tell me does that line work on anyone?" I took a sip of the wine.

"Only on blondes with great figures like yours. You're an eleven out of ten for sure."

"I bet you're all talk. No action." I put down my glass and ran my eyes from his face to his crotch.

"Baby. Action-Man is my middle name."

"How about we go back to the facilities and you show me what you've got. Big boy."

"I gotta be somewhere soon."

"I'm sure it won't take long. But I'm worth it." I took another sip of my drink and licked my lips. Slowly. Dean's nostrils flared, considering the offer.

"That depends on how much."

"I'm feeling generous. "I'll cut you a deal. I'm in the mood for some Italian tonight. How about you? Hungry?"

"A woman who knows what she wants. It's my lucky day. Yeah, I'm hungry." Dean said. He slid off the barstool and headed for the disabled bathroom.

"Oh, you have no idea how lucky you are." I said quietly. I followed him.

As soon as the door was closed Dean leant his back against it and unzipped his pants. "You want to see what I've got. Here you are and it's all yours baby. Some fine Italian sausage. Get those gorgeous lips around this." He held what he thought was an impressive erection in his hand and offered it to me. I wanted to ask him if that was all he had.

I allowed my blonde, curvaceous female appearance to disappear. In its place I allowed my devil face, my horns and all the glory that is the devil's form to be shown for a few seconds. Dean screamed. I quietened him by grabbing his throat and taking a hold of his tongue between my thumb and forefinger.

"You arranged to kidnap a child today. Big mistake. I want to know why?" I let go of his tongue but kept my hand at his throat. He whimpered but spilled his guts in a rush.

"That kid's mine. Just look at him. Dark hair like mine, eyes like mine. He doesn't look like her or the guy she married. My ex-wife has kept him from me. She's pretending that he's only five years old but that kids knows things and does things that no kid of five can do. She must have had him when she was on the job. She lied, she said she didn't want kids, but she must have had that kid when she was in Europe. I want my kid."

"The child is not yours Dean. Believe me when I tell you this. Or not. You chose. But you are never to go anywhere near that family again, or I will find you, and hurt you. You're going to leave California and never return." I allowed him to see my devil face again. I licked his face, leaving a vivid red mark. I got up close and personal, my lips inches from his trembling ones. He closed his eyes.

"This." I said as I grabbed his now flaccid penis. "Is coming off. You don't have any need for it. And the balls. You don't seem to have any need for those either." I knew my grip was tight and my hands were as hot as hell. Any semen would be fried. I gave his balls a little tug. "Hopefully they find you and you won't bleed to death." He passed out.

I left him to consider what he had done, with all his bits still attached, on the cold bathroom floor. I was feeling generous. He was right, it was his lucky day.

16
HARPER

I didn't want to make a big deal about what happened today. Domenic was taking it all in his stride. I had to tell Richard of course, who wanted to go beat the hell out of Dean. Luc talked to him and calmed him down. I have no idea what he said, but I had learned to trust Luc and trust that he knew how to handle things in his own way. Luc told Richard to leave it to him and assured us that Dean was packing up his house and would be leaving California and not be bothering us in the future.

More than ever I had a feeling that Luc was communicating with Domenic in the same way he was communicating with me. I caught Domenic on more than one occasion glancing in Luc's direction, and then Luc smiled as if they shared a private joke.

I made a hot chocolate for both of us, before Domenic's bedtime and brought it to the table.

"Domenic come sit up here. I'd like to ask you a question and I want you to be honest with me. You won't get in trouble, but I really need to know if you are talking to Luc, without opening your mouth." We hadn't discussed telepathy but with a child as intuitive as Domenic, I found there were some things I didn't have to explain in great detail.

"Do you mean in my mind?"

"Yes, in your mind. Can you talk to him, and can he talk to you?"

"Yes."

"How long have you been able to do this?"

"Since I was born."

"But you couldn't speak then. How did you do it."

"I'm not sure. All I know is that Uncle Luc and I could exchange ideas. We're not hurting anyone."

"As I said you're not in trouble. I just wish I had known about it."

"You feel left out."

"Yes. I'm your mother and I should have known about this unique gift. Perhaps we won't tell your father though. It might scare him a little. Okay?"

"It's okay. I understand. I know that Uncle Luc can talk to you too. But you can't talk to him, can you? Not like me. You just think things and he can hear you."

"How do you know this? Can you read my mind too Domenic?"

"Yes."

"Since you were born?"

"Yes. But don't worry it's only when you hold me close or in your arms."

Dear God, what has the child heard me thinking? I couldn't worry about that right now, but at least I am armed with this knowledge in the future. A thought occurred to me.

"Did Luc ask you not to tell me? In case it frightened me, or I didn't understand?"

"Yes. Don't be angry with him. Uncle Luc explained to me that people wouldn't understand, and I would be made to feel like a freak. There are lots of things that I can do that other boys can't."

"Like what?"

"I can touch someone and tell if they are sick. I can't help them. But when I'm older I am going to learn. I'm going to be a doctor."

"Really? Well, I'm glad you've thought of joining such an honorable profession. I'm very proud of you."

"Can I tell my father I want to be a doctor? And Uncle Luc?"

"You certainly can. I'm sure they'll be proud of you too."

"Can I buy some medical books with my birthday money?"

"No need to spend your money. We'll go to the library. It will be lovely to have a doctor in the family."

I left Domenic reading the dictionary. It was his favorite pastime. I went in search of Richard.

"I don't want to alarm you, but it seems our son feels he has the ability to tell if someone is sick by touching them. He wants to be a doctor when he grows up, he tells me. So at least we know now which university to send him to."

"He might change his mind when he gets older. He's a bit young to be deciding don't you think?"

"They say some people are born to be in the medical profession. Maybe this is his path."

"When I was young, I wanted to be a cowboy. That didn't work out as planned."

"When I was young, I wanted to be a ballerina. But if he shows an interest, I will help him any way I can. He has asked for some medical books. I don't see any problem in allowing him to explore this interest."

❧

Since I had given up throwing myself off buildings, and became a mother, I had found another avenue for my creative pursuits. At least the action I encountered these days was all going on in my head and not at the expense of my body. Richard had taken a keen interest in movie production, and I wanted to be involved along with him, but in my own way. I enrolled in a script writing course. Richard's production company had bought the rights to an action movie set here in California, and I thought I would attempt to write a script as practice for my course.

Richard had taken Domenic to school to talk to the principal about the security issue the day before. Which left me free for the day to work from home. We hadn't involved the police, for which they were grateful. We hadn't explained to them exactly what happened either. Richard and Luc had decided to donate funds to the school for security cameras, for the safety of all the students. The school had already discussed putting new security measures in place. No one would be allowed to enter the school without authorization, during school hours. I knew Luc would be extra vigilant where Domenic was concerned.

I poured myself another coffee, returned to my desk, pulled the laptop nearer and tried to envision the action scene, as it was written in the book. I wanted the words to flow, but today I kept seeing other scenes in my head. Maybe it was time to give up and go with the flow. I could return to the action scene later. The sex scene called my name.

Morning at the cabin– In a clearing deep in the woods – a hot sunny day.

Tory appears at the cabin door. An axe slung over his wide shoulders, his hair disheveled, sweat on his brow. His chest is bare, jeans riding low on his hips, and cowboy boots.

TORY

I've chopped all the wood and stacked it against the porch. That should last you for a month.

Mae is drying a pot in the kitchen. Slings the dish towel over her shoulder and pours a large glass of water from the tap. She walks over to the door.

MAE

Here. You look hot.

Tory lowers the axe to his feet, takes the glass. A slow smile spreads across his face. He drinks some water, then pours the rest over his head. It soaks his hair and drips down his chest. Mae's eyes follow the rivulets of water as they descend over ridges of muscle. Mae reaches out, runs the tip of her finger though the water on his stomach, and pops her finger in her mouth.

TORY

Be very careful Mae. I've got a very short fuse.

Mae takes a step closer.

MAE

That's not the story goin' around town. I hear it's plenty big.

Tory pulls Mae into his arms . . .

"What happens next. I'm on the edge of my seat!" Luc asked, leaning over my shoulder.

"Hell Luc. I'm never going to get used to you doing that." I pushed back my chair and turned around. Luc was dressed in dark blue silk pajamas bottoms, slung low on his hips, and matching silk robe. His ridges of muscle were fully on show, a washboard stomach which descended right down to that delicious vee . . .

"You called?"

"No, I didn't."

"I beg to differ. You might have been typing Tory . . . but you were definitely picturing Luc. In all my bare-chested glory. I'm flattered. And here I am . . . to give you more inspiration." Luc fisted his hands on his hips, and tilted his head to the side, in classic super-hero pose. All we needed was the wind machine. And a costume of course. But I didn't really mind the flimsy costume he was wearing. It left nothing to the imagination.

"Thanks, but no thanks." I slammed the Laptop closed.

"I hope you saved that. It was getting good."

"I did save it. I'm practicing. I'd like to write the script for one of Richard's movies, if he'll give me a chance."

"Maybe you should stick to writing romance books."

"Are you telling me I'm pitching above my league, and not to play around with the big boys? Because that is a sexist remark if ever I heard one."

"No. I think you'd make a good romance writer. Honestly."

"Let's change the subject. Did you hear that Domenic wants to be a doctor?"

"Yes, he told me."

"You kept the fact quiet didn't you. The fact that you two have a secret language thing going on. I'm not thrilled about that. What else have you kept to yourself about Domenic?"

"Would you have understood if I had told you that I could communicate with your baby son? Would you have believed me?"

"Given you seem to have the ability to read my mind, and I can summon you with a thought, I shouldn't be at all surprised, should I? Anything's possible when it comes to you. I *have* learned that Luc."

"Does it bother you that I'm always with you Harper?"

"No. It's something I've accepted now."

"Come on, admit it, you rather like it. You'd miss me if I disappeared from your life."

"I admit you have become a part of the family."

"Okay, if you've finished with me, I'll pop back home to my . . . dinner date."

"It's morning."

"What can I say. She stayed the night. And then for breakfast. She's probably missing me now, so I'd better . . ."

"Go."

"You're mad."

"I'm not."

"Oh yes you are. Jealous? Just a tad?" Luc had a smirk on his face, which I wanted to slap.

"Don't be ridiculous."

"You're blushing."

"I'm hot. Go!" I pushed him toward the door, then realized he didn't need a door to exit. He disappeared out of my hands into thin air. Then I heard a low-pitched laugh and a whispered *"goodbye".*

17
LUC

I lingered in the shadow world between here and there. I was in no hurry to return to my bedmate. The truth was, although my own dwelling while on Earth was only a short distance away, I found comfort in being here, in this house where Harper had made a loving home for her family. This place was more home to me than any other place I spent my time. Where Domenic had been encouraged to learn, and where Richard was more in love with the woman he had chosen to be his partner, than when he proposed. At no point would I tell him that the decision to marry Harper had not been entirely his own. But needs must when you are designing a baby who needs more than one parent with the essential DNA to make him my replacement.

Harper settled back to her script writing. I had intended the comment about romance writing to be complimentary, because she does have a romantic soul. I should know. Souls are my forte. My beautiful friend would be waiting patiently for me in my king-sized bed, ready to do my bidding, ready to please me and I knew time was ticking away, and I should go. But I stayed a little longer to admire the way Harper's long blonde hair coiled over one shoulder, and thoughts drifted back to a day, a long, long time ago.

What can I say to Harper that she will understand? How do I explain the connection I have with her, with Richard and now with Domenic?

MEETING HARPER

TIME LINE 1972 – Harper is twelve.

The sky-blue Chevrolet Chevelle was on its side, its windows fractured, with petrol leaking onto the asphalt, when I arrived. A strong smell of death permeated the air. It was a smell very familiar to me. But that did not make it any easier to stomach. I wrenched the driver's door from its hingers and threw it on the road. The woman in the passenger seat had blood oozing from a head wound running down her neck and pooling beneath her on the door and shattered windowpane. Her lifeless eyes stared unseeing at the roof of the car. The man in the driver seat was badly hurt, his chest crushed, his legs caught beneath the twisted metal of the steering column. The engine had been pushed back into the footwell. His eyes were closed, and he was hovering between life and death. It would be minutes before he followed his wife to his forever home. However, Mrs Cole was going to a much better place. She had been a longsuffering wife to a man who cared more about appearances, than he did about kindness. More about money than he did about the people who worked for him. More about stealing from the poor in order to line his own pockets. Mr Cole was coming to Hell with me to be shown the error of his ways. This was the part of the job I enjoyed.

"Wake up." I shook him by the shoulder.

"Help. Help me." His voice quavered. Tears ran down through the blood on his cheeks.

"No can do. There's not much time left. I want you to know you've caused the death of two people on the road tonight. Your wife and the truck driver over there. All because you drank too much, and you were too stupid to let your sober wife drive home. That selfish act has added another few years of torture to a really long list of things you're going to regret in Hell."

I allowed my devil face to be seen. The modern tailored clothes disappeared, and I allowed Johnathon Cole to see me in all my devilish splendor for a few minutes. My fiery red skin, my legs and loins covered in course hair and my horns. He struggled, horrified at the sight before him, and tried to speak. I leant in closer to hear him beg for mercy. I could smell the petrol. It was stronger now. The fire was imminent. I changed back to my human guise.

"My daughter. Is she still alive? The back seat. Help my daughter."

I hadn't noticed the child on the back seat nearly covered in blankets. She was unconscious and had obviously been tossed around in the back of the car. I reached in and pulled the blankets off her. She was barely breathing. Her long blonde curls fanned out on the floor around her. She was so pretty she reminded me of an angel.

"Correction, the count is going to be three lives lost tonight because of your carelessness"

"Help her. She's just a child. Help her."

The fire ignited in the damaged engine and the cabin filled with smoke. I peeled back the metal rear door and lifted the girl to safety seconds before the car erupted in flames. I turned my back on the fiery wreck to protect her, laid her on the grass under the tree, and away from the carnage. She was such a delicate young thing, and so pale, she looked as if she had been a sick child. I laid my hand on her chest, over her heart. It was beating very irregularly. I knew I could help her. I had done this before, but never with someone so young. With lightning speed I cut open her chest with my finger, yanked open my shirt, dug my fingers beneath my ribcage and extracted a small piece of my own beating heart, which I placed on top of hers. The piece of my heart was full of dark red blood vessels pulsating with energy. Within moments it had grown and encased her small fragile one. I sealed up the incision in her chest. It would leave a small scar, but that couldn't be helped. The cavity in mine closed over in minutes. My heart would recover and heal quickly. That was one of the perks of being the Devil.

The girl was still unconscious and required proper medical help, and family to come to her aid. I placed her on the back seat of my Cadillac and headed for the nearest hospital. We passed a fire truck on the way to the accident. I informed the nurse who took her from my arms and placed her on a gurney, that she had been in a car accident. They rushed her into the Emergency Room.

I disappeared before anyone asked any questions. I had to admit I rather liked playing God. I watched over her every day in the guise of a nurse and on her last night I entered her room when she was asleep and promised her that I would check in on her from time to time.

I have kept my word for all these years. What I didn't expect was that one day, when she was all grown up, when she could jump from a building, or race a sports car through heavy traffic, or perform some death defying stunt to amuse the masses, my heart would beat faster whenever she was near, and that I would fall in love with Harper Cole.

18

LUC

OCTOBER 1998

Most humans have an alarm clock, which will awaken them day or night, from the deepest slumber. I had a built-in alarm, wired straight to my brain, and it went off now and then at the most inopportune moments, causing a great deal of angst in my private life. But can anyone who is the Devil have a private life, you may ask? Not as far as The Big Man is concerned. I'm directed to Hell without choice by this alarm, to greet those souls who need a little extra TLC, a little extra assurance that their suffering will never end in that Hell hole called purgatory. Sometimes I enjoy this part more than others. I like to witness them recoil in horror, I like to watch them backing away into a corner, afraid of my implements of torture. It is not until they see me and actually put two and two together that they realize they are not in some macabre nightmare. Then their Hellish experience officially begins. What can I say? No need to be modest. I'm good at my job.

. . .

However, if they were giving out awards for my attendance, I wouldn't be receiving one this year. I've been spending a lot of my time on earth with humans. Small humans actually. Since Domenic was taken from school in broad daylight, I made it my business to keep an eye on that school and its occupants. It wasn't hard to find out that the school secretary was dating Dean Natoli and supplied him with the details about Domenic's advanced intelligence. I wiped her memory of Domenic, of Dean and of her life here and made sure she found other employment in a maximum-security prison on the other side of the country. Now she knows what it feels like to be in a constant state of anxiety. The prisoners can't wait to show their appreciation of a beautiful female.

Domenic has made friends at school, and I'm proud of his progress. His gifts are only just beginning to reveal themselves. I don't know if he fully realizes how different he is from the children around him, gifted or otherwise. Due to my blood mixing with his father's and a piece of my heart living within Harper, he has some of my DNA. Therefore he has some very unusual traits. I've been able to communicate with him telepathically since birth, but I am not aware he can do that with anyone else.

When his mother touches him, Domenic can read his mother's mind. I can read Harper's mind whether I am with her or not. Whereas I have the ability to know a human's weaknesses by merely being in their presence, Domenic must touch someone to sense they are unwell. I have strength superior to most humans, but until now Domenic hasn't shown any signs of this. But time will tell if other traits appear.

It doesn't surprise me that Domenic wants to be a doctor. His parents are caring and nurturing, and he had never known anything other than kindness and love. I've seen the way they look at him, the way

Richard plays with him and the way Harper tirelessly explains and answers the many questions Domenic puts to her every single day. And if I have to admit it, I also enjoy spending time with him. His brain is expanding so fast, the knowledge that he soaks in like a sponge, far exceeds that of a child his age.

Richard is taking up yacht racing again, regaining his skill on the water, and trying to assist when possible if Domenic shows an interest in anything outdoors. He spends so much time reading and learning, his father would love him to experience the exhilaration in team sports and activities. He's also talking about buying a small yacht for the family and teaching Domenic to sail. Harper is all for it, her social life has taken a back seat since she became a mother. She is imagining cocktails at the Yacht Club and meeting people who enjoy the outdoor life, rather than the crew and production team who spend all their time indoors making movies. She is imagining sailing into the sunset, with Richard at the helm and Domenic by his side, learning to love the outdoors as much as she once did.

19

RICHARD

MID-OCTOBER 1998

I'd almost forgotten how much I loved being on the water. Thank god it all came back to me as soon as I climbed aboard. Invigorating fresh air, salt-water spray, and the camaraderie of working with a team of like-minded sailors. Magic. I want to bring Harper and Domenic out on a yacht to experience this. Who knows, we may have another sailor on our hands if I play my cards right. Domenic has shown a lot of interest in yachts and the sea of late. I found him watching a documentary and asking his mother an unusual amount of questions, even for him.

We sailed out of Del Ray Yacht club. The weather forecast had predicted only 10 to 15 knots, which is pretty benign. Irrespective of the weather we're on Lionheart, a Swan 48, which can handle any conditions thrown at her. We're fairly short on the crew, but as the forecast is light I can't see it being an issue.

Racing was well underway as we rounded the downhill mark, when the wind whipped up to 30 knots gusting to 40 knots. Even an experienced sailor given the conditions, would take precautions, so I tethered on to the jackstays. We have too much canvas up now, so I make my way up to the bow to do a quick sail change. The boat is currently heeling too much for the skipper and he's losing control. We don't have enough people on board who are capable and competent enough. I must do the job myself. I deploy a smaller headsail and the sail I pulled down, I lash to the lifelines, to stop it flogging in the wind. The crash of waves against the hull and the screeching wind is deafening.

As we round the mark, the boat dives down a wave. I find nothing underneath my feet but water, and I realize I've been thrown over the lifelines.

I grab onto the gunnel trying to reach the lifelines, but the waves are pulling me under. Every wave that hits the boat fills my wet weather gear and my sea boots. My body weight has now doubled and is being slammed repeatedly against the leeward side of the boat like a ragdoll. Tension on the tether increases exponentially. The water activated personal floatation device has self-deployed, but it's in my way. It's restricting my ability to reach the lifelines.

The saltwater is burning my throat and nasal passageways. In an attempt to get in as much air as possible, I'm gagging. Choking. I'm battling between trying to get air in and my body's need to expel all the foreign saltwater. I am losing this battle. How can I? I'm fifty-three, I'm in the prime of my life. I'm fit. I've been faced with more challenges than this in my stunt career.

Despite everything I'm losing strength and it has now been 90 seconds and I haven't been able to reach the lifelines. How has no one seen me, or not seen me? I am not on the boat. What are they doing? What about other boat crews?

I don't know how much longer I can do this. I give up trying to reach the lifelines, now I reach for my tether to release myself from the very safety I have been seeking. But I can't see. My PFD is obstructing my view. I feel my way and I try to pull myself against the tether and the boat to release myself, but I can't. The device that is meant to be saving me is in my way. I have no body strength left to pull against the tether clip to release myself. I reach for my sailing knife, which hangs around my neck on a line of spectra in a double fisherman's knot. But I can't reach it, as my PFD is deployed. If I could cut my tether, I could take my chances in the waves. Perhaps they would see me or turn the boat around to search . . . But I've run out of time.

All these safety measures are the things that are killing me, taking my life, taking away my ability to see Harper and Domenic again.

Well this is it! I have no strength left to fight. The ocean is calling me home.

Domenic, my son, take care of your mother.

Harper my love, my soulmate. Goodbye.

20

HARPER

Not long after I had tucked Domenic into bed, the doorbell announced a visitor. I checked through the window, before I opened the door. There were two uniformed officers on the front porch, one male one female.

"Yes, can I help you?"

"Mrs Erickson?" The male officer said.

"Yes, I'm Harper Erickson."

"Can we come inside ma'am?"

"Yes. Please come in." I stood aside and ushered the officers into the living room.

"Are you here alone ma'am?"

"No, my five-year-old son is in bed. What's this about?"

"Is there a relative, a friend you can call?" The female office asked.

"No. What's going on. You're frightening me."

"There was an accident. Your husband."

"Richard. Where is he? What happened? Is he in hospital?"

"No ma'am. I'm sorry to inform you, your husband had a boating accident at sea. He's deceased."

"No. It's a mistake. Not my husband. Richard knows the water.

He's a sailor. He would have taken precautions. There *has to be* some mistake."

"Is there someone we can call to be with you? A Neighbor? A friend."

"Luc." I thought about Luc. *Oh my god Luc.*

"What's his number?"

"No need." The floor is tilting. I'm finding it hard to breathe. Domenic appears by my side, his eyes big and round. He's taking hold of my hand. Tears as big as raindrops are falling on the floor. We summon Luc together.

The front door flew open. Luc appears, striding down the hall, concern etched in his expression. When he saw my tear stained face, he reached for me, and wrapped me in his arms. I held onto Domenic's hand. I thankfully laid my head against Luc's chest and held on tight as my world dissolved around me. No need to tell him what had happened, his expression said it all. But I wanted answers. He can move mountains, he can change his appearance, he can appear beside me in an instant, he can send me back in time. So, what happened? *Richard is dead, Luc. Why didn't you help him? Save him? Why?*

He placed his large hand over my cheek and ear, his thumb resting on my temple, and voices in the room became muted. All I could hear was my sobbing and the rapid beating of my heart. Which, the longer Luc held me to his chest, began to slow in time with his. Somehow his embrace calmed me a little. That plus the warmth of the tiny hand in mine. I closed my eyes and sank into the tears as they spilled over. The officers left, with assurances that they would return tomorrow. Luc took my hand and led me to sit beside him on the couch. I laid my head against his shoulder, and he let me cry. Domenic hopped up beside me, his head on my knee, his tears soaking through my skirt. I have no idea how long we stayed there, but when I opened my eyes, I was in bed, fully clothed, and the sun was streaming through the window. I could hear no sounds throughout the house. I stepped into the shower and allowed the hot water to wash over me. Exhaustion pulled at my limbs, making every movement awkward and slow. I felt one hundred years old. I saw Richard's razor and the tears began again. Richard was my anchor, my partner in life and work. The father of my son. What will happen now?

I dressed and ventured into the kitchen to find Luc quietly making eggs for Domenic's breakfast. They looked at each other, and then at me. They were communicating again. I felt left out.

"Good Morning. Would you like some breakfast? I'm making Domenic's favorite. Deviled scrambled eggs." Luc whipped some chili flakes into the egg and butter mixture. "Well the eggs are his favorite and the devilled part is my favorite, but he's chosen to try them. Don't worry it's not too hot for him."

"No. I'm not hungry."

"Coffee then. I've made a pot."

"Coffee? Yes. I'll have some coffee. Do you want some?"

"Sit, I'll get it. There's fresh juice on the counter. Pineapple and orange. Your favorite combination."

"Thank you for looking after Domenic." I kissed the top of my son's dark head, cupped his face in my hands and looked into his big eyes. "Are you alright?" I hugged him to my bosom. Then I slid onto the stool beside him.

"I'm alright." Domenic said.

"I'll call the school and let them know you'll be staying home."

"I've already done that." Luc said.

"Oh. Thank you. What did you say?"

"I explained the situation. I told them you'll notify the school when Domenic will return."

"Oh. Thank you. What time did those officers say they would be back? I think I heard them say I would be needed to identify Richard's body."

"I can do that for you." Luc said.

"No. I want to see him. Say goodbye. I need to . . . I won't believe it until. . . ". Tears welled in my eyes and splashed on the marble counter. Domenic took my hand in his and rubbed his thumb over the back of my hand. My tears slowed. I took a huge shuddering breath in and felt calmer. This child of mine was able to calm me by touch. Luc and Domenic exchanged a glance.

"You need to stop doing that. Talk to me."

"You're wondering why Domenic has the ability to calm you."

"Yes. I'm also wondering what else is going on. Because I know there's more to this than you two being able to communicate."

"Domenic has displayed a unique ability to sense when someone is sick, by touch. He has also been able to instill a level of calm, or peace, by touch. Much like I can. You've experienced this on occasions with me before Harper, have you not?"

"Yes I have. But why does my son have this ability?"

"It's complicated." Luc said.

"People only say that when they don't want to talk about it. Out with it. Why does my son have this ability?"

"Domenic has some of my DNA."

"What? Don't talk rubbish. Richard is Domenic's father. . . *was* Domenic's father."

"It's a long story"

"I have time. Tell me what's going on. What did you do to my son?"

"I didn't do anything to him. This goes back many years. Before you met Richard."

"I'm listening."

"Many years ago, when Richard was a young man, he tried to stop someone attacking me, and in the process, he was injured. He was stabbed. The knife penetrated his liver and he was bleeding very badly. No one had ever put themselves at risk for me before. I was grateful and I helped him by giving him some of my blood. Just a few drops into the wound, to help heal his injury. But my blood is very powerful, and he survived and grew strong and became more of a man than he would ever have been without my DNA. He became a stunt actor. He became a dare devil, an action hero, a clever and resourceful businessman."

"So, you helped him, and your DNA has now been passed on to Domenic. Is that why he is connected to you?"

"Yes."

"So then tell me why I'm connected to you. It's not just about the deal we had. Is it?"

"No. You're connected to me because you were also injured, and I helped you too."

"Injured in what way?"

"You were in a car accident when you were twelve. The same accident where you parents were killed."

"Yes. I remember."

"Do you remember the night nurse in the hospital who came to your room and read to you when you couldn't sleep?"

"Yes. I remember. Wait. How do you . . . was that you?"

"Yes."

"Why?"

"I promised you I would check up on you."

"There is more to this story. Tell me."

"You were a sick child, with a bad heart. I helped you."

"How?"

"I gave you a small piece of mine."

"You gave me a piece of your heart. I don't believe you."

"You have a small crescent shaped scar on your chest. I had to open you up. It left a small scar. If you check under Richard's rib cage you will find the same crescent shaped scar."

"Let me get this clear. You donated parts of your body to Richard and I, so we have your DNA."

"A tiny bit. Yes"

"And Richard and I were both dare devils. Was that why we both were drawn to dangerous stunts?"

"It seems that way."

"Oh . . . hang on . . . you engineered this? You brought us together, you told me as much. You wanted us to have a child together. You engineered a child. Domenic is . . . is. . . "

"Genetically, related to me. Yes."

I stood up and paced to the window to think about what I had just learned. I turned and looked at Domenic who was calmly eating his breakfast, and then at Luc.

"He knows." I said.

"Yes, he's known for a very long time."

"I'm finding this hard to believe. Your heart is beating inside me?"

"A little bit of it. Yes."

"And that's why you can read my thoughts?"

"That, and I know when you're troubled, upset or anxious."

"And when I'm near you, and you touch me, I'm calm. And when I'm near Domenic, and he touches me, I'm calm."

"Yes. I believe that's the case."

"What else?"

"What do you mean."

"What else are you hiding from me?"

"Nothing else."

"Why should I believe you?"

"Have I ever done anything to hurt you?"

"You could've saved Richard."

"No, I didn't have the same connection to Richard. He had a few drops of my blood. I couldn't hear his thoughts. I couldn't tell if he was troubled, upset or anxious. I didn't know he was in trouble at sea."

"This is all too much to take in."

"Don't be upset Mom. It will be alright. You'll see." Domenic said.

"Out of the mouths of babes. I hope so Domenic. Because right now I am feeling very lost, and very tired."

"Drink your juice." Luc said.

"I don't want my damned juice." I threw the glass across the counter. Everything slowed down. Luc reached out and caught it before it hit the wall, and in slow motion the juice returned to the glass, and the glass returned to the counter. Time speed back up again.

"Neat trick. Can you go back in time to before my husband was killed and fix that too?"

"He's dead. I cannot resurrect the dead, Harper. That's not in my job description. Even if I went back in time, Richard's time was up, believe me. His path was set before you and I came together. You have to find a way to get over this."

"How do you know this? You're not God."

"No. But I do have a direct line to that department. And my information has been confirmed. Nothing I would've done would've stopped this."

"And I have to take your word for it?"

"I have never lied to you Harper."

"You've lied by omission. You've kept things from me. You've engineered a baby for god's sake. My baby."

"And we had a deal if you remember. You're not an innocent in all this. You shook my hand. You committed to seeing this though."

"I didn't know what was at stake. And I fell in love . . . oh. . . please don't tell me that wasn't real."

"It was real. I just brought the two people together I knew would be good for each other. Who would make good parents."

"Parents who would give you the child you wanted! The child you designed. I want you to leave. I can't even look at you right now. You've kept things from me. I feel used. Betrayed. I feel like some chess piece on a giant board game."

Luc's eyes bored into mine. I could feel tentacles reaching into my mind, searching, probing. And what he would have found was anger and betrayal and disgust, and a million "what if" questions I was asking myself.

"If that's how you really feel. I'm gone."

Luc disappeared before my eyes. The enormity of what he had told me began to sink in. I had been a sick child, spending long periods of time in the hospital with congenital heart disease. But after the car accident I hadn't had a sick day in all that time. When I had an injury on set, I healed pretty quickly. The pregnancy had been perfect, apart from some strange cravings. The fact that the three of us are all linked began to make sense. Domenic slid off the stool and came to stand beside me. He took my hand.

"Don't be mad at Uncle Luc, Mom. He's trying very hard to help us. He's upset about Dad too, and he's been explaining things to me. He understands me better than anyone else. Other people would not understand what he's done, and why. But I understand. I know who he is, and I'm not afraid."

"Oh Domenic. You are so young to be weighed down with all this."

"I'm not like any other six-year-old boy Mom, trust me. Trust Uncle Luc. He loves us." Domenic took my hand, and I knew what he was doing.

I pulled my hand away. "No. I have to think clearly. I need some time alone. Can you go to your room for a little while, please honey?"

"Sure. If that's what you want." Domenic left the room and closed his bedroom door quietly behind him.

I sank onto the couch and closed my eyes. My world had shifted in the last twenty-four hours and I was finding it hard to come to terms with what this would mean for me and for Domenic. But I had to pull myself together, for my son.

I made the call to arrange to identify my husband's body. I had never felt more alone in my life.

21
HARPER

I can honestly say the days bleed together now, and the nights are long and unbearable without Richard in my bed. I am coping with the school run, the office and the grocery shopping but I am not coping without someone to talk to when Domenic goes to bed. Truth be told I have lost two very important people in my life. I miss Luc. But I am still too upset and confused to reach out to him. Even thinking about him now means he knows, but he also knows that I am still hurting, and he won't come to me. I'm not ready to forgive him. Halloween, Thanksgiving and Christmas came and went, and celebrations were hollow. But I had to do something for Domenic's sake. Taking down the Christmas tree and putting away the ornaments gave me more pleasure than putting it up. If only I could pack up and fold away all my anxiety and concerns as easily.

The female police officer had given me the name of a grief counselor and I am ready to talk to her. Jaime Gordon's office is only a short walk from my building, and I've scheduled a session before I pick up Domenic.

"Please come in Mrs Ericson. Take a seat. Would you like some water before we begin?"

"No thank you, I'm okay."

"As we've already talked briefly on the phone, I would like to talk in more detail now if you're comfortable? May I call you Harper."

"Yes. That's fine."

"Good. You may call me Jaime. How are you feeling now that it's been several weeks since your husband has passed?"

"I'm tired all the time. I find it hard to concentrate after I put my son to bed. I usually go to bed too. But I'm not sleeping."

"Would you like me to prescribe something to help you sleep?"

"No. I don't want to become addicted to meds."

"Can I recommend some tapes? Some breathing exercises?"

"Yes, that might be better."

"How is your son. Domenic, isn't it? How is he managing?"

"He's handling this better than I am. He's a bright child."

"I understand he's gifted."

"Yes."

"Gifted children are often emotionally better able to cope with these situations." Jaime said.

"I don't want to use him as a crutch for my suffering. I wanted him to have as near to a normal childhood as possible, given his intelligence. He's already up against so many hurdles. Even the children at his special school find him too different."

"Is there a financial burden on you now?"

"No. Richard had life insurance. He made sure we were well taken care of if anything happened. But I've gone back to work during school hours. I have very good office staff, and they're taking care of the business very well. But I'm needed there. I also think it's doing me good to get back to work."

"Yes. I agree. Having a purpose is very important. I sense you are also very angry about something. Are you blaming Richard for his death? Or are you blaming yourself?"

"No. I'm not blaming Richard. Maybe I am blaming myself. I've also been angry at a close family friend. Domenic's godfather actually."

"Why is that?"

"He kept things from me. Things he knew about Richard."

"But Richard has passed now Harper. Perhaps it is time to let all that anger go?"

"Maybe."

"You're not convinced, are you? Let me tell you that what you are experiencing is normal. You are up against a grief roadblock. You are going over and over things in your mind, and the end is not in sight. There is no specific time period for this. It will end when it is right for you. Feeling anger, guilt, regret is normal. But at some stage you will have to forgive. Forgive Richard for leaving, forgive yourself for not being able to prevent it, forgive your family friend for keeping things from you. You need to forgive to move on. When the time is right."

Jaime's words echoed in my brain. Perhaps I was blaming everyone for Richard's death. Blaming myself for not going with him that day. Blaming Luc, when it wasn't Luc's fault. Maybe it was time to forgive. Maybe then I could get some sleep.

22

LUC

LATE FEBRUARY 1999

I stayed in between the here and there, the shadow world where I could watch and listen, and still keep my eye on Harper and Domenic. Occasionally I had to pop over to the dark side to deal with business. But really, how could Harper expect me to just leave her when she needed me more than ever now. Understandably I was giving her time to adjust. Time to see that she was strong enough to manage a business and a family by herself. Well almost by herself. I would of course, help when needed. I lived so close that I was practically on her doorstep, I could be there, in her kitchen, in a matter of seconds. She would see how much assistance I could be to Domenic. He needs his Godfather more than ever now. He needs a strong male figure in his life.

We've been talking at night. Oh, I know his mother said to leave the house. But she cannot stop me talking to Domenic, or Domenic talking to me. It's as natural to him as breathing. He's told me he's worried about his mother, but she's going to see a counselor. I didn't tell him I know all about the counseling sessions. I didn't tell him that Jaime Gordon and I are very well acquainted. Jaime has another occupation, other than a conventional role as a grief counselor. She is a very well-paid Dominatrix in a Hellfire Club, where I'm a full paid up member. She called on me a long time ago to make her favorite pastime more pleasurable. Being possessed by the devil is not always as bad as everyone thinks. It sometimes does have benefits. I entered Jaime's body to engage with Harper and give her the best advice available . . . which was to forgive me. Quickly. When I slipped out of Jaime's body, after Harper left her consulting rooms, Jaime had the best orgasm of her life. I left her gasping for breath on the couch. Believe me when I tell you I didn't have to twist her arm to persuade her to participate. We are old friends when it comes to sensual pleasure. Jaime gets her kicks in all sorts of deviant ways, in complete contrast to her socially acceptable day job. Needless to say, I respect the Hell out of the woman. She is a remarkable human.

I need Harper to get over this lethargy, get over this sadness in her life and realize that it's best to move on. Perhaps I could give her something to look after. A puppy. Yes, a puppy would do her and Domenic good. Or maybe a fully-grown dog might be better, to look after *them*. I remember talk of a dog somewhere in their past, and they never got around to it. I will have to find the right dog of course. A trustworthy, obedient specimen. A dog that I can rely on to protect the two people who have become very important to me.

MARCH 1999

I rang the doorbell and instructed Max to sit with a hand action. He obeyed. Max was a sleek, black, four-year-old Doberman, with an impeccable pedigree. His owner had recently passed away, and he was in need of a new family. The animal shelter had assured me of Max's intelligence and good nature. But they did not need to convince me as

I had investigated Max's history and was sure he would be the perfect family pet and diligent protector for Harper and Domenic.

Harper looked out the side window before she opened up the door. Did I detect a look of relief?

"Hello Luc. I should've guessed you'd turn up tonight."

"Because?"

"I'd been thinking it was time."

"Time to . . . forgive me?"

"Yes."

"Wow I wasn't expecting you to agree so quickly. But let it be noted I am thrilled."

Who's your friend?"

"This is Max. Shake Max."

Harper took Max's raised paw and shook it. "Good manners Max. Come in Luc. . . and Max"

Domenic came rushing through the house.

"Mom, a dog. Is this your dog Uncle Luc?"

"No. I brought Max for you Domenic. If your mother says it's okay. He's very loyal, and protective."

"A dog Luc? I don't know if we can have a dog." Harper said.

"Why? It will be good for Domenic to have an animal to care for. Teach him responsibility. Animals give unconditional love. See."

Domenic was kneeling bedside Max, patting him, giggling like any other five-year-old and enjoying head nudges and licks.

"I've got food and bedding and all he needs in the car. If you say he can stay, I'll bring it in. If not, I'll have to take him back to the shelter. And I don't know how long he'll be there before someone picks him again. They euthanize dogs after a time, you know. Large dogs take longer to find a good home. Some people don't trust Dobermans, but I can assure you Max is the perfect house guest." I was relying on her soft heart to say yes.

"Why was he in the shelter?"

"His elderly owner passed away. Max was a service dog. He's well trained, knows lots of commands. I'll feel better knowing he's here with you. No one will get past Max. Will they boy?" I snapped my fingers and Max returned to my side. I signaled to sit. I laid my hand on his head as reward. He sat up very straight, ears alert, watching me, waiting for the next command.

"Mom. Can we keep him? Please. I'll walk him. I'll feed him. He can sleep with me."

"No Domenic he's not sleeping with you."

"So we can keep him?"

"On trial. If he displays any negative qualities, he's out of here."

"Cool Mom. Max you can stay. Come on boy."

Max did not move from my side. "Go on. Go to your new master, Max. Take care of him." Max glanced up at me, then joined Domenic, and together they walked into Domenic's bedroom.

"I mean it Luc. If that dog does anything, nips Domenic's fingers, or destroys anything in the house, I'll be asking you to take him back to the shelter."

"Trust me. Max will be good for Domenic and for you. He's very protective. Show him love, show him who's boss, and you'll be fine. I've told Max all about you. He knows what his job will entail in your home."

"What his job will entail?"

"Yes he has a job to do. I expect him to be a friend to Domenic, but I expect him to be the best protector he can be, to you both. He will guard you with his life. He has assured me of that?"

"You can communicate with the dog? . . . no don't answer that. . . of course you can."

"It has its advantages. Don't knock it."

"I wasn't going to. I will trust that Max will follow your orders. Domenic is already sold, so I will give Max a chance. Would you like to stay for dinner? Lasagna and salad?"

"Yes. I've missed your cooking."

"I'm sorry I was upset and angry with you. I've missed you. It's been very hard losing Richard, and lonely, but I was also missing my friend, and feeling very sad about that too."

"We're friends?"

"Yes, we're friends Luc. Regardless of who you are, and how you came into my life, I think of you as a friend. Richard thought of you as a close friend, more like a brother really. We never had a big family, and now that there's just the two of us . . . I'm glad you're back. I know Domenic has missed his Uncle Luc."

"You've brought a tear to my eye. No one has ever called me a friend before."

"There is one thing that I would ask. When you and Domenic are with me, please don't shut me out. Don't make me feel that I'm not in the same league as you both. Talk out loud. Okay. Private conversations make me uncomfortable. It's like two people taking in a foreign language when you're in the room, and you can't understand them, but you're sure they are talking *about* you."

"Understood."

Harper approached and put her arms around my waist. She laid her head on my chest. I raised my arms and wrapped them around her, a little awkwardly I must admit. I had to keep myself in check to stop that tear I had in my eye from falling. I had the strangest feeling of coming home. I had missed this, my surrogate family, I had not realized how much until this moment. Harper raised her face to mine and kissed my cheek. She smiled at me and in turn I found myself beaming at her. We walked to the kitchen with her arm linked in mine.

"Pour us some red wine and help me make the salad. The lasagna is nearly ready."

"Yes ma'am."

Harper yelled down the hall. "Domenic. Wash your hands and bring Max back to the kitchen. Dinner's nearly ready."

And so it began. A new era. A new norm with Harper and Domenic and now Max. I left him pretty explicit instructions when I bid them all goodnight and reluctantly returned home.

Domenic and I talked before he went to sleep. He was thrilled to have Max, and Max was thrilled to have a secure home, with people to love and protect. I was thrilled to be back in their lives. A win-win situation for all of us.

23

HARPER

MARCH 1999

The dreams about Luc began again last night. Recurring dreams that I had after Domenic was born, where I was with Luc in another dimension, and he was kissing me, and he was touching me. But we never actually got down to the nitty gritty. I was in a complete lather when I woke up. Now was not the time to delve into why this was happening again. I had to prepare breakfast and get Domenic off to school.

When I turned around from the fridge and saw Luc sitting at my kitchen counter, impeccably dressed and calmly drinking a cup of coffee, I jumped out of my skin and nearly dropped the bottle of orange juice.

"My God, Luc."

"No. . . I'm your Devil. . . but you can call me "My Lord of Darkness" if you like."

"Never gonna' happen."

"Suit yourself."

"What are you doing here?"

"I came to check up on Max. Make sure everything was running smoothly."

"Domenic has taken Max out to walk around the garden before breakfast. He's enjoying having him. Thank you. It's been a while since I've seen my son smile as much."

"You're telling me I did something right?"

"I guess I am."

"We need to make note of this momentous occasion."

"Now you're being condescending."

"It's not every day you thank me. *And* tell me I did something right. I'm making the most of it."

"Smug does not suit you with that complexion. Go back to being apologetic."

"Don't pretend you haven't missed my teasing. I can see a smile trying to break free, and a mischievous twinkle in your eye."

"The only mischievous twinkle is in *your* eye. Now I have to get on with making breakfast and getting Domenic off to school."

"Would you like me to take him?"

Domenic burst through the sliding doors, with Max at his heel. "Mom, can he? Can uncle Luc take me to school with Max? I can show him to my friends. I can show them all the tricks Max can do. He can sit, and he can shake, and he can drop, and he can fetch. He does everything I tell him. Can uncle Luc take me and Max?"

"Luc?" I asked.

"Sure, we can take Max along for the ride." Luc said

"Go wash your hands then hop up here and have your breakfast."

Domenic disappeared and Max followed.

"You're sure you have the time to take them? You don't have to, you know? I bet you have more important things to do."

"You and Domenic are important in my life."

Luc locked eyes with me, and I felt the tentacles reaching out, searching my brain for what? Validation that he was also important in our lives. Surely, he knows this already. I often get frustrated and annoyed with him, but there is no doubt he's a big part of what matters to Domenic and to me.

I poured milk into the bowl of cereal on the counter top. "Domenic, come get your cereal."

"When I bring Max back, perhaps you would like to go for a drive with me?" Luc asked.

"Why."

"To feel the wind blowing in your hair, to feel the sun on your face. I'll put the top down."

"It's a bit chilly out there."

"Wear a coat. Come on. It will do you good to get out."

"Go on Mom. Luc has heated seats in his car." Domenic shoveled cereal into his mouth, in a hurry to get to school, no doubt to show Max off.

Domenic, Max and Luc left, and I quickly dressed for the outing. I was applying lipstick in front of the bathroom mirror when Luc returned. I heard the car pull into the drive. I walked to the lounge and watched through the window until he secured Max in behind the fence and gave him clean water. His movements were measured, his body athletic as he strode back to the house. Butterflies fluttered in my stomach at the thought of an outing with Luc. I shook my head at my imaginings. *Stop it. He's your friend, nothing more.*

We drove from Santa Monica, down the Pacific Coast Highway to Newport Beach and back and I felt lighter somehow, refreshed and able to see a light at the end of the tunnel. There had been too many gray days in my life lately.

"How is it that you seem to know what to do to make me feel better?" I asked.

"No one can make you feel better. I am only providing the means for you to see beyond the confines of your four walls. There's a big world outside, and you have to get back into it. I must admit I like seeing you smile again."

"No matter what, you never give up on me."

"And that surprises you?"

"Yes. What's in it for you?"

"You said a short while ago that we were friends. That surprised me, because as far as I know, the Devil didn't have any friends."

"Richard also thought of you as a friend. He thought enough of you to want you to be Domenic's Godfather."

"A role which has surprised me. Domenic is an interesting young man."

"He's growing up fast. It's been lovely to see him behaving like a normal kid with Max. I know these are early days yet, but you did a really good thing bringing Max into our lives. I hope I'm not going to regret that admission."

We pulled up in front of the house. I didn't want this outing to end. Luc and I had been through some tough times, and I had found it hard to forgive him in the past. But if we were to continue on this positive footing, I had to let go of all that bitterness.

"Thank you for taking the time this morning. I needed the fresh air. I needed the sun and the sky and the beach views. But most of all I needed to spend time with my friend." I leant across the car and kissed Luc on the cheek. As I pulled back our eyes locked. Thoughts were whirring around in my head, but the one that was most consistent, was the one that wanted his lips on mine. I jumped out of the car before I turned that thought into action, and risk rejection again.

24

LUC

Another day in the life of the devil.

I followed the scrawny homeless man named Jake, as he dodged in and out of doorways. His filthy black bedraggled clothing and wool cap made him practically invisible on this cold and windy night. He could not see me, but had he turned around he would only have seen some leaves being torn from the trees by a gust of wind and scattered along the dark sidewalk. Jake in turn was following a smartly dressed elderly man named Jeffrey Rusden, who had appeared from a drugstore with a package under his arm. Jeffrey was a good customer of the drugstore in his neighborhood and required regular pain medication for his arthritis. Tonight, he was also picking up sleeping pills and medication for his bed-ridden wife. I knew this because I was standing next to him in the drug store when he collected his prescription orders.

I had been sent to this location tonight to monitor the behavior of a serial attacker, who targeted the elderly and infirm, and make sure he got his comeuppance.

The arthritic old man had difficulty negotiating the wide stone steps from the sidewalk to his building and made his way slowly to the top. He paused on the stoop two feet away from his front door to collect his breath. The homeless man sprinted up the steps and grabbed the frail gentleman. Jake grappled with Jeffrey and yanked the package free from his arms. Jake pushed the old man and just as Jeffrey was losing his footing and would have toppled down the steps headfirst, I froze time, and moved Jeffrey to the safety of his front step. I took the package from Jake's grip and placed it at Jeffrey's feet. Then I grabbed a handful of the back of Jake's sweatshirt, flew up to the roof and dangled him off the edge on the other side of the building overlooking the alley. I unfroze time.

Jake flayed about, panicking, no doubt wondering how he had arrived in this precarious position. He really was the scum of the earth. I had been informed he had maimed and caused the death of some elderly people unable to defend themselves. It was time he paid for his sins.

"How do you like being the one who's afraid. You don't know if I will let you go. You don't know who I am. You don't know what I want of you. Do you?" I hissed in his ear.

"No."

"Just like the poor souls you've attacked. For money. Or drugs. Or booze. You didn't know them. You didn't care. You tossed them aside once you stole from them, like the scum that you are."

"Let me go." Jake pleaded.

"Oh. . . let you go? With pleasure." I let Jake go and he plummeted to the ground. I watched his body hit the concrete and heard his skull crack. In the few moments before he died, I informed him where he was going to spend the rest of eternity. With the other low lives who deserved to be in Hell.

25

HARPER

MID-APRIL 1999

I asked Luc to babysit Domenic for a few hours. Max and Domenic were playing on the deck beside the pool. I had made a tuna casserole for dinner, with garlic bread, two of Domenic's favorites. I served up the food and called him in to eat. Luc let himself in through the front door and came to sit at the table.

"Any left for me?"

"Yes, there's plenty. I'll get another plate."

"Where's your plate? Why aren't you eating."

"I'm going out for dinner."

"With whom."

"Paul Stone. One of the producers who worked with Richard on his last movie."

"I thought you said you had work to do, and that's why I'm babysitting."

"This is work. I want to be involved in the movie that Richard was working on with Paul."

"So, you're going out to eat with this Paul guy to persuade him to let you take over Richard's share?"

"Yes."

"And you're dressed to impress to use your womanly charm to get him to agree."

"That probably sums it up."

"Not going to happen."

"What do you mean?"

"He won't let a woman take over Richard's role. He has no time for women other than in the. . ." Luc hesitated and glanced at Domenic. "boudoir" He has a reputation."

"You do know I understand French, don't you?" Domenic said, lifting another forkful of pasta to his mouth.

"Since when?" I asked.

"Last Sunday." Domenic said. "There was a French documentary I wanted to watch, so I took an online course."

"How much French?' Luc asked.

"Enough to know you mean bedroom. And sex. You're not going to have sex with him are you Mom?"

"No. I am *not*. Thanks Luc." I folded my arms and glared at Luc.

"I don't want you anywhere near this sleaze ball. I forbid it." Luc said, banging his first on the table.

"Oh, *you* forbid it. That's rich. You are *not* my husband. And I am perfectly capable of looking after myself." I cleared away the serving spoons and washed my hands. "I'm going to get ready. If you don't want to look after Domenic, I can call Ruby and drop him off at her house on the way. I'm sure she'd love to have him for a few hours."

❧

I was glad Luc had relented and decided to stay. Domenic would sleep in his own bed and Luc would . . . actually I had no idea what Luc would do. I'd never asked him to babysit at home for me before. He's taken Domenic out for the day, to his house, or to the movies and paid for entertainment, but I've never specifically asked Domenic what they did when Luc spent time with him. They were happy in each other's company, that's all I cared about.

Paul was already seated when I arrived at the restaurant. The Maître D' escorted me to the table. Paul rose, hugged me, kissed my cheek and gave me his condolences. Again. He lingered a little too long in that hug. Maybe what Luc said had merit. Or maybe it was my insecurities. I'd become uncomfortable with physical contact since Richard has passed. So many people felt the need to hug or kiss or take my hand. I wanted to yell "Just leave me alone. I'm fine thank you. No need to touch me." But I didn't want to cause a scene.

The conversation went well all through dinner. I was thrilled when Paul said he would consider my proposal, and suggested we look at some manuscripts back at his place, which wasn't too far from the restaurant. He paid the bill and I followed him in my car. As we drove, I noticed dark clouds had formed above the city, and it looked like a storm was gathering.

"How about a glass of wine to celebrate our collaboration?" Paul moved behind the bar in the corner of the living room.

"A small one. I have to get home soon." I said. I glanced out the window and saw rain was falling. Thunder rolled over the earth and flashes of lightning split the sky immediately. The storm was above us.

Paul removed a half full bottle of white wine from the bar fridge, took down a wine glass from the shelf, and began to pour.

"Stop. That's enough."

"There's hardly enough there to enjoy the taste." He added a little more and returned the cork to the bottle.

"Aren't you having any?"

"I'll have a scotch." He selected a short cut crystal glass from the shelf, added some whiskey and dropped in two cubes of ice, from an ice bucket.

"Let's sit down and we can go over the project."

As we walked to the couch, Paul placed his hand on my lower back and then slid his hand lower to the curve of my buttock. I stepped away out of his reach and sat down. He sat beside me. He pulled two manuscripts toward our side of the coffee table and handed me one. I placed my drink on the table and placed the manuscript on my knee to read. As he moved forward on the couch to reach across me and pick up the other manuscript, his thigh pushed against mine. I bent my head and studied the pages.

"It must be lonely without Richard. I bet you could do with some company."

"Actually, I have company. Our son, Domenic."

"I meant someone you could talk to, share things with."

"I have friends for that. Which one of these manuscripts would you like to look at first?"

"I was hoping we might come to some arrangement." Paul had edged closer. "You look like a woman who knows how to have a good time. I heard you were a stunt actress on Mindy Michaels films back in the day. She sure knew how to throw a party."

"I wasn't invited to her parties. I was the hired help."

"Booze, drugs and rock and roll at those parties, so I heard." Paul turned toward me, took a sip of his scotch and licked his lips. "Pool parties, skinny dipping, cocaine snorting parties." His eyes lowered to my modest cleavage. The dress I wore showed very little, but his eyes seemed to be boring right through the fabric.

"I would say a lot of that was hype for the media." I said.

"I've got some good stuff here if you're interested?"

"No. I don't do drugs. Now, about this manuscript . . .?"

Paul had moved even closer on the couch. I knew the moves and reached down and lifted my drink to my lips, to avoid his. Paul Stone had a look of a man who wouldn't easily take no for an answer. It was time to cut my loses and leave.

A huge crash of thunder and flashes of lightning illuminated the room through the archway and had me jumping up off the couch, and slopping my wine over my dress. Several short sharp flashes of light appeared to be coming from the front door. A red mist wafted down the hall into the living room. The air warmed up to a thousand degrees, and Luc appeared marching through the red fog, dressed from head to foot in black. I barely recognized him. The tops of two huge ivory wings, sprouting from his shoulder blades nearly touched the cathedral ceiling. They were glistening with rain. His black hair was slicked back, his eyes glowed blood red, and his nostrils flared. His fury was palpable. He flicked open his wings, the room shook with the sudden vibration, and raindrops flew over all the surfaces. His presence filled the room. All of the oxygen seemed to have been sucked out, making it hard to breathe. Electricity sparked from his hands as he clenched and unclenched his fists at his sides. He pointed at my glass.

"Don't drink that." Luc yelled. A bolt of lightning shot from his fingertip and the glass flew from my hand, hit the tiled floor and shattered. He turned his gaze on Paul, who was standing beside me . . . "Get away from her." Luc snarled. He took two giant steps toward Paul, grabbed his throat and lifted him off the floor. Luc held him aloft with one hand, and Paul thrashed about trying in vain to release Luc's grip. Luc wasn't even looking at him. He was looking at me, with obvious anger etched into his expression.

"Luc. What are you doing?" I had never seen this side of him before. The full Devil persona.

"I warned you not to go near this low life. But you didn't listen."

"You can't tell me what to do."

"Can't I? You're the mother of my Godson. You have responsibilities. Taking drugs and being involved in heaven knows what with this deviant . . . "

"There are no drugs . . ."

"You are so naïve . . . he spiked your drink. Give it about ten minutes in your system and you would've done whatever he wanted. With no memory of the events"

"No." I said.

"You don't believe me?" He shook Paul and his teeth rattled. "Tell her!" Luc snarled. "Did you spike her drink?"

"Yes." Paul whimpered. He was turning purple.

"Louder!"

"Yes." Paul attempted to yell and coughed and spluttered instead. His feet were high off the ground and he was twitching.

"Put him down. You're choking him."

"That *is* the purpose of my hand around his throat."

"You can't do this."

"Oh, but I can, and I will. You are one of many. The end of a long list of women he has used and thrown aside. But tonight, it ends."

"Please, Luc, don't do this."

"Harper. You're forgetting who I am. This. Is. My. Job. He has caused Hell on earth for many. He chose the wrong person to try it with tonight. Now it's his turn to suffer."

Luc lowered Paul to his stand on his own two feet but kept a hold of him. He dragged him to the bar to retrieve the bottle of wine, uncorked it and poured it into Paul's mouth. He gagged and spluttered, but a fair amount of the alcohol went down his throat. Luc patted his pockets, found more pills, stuffed a handful into Paul's mouth, and topped them off with more wine from the bottle. He held his mouth closed until he swallowed. He clawed at Luc's hand until he dropped him. Paul gasped for air.

"Now watch. *Watch!*"

Paul twitched and began to fit.

"Stop it. Please."

"This is what he was going to give you. Rohypnol. The date-rape drug. Oh, maybe not as much, but you wouldn't have remembered anything tomorrow. There may have been some other pills in his pocket, which I stuffed in his mouth, judging by the seizures."

"I can't look."

"Go home. Get in your car and go home to your son. Forget you were ever here."

"You expect me to go home and just forget about this?"

"Yes. I expect you to go home . . . and let me do my job!"

"I . . ."

"Now Harper!" Luc barked the order.

. . .

With tears in my eyes, I grabbed my purse and car keys and ran out the front door without a backward glance. Luc's avenging, protective angel had shocked me tonight. But there was a part of me that was turned on by it at the same time. Just how sick had I become?

I was in the car when I remembered that Luc was supposed to be babysitting. Who was looking after my son? I was glad I didn't live far away. I raced through the streets and rushed inside my house to find Luc . . . the Luc I knew and was familiar with. . . reading a book, looking relaxed, with his feet up on the sofa. I checked the bedroom and Domenic was sound asleep, and Max lay beside the bed. Max lifted his regal head when I approached, tilted his head from left to right, and back again, and resumed his comfortable position. Everyone and everything in the house was quiet and calm. I was the only one in turmoil. I marched back to the lounge room.

"When you were out showing off your avenging angel. Who was looking after Domenic?" I said through clenched teeth.

"Max."

"You left my child with a *dog*?"

"I left him asleep, with the best guard dog possible, for approximately twenty minutes."

"A *dog*, Luc. What if something had happened? What if he had wakened up?'

"Then Max would have let me know, and I would have been back here in milliseconds."

"You have no idea. You don't leave a child you have been given to care for, to a dog."

"I thought that *you* were in more danger than the sleeping child. If I could have sent Max to do my job for me, then I would've."

"I'm having trouble with *everything* that happened tonight. I feel as if I've stepped into an alternate universe."

"Come sit down." Luc swung his legs down onto the floor and patted the sofa beside him. I sat. Ramrod straight and tense.

"You need to put this behind you." Luc placed his hand on my shoulder. Immediately my body relaxed.

"You frightened me tonight." I turned to see concern etched on Luc's face.

"You need never be afraid of me, Harper. I would never harm you. Or let anyone else harm you."

"I'm not afraid of you. I'm afraid of what you can do. I'm worn out. I think I should go to bed."

"Good idea. I'll go home now." Luc snapped his fingers. Max appeared down the hall within seconds. "Max, I'm leaving you in charge. I think you should sleep in Harper's room tonight. She needs you."

And with that Luc disappeared into thin air.

❧

The newspapers said Paul Stone was "allegedly" wanted by the police in relation to statutory rape, coercion, drug trafficking, blackmail, and other numerous offences. Unfortunately, detectives had turned up at his house too late to arrest him. He had disappeared without a trace. His car was parked in the driveway. The lights in his house were on, and the house was in a bit of disarray. It appeared as if he had left quickly. However, no one knew where he was, or where he had gone. His business partners took over the job of looking after his production company. I advised my solicitor to cut all ties with Stone Productions. It was time to put all that behind me and find someone else willing to take me on as co-producer.

26
LUC

I have often wondered about human desires. Sure, everyone wants money, most people want a big house and fancy car. But no one really wants to work for it. They dream of winning the lottery, or a long lost rich relative dying and leaving them millions. But interestingly enough the most desired item is power. The power to choose their lifestyle, to make their own decisions. The ultimate power of controlling the lives of others around and beneath them. They think that power will intrinsically provide them with all the things they need, and money will follow.

Unfortunately, many people in power abuse their positions. Most have no regrets, and continue to live a life of corruption, leaving casualties in their wake, without so much as a backward glance. Tonight, I am seeking out a woman who has stood idly by and watched her husband ruin hundreds of innocent lives by his fraudulent financial advisory service. He ended his life earlier that day. He is currently being processed in Hell. I had a brief meeting with him to get some of the juicy details, but I wanted to meet the wife who lived off the proceeds and the misery of others.

I approached Francesca di Mare, on the sidewalk outside of The

Sunset Tower Hotel, on Sunset Boulevard and offered her a business card from a fake funeral service. She took the proffered card, and in doing so, brushed against my fingers. She lifted her dark hazel eyes and glanced at me, and I could see the arrogance and entitlement reflected there. This woman was no obsequious wife. She was no innocent. I had misunderstood the relationship in their union. She was the mastermind behind all of her husband's dealings, from the top of her perfectly styled shoulder length sleek brown hair, to the toes of her expensive high heels. In the few seconds I had been in her presence, touching her hand, I had drawn countless case histories from her memories.

Her large parties were a cover for her husband's deviant sexual proclivity. You couldn't really call it infidelity, since both parties consented. He collected young starlets, actors, male or female, actresses, anyone attractive who wanted to climb the ladder to success and didn't mind what they had to do to get there. Quickly. He provided them with the means, the connections, the funding, and then he reaped the rewards in sexual favors when they couldn't pay it back on his terms. She provided the lavish settings for his seductions in penthouses, on private yachts, and holiday homes on private islands. All paid for by money her husband had promised to invest and look after for his clients. When the IRS got involved and it all caught up with him, he preferred to swan dive from their Penthouse balcony than change his life.

"Perhaps I can be of some assistance. Luc Nightingale, from Final Moments Funerals. My staff would take very good care of your late husband."

"My husband is already being taken care of. Thank you." Francesca said. Her eyes flicked over my body, assessing me. I noticed a subtle change in her stance, and then she locked eyes with me. Staring into those eyes I had witnessed pure evil in their depths. And I know all about pure evil.

"Maybe we could discuss this upstairs in your suite?" I smiled. I had piqued her interest. I watched her expression change as she calculated what she was going to do to me behind closed doors. She had balls I had to give her that, contemplating fucking a stranger, a Funeral Director as far as she was concerned, not 24 hours after her husband had been found dead. Of course, she was staying at this hotel rather than her apartment because the police would have been crawling all over it today.

"Come up. We'll talk." Francesca sashayed ahead of me, heading toward the elevators in the foyer.

I followed, acutely aware of heads turning as she passed by. She was a striking woman, tall and elegant, with long shapely legs in her heels. The black fitted dress she had chosen for her grieving widow weeds, could not have been less mournful. She had selected something to celebrate her curves, which showcased to perfection her hips and the ample bosom she undoubtedly paid a fortune for. I couldn't wait to unwrap this gift. A soon as the suite door was closed, she marched over to the mini-bar and poured herself a shot of brandy.

"Do you want one? I need this. I've had a Hell of a day." Francesca knocked back the drink and poured another.

"Sure. I've had a day in Hell. Hit me up."

She stepped out of her heels and padded across the carpeted floor to give me the glass. She watched me watching her, and her lip curled up at the edge. She was so sure of herself.

"You look like a man who appreciates women."

"Men, women, and all manner of creatures actually."

"Well, it takes all kinds. I prefer men. Strong, sexy men, who know how to fuck. Tell me, are you someone who knows how fuck Mr Nightingale?

"I have been told I know my way around the clitoris, if that is what you're asking."

Francesca laughed. A sensual throaty laugh. Her eyes crinkled at the corners. She assessed me, from the top of my well-groomed head, to the tips of my highly polished black shoes, then back up to my groin area. Her eyes narrowed and her smile widened when she saw I was indeed ready for action.

"Bottoms up." We both knocked back the alcohol and put our empty glasses down on the side table. Francesca was only inches away from me. I knew what she wanted. But I wanted her to show her cards first. It shouldn't have surprised me when her hand shot forward and she cupped my package.

"Not shy, are you?" I said.

"You don't get anywhere in this world unless you take what you want. Strip."

"Ladies first. I insist."

Francesca reached behind her and unzipped her dress, shrugged her shoulders, and it slid to her hips. She pushed the fabric down with both hands over her generous curves and it slithered to the floor. She unclipped her bra and let it drop. I was right. Those beauties stayed up all by themselves, which was against both nature and gravity, given their shape and size. Her dark nipples protruded like bullets against her enhanced breasts. Coincidentally large breasts are a favorite of mine, and I have always been someone who does not look a gift horse in the mouth. So no complaints from me. All that remained was a pair of black lace top stockings and a landing strip of dark hair.

"No underwear?"

"Why bother? I've never been a fan. Now you." She placed her hand on her right hip and took a step back.

I removed my clothes and enjoyed her admiration.

"Now what were you saying about knowing your way around . . . "

Her mouth slammed into mine. I lifted her off her feet and threw her on the couch. She bounced, her breasts jiggled, and the throaty laugh cascaded from her again. I had picked up that she liked a bit of rough play.

"Oh, I know my way around. Up and down, in and out. And you are about to find out just how well." I climbed on top of her and enjoyed her moans of pleasure.

I closed the door to her hotel suite after a few hours of very athletic fornication. I could tell I had not disappointed her on the couch, on the bar, or on the bed. I left her with a smile on her face, and as soon as she fell asleep, I made sure she had no memory of our encounter.

I emailed a long list of very damning evidence of Francesca's involvement in the Financial Scams to all the interested parties. Plus, a reporter that I knew. Intimately. Francesca's time was coming, rushing at her like a freight train.

Sometimes I love my job. What can I say.

27

HARPER

1st MAY 1999

I couldn't bring myself to summon Luc since the incident and tried very hard not to think of him during my waking hours, or at work. But that was almost impossible. I knew wherever he was, he'd be aware I was thinking of him. He had disposed of Paul Stone of that I was sure. Whether he'd taken him to Hell with him or burned his body to a crisp and taken his soul, the end result was the same. The police investigation into Paul's behavior uncovered a very seedy past and wasn't painting a pretty picture of the man in question. Women were coming out of the woodwork to tell their story of how he had abused his position of power within the industry over many years. There was even a rumor going around that a boyfriend or husband or friend of one of his victims had taken matters into their own hands, and the authorities would never find the body. Ain't that the truth.

Nighttime was a totally different matter. I had no control over my dreams, and they were vivid and explicit. In each one of them, the scenario was slightly different, but the theme was the same. Luc watched Paul die and then came toward me and slowly morphed into the Luc I knew, impeccably dressed and without the wings, without the blood red eyes, and when he touched me . . . god help me . . . I wanted him. His kisses lit me on fire, his arms were strong when he lifted me up and placed me on the couch or the bed or the table and began to make love to me. There was never a conclusion though, he never entered my body. It was as if my imagination could go so far and then go no further. I knew it was so very wrong of me to want him this badly after what I had witnessed. The logical part of my brain kept pointing out that he was protecting me, but in doing so, he had done something horrific. However, the biological part of me sent surges of desire through to my very core and had me shaking with need when I awoke in the early hours before dawn. Something had to give. It appears that something was me.

❧

Even Domenic had noticed the dark circles around my eyes and had begun to ask questions about my health and wellbeing. I knew he was in contact with Luc, because he hadn't questioned me as to why Luc was absent from the house. I guessed that my current rundown state would be reported through my child's eyes. I was very careful not to think of Luc whenever I touched or hugged Domenic.

I had been working from home the day the two detectives came to ask questions about the last night anyone had seen Paul Stone. Someone from the restaurant had recognized me from my past movies. Or rather they had recognized someone who looked like Mindy Michaels, and the police investigation led them to me. That, and my car registration, the valet parking had provided. They flashed their ID before I opened the door to them. Detective Reed was over six feet tall and thin and looked to be mid-forties, and Detective Moretti was shorter and stocky and probably in his late thirties. They both wore black suits, white shirts, dark ties, and somber expressions. I immediately thought of the movie Men In Black and tried not to smile.

Max stood on guard beside me at the door and growled at the two men in suits who he did not recognize, or trust. His pointed ears stood tall, taking in every sound, his eyes were watchful of every movement, every nuance these uninvited visitors portrayed. I laid my hand on his head reassuringly. He growled softly and the vibration passed through my palm. I took a step back and invited them into the house, the neighbors did not have to witness this. Max did not want to give up his post. Domenic appeared in the hall and called Max to his side. I gave the command to go to Domenic. It took a couple of attempts for Max to move from his protective stance.

I asked Domenic to take Max to his room. He had to hold onto Max's collar, the dog kept looking back and growling. I should have put two and two together, because as I invited them in and directed them to the living room, Luc came strolling through the house, with Max at his side. I could tell the detectives were nervous around the dog. Luc had probably bargained on that too. I did not ask them to sit. We all stood in the middle of the room.

"What can we do for you gentleman." Luc asked. He came to stand beside me and put his arm protectively around my shoulder. Max followed and stood by my other side.

"We just want to ask Mrs Ericson a few questions about the night of Paul Stone's disappearance." Detective Reed said.

"And that would be because . . ." Luc asked.

"Mrs Ericson was seen with him at dinner on the night he disappeared, and they left together. The valet remembers Mrs Ericson getting into her car." Detective Reed said.

"I was babysitting Domenic that night." Luc said. "Mrs Ericson came home after her diner at the restaurant to relieve me of my babysitting duty."

"And you are. . .?" Detective Reed asked.

"A friend of the family." Luc said.

"Luc is my son's godfather." I said. "As well as a family friend."

Detective Reed gave Luc a steely eyed stare. Luc matched it. It was a stand-off, and no one was game to look away first.

"How did Mr Stone seem when you left the restaurant that night?" Detective Moretti asked me.

"He seemed fine." I said.

"Had he been drinking?" Detective Moretti asked.

"Yes, but not a lot. He ordered wine at dinner, but I think he only had two glasses, and I had one." I said.

"Did he say where he was going after he left the restaurant?" Detective Reed asked. He had finally let Luc off the hook and turned back to me.

"He was going home." I said.

"Are you sure?" Detective Reed asked.

"Yes I'm sure. He was going home after we had dinner." I said.

"And your late husband had dealings with him?" Detective Reed asked.

"Yes they worked on movies together." Luc said.

"And you were here on the night Mrs Ericson was dining with Mr Stone?" Detective Reed asked Luc.

"Yes. I had dinner with Domenic, and we watched a movie together till his bedtime. Then when Harper came home about ten o'clock, I left." Luc said.

"And where do you live Mr . . .?" Detective Reed asked.

"Nightingale. Luc Nightingale. I live at the top of the Hill, Northview Grove." Luke said. "About five minutes away."

Detective Reed took a step toward Luc. Max began to growl. Low, but enough that everyone in the room could hear.

"Shh Max." I laid my hand on his collar.

"If that's all gentlemen. We're about to go out for dinner." Luc said.

"If you can think of anything that might be useful. Something he said or . . ." Detective Moretti said.

"Yes. We'll be in touch. I'll see you out. Come Max" Luc gestured down the hall to the front door. "After you Detectives." The two detectives left the room first. Max came to heel beside Luc, and then walked regally to the front door behind the detectives, every muscle in his body ready to jump into action. Luc followed them.

When Luc returned to the kitchen, I had already taken a bottle of white wine out of the fridge. I poured two generous glasses and handed one to Luc. My hands were shaking. I took a swig of my wine and inhaled deeply.

"Thank you for the support." I said. I lifted the glass in salute and took a long drink. "And Max"

"You're welcome." Luc took a drink

"What's going to happen now?" I asked.

"They are going back to the station to file a report that clears you of any more questions."

"How can you be so sure? They looked pretty serious when they left."

Luc tilted his head to the side, held my gaze and looked deep into my eyes. "What was the last thing you said to me?"

"What's going to happen now?"

"No. The last sentence you said."

"I think that was the last sentence."

"No. I wiped a few seconds of your memory. You said 'How can you be so sure. They looked pretty serious when they left'."

"How did you do that?"

"Think of it like a cassette recording. . . you can go back and forth, you can delete, you can edit. I edited a little of what they learned, and I planted new information. They left satisfied that you had nothing to do with his disappearance. Which we both know you did not. But they won't be back. I made sure of that."

"They were afraid of Max."

"As well they should be. He's a killer. Aren't you Max?" Luc rubbed Max's ears and neck. Max leaned into the affection in Luc's touch, and blissfully closed his eyes. *Oh, to be Max right about now.*

"Oh, that makes me feel very *comfortable,* knowing a killer dog is best friends with my son."

"Max would never hurt Domenic. I've given him very explicit instructions in regard to you and Domenic. You needn't worry. Trust me."

"I keep reminding you he is a dog."

"And *I* keep reminding *you* he's a service dog, highly trained to care for and help ex-army personnel going through post-traumatic stress disorder. Max is my eyes and ears when I'm not here. He's watching over you both every moment he's with you. Haven't you noticed Domenic is calmer since Max arrived. He no longer has the bad dreams he was having after his father died. He's not waking up at night, he's not coming into your bed for comfort."

"Yes. I had noticed Max often sleeps on the bottom of Domenic's bed, curled up at his feet. And my son is a lot calmer."

"Then believe me when I say that Max will defend you both from harm but will never hurt you."

"You told them we're going out for dinner."

"I did. To get rid of them."

"Would you like to stay and have dinner with us? Unless you have plans?"

"I would be delighted to stay and have dinner with the Ericsons"

That casual comment stopped me in my tracks. Luc used to say that when Richard was alive. It gave me pause to think, and suddenly I missed my husband, and the tears readily sprung to my eyes. Luc realized what he had said, sorrow etched on his face.

"Oh, Harper I'm sorry, that was stupid of me. Come here." Luc took two big steps and enveloped me in a bear hug.

"I miss him, Luc."

"I know you do."

"Where's Domenic, I don't want him to see me upset." I withdrew from Luc's arms, dashed away the tears, found a tissue in my pocket and blew my nose. "Give me a few minutes and I'll get dinner started.

"How about this. I pour you another wine and you sit at the table, and I'll prepare dinner"

"What are we having?"

"Veal scaloppini."

"Really?"

"Yes. Close your eyes and count to one hundred."

"Veal Scaloppini? You promise?" I closed my eyes "One, two, three . . ." There was no noise in the room. I opened them a fraction to confirm my suspicions. Luc had disappeared. I got up and found silverware and placemats and called to Domenic to wash up for dinner. Domenic appeared and sat at the table and Max, his faithful companion, sat at his feet, hoping for scraps. I pretended to disapprove of this practice, but I loved the fact that they relied on each other and thought they were getting away with something under my nose.

Luc appeared through the front door a short time later holding a tray laden with covered dishes. He had brought all my favorite dishes from a local restaurant.

"This is how you prepare a meal?"

"This is the best way I find. It saves me a lot of stress. Not to mention it tastes so much better when Alfredo cooks my meals."

Luc served up a big helping for each of us. He pulled out my chair and I sat at the table. He took his usual place opposite to me, and beside Domenic. He didn't sit at the head of the table because that was Richard's place. Since Richard's death we had fallen into a pattern that was familiar to us and comfortable.

"I love Alfredo's meals Mom. Luc took me to Alfredo's when he looked after me." Domenic said. His enthusiasm for the food in front of him was surprising. "Can I have dessert if I finish this?"

"Do you have room for ice cream?" I asked.

"There's always room for ice cream." Luc said and winked. Luc and Domenic looked at each other and laughed. It was good to see my son happy again. I realized I'd been selfish keeping Luc away from Domenic. I realized I had been stupid keeping Luc away from me and denying the attraction that had always been there. He made me feel good. I realized he was a part of my family, and I loved him. There, I said it. Just being around Luc made our lives a bit easier.

After I had tucked a very sleepy Domenic into bed, patted Max on the head as he settled himself on the end of Domenic's bed, and said goodnight, I returned to the living room to find it empty. I had been hoping that Luc would still be there, and we could talk about what had happened, and this new situation I found myself in. That of being torn between the grief I felt for losing my husband and the attraction that had always simmered beneath the surface for Luc. I had dearly loved my husband. We had brought a beautiful boy into this world whom we loved and adored, and we had enjoyed over seven years together. But I had always known there was a part of me that belonged to Luc. When he told me about a piece of his heart beating in mine, it did not come as such a shock, strangely enough. The strong connection I had felt whenever he appeared, the way my anxiety diminished when he was near. The reasons now seemed pretty clear

I finished my glass of wine and flicked off the light switch on the wall. I bent down to turn off the remaining table lamp, which threw the room into semi darkness, when I sensed a presence behind me. I turned to see Luc, backlit by the soft glow from my bedside lamp, standing at the end of the passageway to my bedroom. He was holding out his hand to me. I walked toward him, took his hand, and he led me to my room and softly closed and locked the door. My bedroom was at the other end of the house to Domenic's, but he was obviously being cautious. I turned to him and was about to speak, but he took a step closer and placed a finger over my lips to quieten me. The heat from his chest warmed me, and the few inches separating us vibrated with energy. He cupped my face in his hands and gently kissed my forehead and each cheek in turn, then placed slow tender kisses along my jawline and down the column of my throat. I swallowed, and then sighed. He slipped the jacket from my shoulders and it slid to the floor. His thumb hooked under the shoulder strap of my dress, edging it aside. His lips applied the softest pressure on my collar bone, his tongue darting out to taste my skin. Liquid heat flowed from his tongue. I quivered. My nipples had puckered into tight bullets, pushing into the soft cotton of my bra, stretching out and peaking my fitted blue jersey dress. I ventured a little closer. I wanted, no I needed, pressure on those hard nipples and as he was taking his time exploring my neck with delicious precision, I didn't want to stop that progress. My breathing was shallow and rapid, in anticipation. When we connected chest to thigh, with his manhood pressed up against my mound and stomach, electric pulses shot to my core. His arms wrapped around me holding me close. The pressure proved to be worthwhile. Luc's chest was lava, and I was on fire. His kisses had progressed up under my ear, and when he sucked my earlobe between his lips, the pressure on my nipples, and the rhythmic sucking sensation of his mouth sent me over the edge into a pleasure spiral I had only dreamt about. I came and he wasn't even inside me! Oh my god no one had ever done that to me before. My legs turned to jelly, and swiftly I was swept up into his arms, placed on my back on the bed. Luc was above me and I was looking into his magnificent midnight blue eyes. A lock of black hair had fallen over his brow, his mouth quirked up at one edge. He looked captivatingly roguish. The strap of my dress and bra had fallen down and one of my breasts was partly exposed, the nipple peeping out provocatively. He glanced down, the smile spreading across his face, nipped my wayward nipple with his teeth and lathed it with his hot tongue. I bucked on the bed. He pulled back and smiled. His mouth hovered, not even an inch away from mine, and I longed for his lips. I longed for the sensation I had experienced only twice before, many years ago, when I was swept into a tornado of emotions with merely the press of his lips on mine. He bent his head and kissed down the column of my throat. The whiskers from his five o'clock shadow rasped along my skin.

"Kiss me. Kiss me properly, on the lips. Please."

"If I kiss you, *really* kiss you . . . I'm afraid I cannot control what happens next."

"I want you to kiss me. I have wanted you to kiss me for a very long time. I'm not afraid. I've seen all sides of you Luc, and I still want you. Desperately."

"Harper, I don't want to hurt you. I'm aware of the need I have for you, and you for me. But I have to contain this. . . this heat I produce . . .or . . "

"Or what? I might burn. I'll risk it." I raised my head and took command of his lips. He leaned into the kiss his lips parting a little and the heat washed through me in a wave and enveloped me. I pulled back gasping for air. I still wanted more.

"Again." I pleaded. "Please."

I could do this. I knew I could. I arched my back, and he moved to cover my body with his. My skirt had risen, and the heat seared my skin even though his clothes. His lips found mine, his tongue ran along the seam of my lips and another surge of heat transferred to me. Pleasure pulsed though my body with a steady beat.

"If I'm going to die, I may as well experience it all the way. Make love to me." It wasn't all talk, I wasn't afraid. I knew I could take this. Fate surely would not have brought me to this point if I couldn't go any further.

I could feel Luc's arousal between the apex of my thighs. I wriggled a little lower in the bed in an attempt to get closer and my skirt rode up higher. There was nothing between us except his trousers and underwear and my thin cotton bikini briefs, and I wanted them gone.

I reached between our bodies and unzipped his trousers and pushed his clothes down over his hips to his thighs. I wrapped as much of my hand around his girth that I could, reveled in his quick intake of breath, and also took pleasure in the swift removal of the cotton barrier, when he grabbed the side seam and ripped my underwear from my body. He was much bigger than I could have imagined, but I wasn't turning back now. I guided him to my entrance and rose to meet him. He edged in slowly. I tried not to think about the heat, I tried not to think about the pain, for I had crossed the pain barrier as soon as he entered me, and I was still breathing, still alive, still pulsing with a need I couldn't control. He filled me to capacity, and my body stretched to accommodate as much of him as I could. I could tell there was more he was not sharing for fear he would hurt me. Luc balanced his weight on his forearms so as to not crush me, leant down and whispered words, which I could not understand, into my ear. Soft endearments of another language, another time, and with each stroke he flexed his hips and dove a little deeper.

I closed my eyes and imagined flames surrounding us. Or maybe it wasn't my imagination as tongues of heat licked at my thighs. My fingers dug into his shoulders through his white cotton shirt, and I held on tight. His pace quickened and the thrumming, constant beat of my heart became faster, louder, in time with his, until I couldn't tell whose heart I could feel, whose blood was pumping through whose body, whose pleasure was climbing higher and higher. His breath was my breath. His skin was my skin, glowing and slippery to the touch. Each thrust brought me closer to him, until the building pressure was released, and a thousand stars exploded in my head. My body splintered into a kaleidoscope of colors, and sharp metallic pieces, which in my mind's eye, appeared to be floating in the air. I saw in the middle of all of these pieces of me, his heart entwined with mine, beating and pulsating with dark red blood, and then suddenly I was whole again, and I didn't feel the heat, I didn't feel the pain and I called out his name over and over again until he covered my mouth with his and joined me.

28

HARPER

The birds sang in the tree outside my bedroom window, and I opened my eyes to the early morning sun rising up through the clouds. I came back to earth in the knowledge that I had changed, dramatically and undeniably different to the woman of the day before. I sensed I was more alert, as if I had awakened from years in a drugged sleep. I ran my hands down my naked body, over the tender swollen nipples, and the sore muscles to the place where I could still feel the vibration of last night's love making. The self-satisfied smile spreading across my face was reminiscent of the cat that got the cream. I stretched out my sore limbs to embrace the cool cotton sheets, turned on my side, pulled the other pillow to my chest and hugged it tight. I pressed my face into the pillow searching for the last vestige of Luc's cologne.

I had done it. I had made love to Luc, and he to me. I had given him my body and he had taken me to a place I had never experienced before. Every muscle remembered the hours, yes hours, he worshipped my body. I had never felt more alive in my life, I had never felt more like myself than when I was in Luc's arms and his body joined with mine. The realization that he could not hurt me, that due to a part of his heart inhabiting my body I was able to withstand the heat his body generated, brought us closer together. He appeared to rejoice in the knowledge that he need never worry about how passionately he made love to me. I had found my soulmate.

It was time to get up and face the day. I stood under the shower and allowed the hot water to flow over me, and yet I didn't want to wash away what had happened. I wanted to keep the smell and the taste of Luc on my skin. I wanted to hold his seed within my body, that was now undoubtedly flowing down the drain. What if I became pregnant? I laid my hands against my stomach protectively. What if I already am pregnant. I felt different. What happens when you have a child of the Devil inside you? That was something I had not considered last night. I had been on the pill for many years for health reasons, but since Richard's death I hadn't been as diligent with any of my daily routines. Some days were diamonds, as they say. . . and some were not. It was hard to get back on track, but I had tried as much as I could because of Domenic. Children need stability and routine.

I turned off the taps and reached for the bath towel. Luc stood on the other side of the glass door holding the towel. I stepped into it, and into his arms. He hugged me to his chest.

"I hear you. If you are pregnant with my child, I would be the proudest father in the world. Don't worry I will take good care of you. You are not alone."

"Is it possible to feel so different this soon? I've heard people say they knew the moment that they conceived, but I thought that was a myth."

"I have no idea. This has never happened before. I have always taken great care for this *not* to happen. I have always held myself back. But not with you."

"Why me?"

"Oh, my beautiful girl, that's an easy answer. Because I love you. Until you came into my life, I was angry, and everything around me was bleak and dark. Watching you grow into a woman, following your journey, seeing the world through your eyes changed me. You've had a piece of my heart all these years. But now you have all of my heart. I am yours, wholly and completely."

Tears formed in my eyes and threatened to spill. "I cannot remember a time in my life where I have felt more myself than with you. I love you Luc."

"And I love you." He peppered my face with kisses. I leaned into his body, realizing that until this moment I had not been fully aware of the true meaning of belonging.

"As much as it pains me to leave on this note, I have to get dressed and prepare breakfast for Domenic. Will you stay and have breakfast with us."

"I'm sorry I have something I have to take care of. I'll be back tonight if I can. But it might take a few days."

"I understand. I'm not going anywhere." I smiled up at him.

"There is nowhere you can go that I won't find you." Luc laughed.

"That's true." I looked up into his eyes and knew that he meant it. He would go to the ends of the earth to find me, and that fact alone made my heart sing.

One kiss on the cheek and he was gone. I wonder if I will ever get used to him disappearing into thin air.

❧

Three days passed, and Luc had not appeared. I kept him in my thoughts, and I knew he would hear me. I jumped into bed at the end of a very tiring day and laid my hand against my stomach. Nothing had changed, yet everything had changed. I could be carrying a child of the future. Luc was after all, a fallen angel. I knew his good points. I knew his heart, intimately. Was it wrong for me to long for a part of Luc? Was it wrong for me to want to have conceived and be carrying his child? Instinctively I knew my body was different.

Could I cope with the outcome if this child looked nothing like a human child? I pushed that though into the back of my mind. This child would be beautiful and brave because it came from love. I had to believe that.

29

LUC

I had been aware of changes, or vibrations around the globe, an underlying threat to the status quo, the Veil between the underworld and Earth had been compromised. Evil souls had returned from Hell, and I had to fix this situation before more damage was done.

In a dingy bar just outside the city, the bartender announced "last drinks". The middle-aged waitress, eager for her shift to be over, cleared the tables and carried a full tray out through the swinging doors to the kitchen. Nearly everyone had left. A loved-up couple rose from the table, put their arms around each other and laughed as they both tried to get through the door at the same time. I sat at the rear of the deserted room, unseen by those around me, and watched the transaction at the bar. The bartender refused to give the customer another drink stating that he didn't supply alcohol to drunk patrons. The man became agitated, rose up from his seat, swaying on his feet, raised his left hand and pointed a revolver at the barman's chest. A bullet pierced his chest and the barman crumpled to the floor. He reached over and poured himself another shot from the bottle, whipped his mouth with the back of his hand and left the premises with the bottle firmly in his grip.

As he entered the alley beside the building, I caught up with him, and laid a hand on his shoulder.

"Hey. Big shot. You left a man lying on the floor back there with a hole in his chest."

"What's it to you, get lost." The man shrugged off my hand and swayed on his feet

"All that for a bottle of whisky. I don't get it."

"Mind your own business" He turned and lifted his left hand with the revolver. I dodged out of his way. He was having difficulty standing and dropped down heavily onto his knees. I heard the crack of bone on concrete. He took another swig from the bottle, oblivious of the pain. I took a good look at him. His clothes were not from this time. Maybe from a century before.

"This is my business. I don't think you belong here. I think I should take you back to where you do belong." I took a hold of his collar and yanked him through the Veil to the underworld. I handed him over to the night patrol, who slapped chains on him. I went in search of Rourke, my second in charge.

Before I could even find him, several messages had reached me. More of these troublemakers had appeared all over the country, and the information I was receiving was that they were souls which had left Earth long ago for their forever home down below. Rounding them up was taking time. Time that I should have been spending with Harper. But there was nothing I could do about it. I hadn't been able to find out who had been returning these demons to Earth. Someone was using pretty powerful magic to keep that information secret.

30

HARPER

MID-MAY 1999

Two weeks had passed and no sign of Luc. I'd kept myself busy working from home as much as possible. The agency had been surprisingly busy of late. The agency staff had all been wonderful since Richard's death, and I had appointed someone Luc found to take over Richard's position as Managing Director. His name was Peter de Haviland and he had proved to be invaluable with his knowledge of motion picture history as well as the stunt business and current movies. The movie Richard and his assistant had been working on had been set aside, to a time in the future when we could bring in new writers and source more funding.

I'd slept in this morning. Not unusual when you turn off the alarm and pull the covers up for five more minutes, which turns into an hour. It's amazing what you can achieve in a short amount of time when there's no choice. I poured milk onto cereal for Domenic and got dressed quickly while he ate. We were out the door in thirty minutes flat. I left him at school with his friends, watched him walk up the steps and into the building and raced off to grab a sandwich to take to the office for lunch. I was standing at the counter of a café waiting to receive my take-out order, when a woman yelled out from across the room.

"Behold. She has the spawn of Satan inside her. Stand back. She's unclean." I turned toward the woman who appeared very dowdy and ordinary, apart from her outburst. She wore a dark blue dress and jacket, had shoulder length grey hair, her eyes were wide, with a horrified expression on her face.

The manager approached the woman. "Madam. I'm asking you to quiet down or leave." She pushed him away.

"She's a harlot. The slut of the devil. See how her skin glows. See how her stomach bulges with his progeny. She's cursed." The woman yelled louder, pointing her finger at my stomach. I took a step back in reflex and knocked over a chair.

The manager took her by the arm and forcibly removed her to the street. She walked away still yelling and raising her hands to the heavens. A few minutes later the assistant handed over a paper sack with my lunch order. I left the store and quickly got into my car parked at the curb. Suddenly the woman appeared at my window, yelling more insults. I quickly locked my door, stepped on the gas pedal and took off. I didn't stop until I was safely through the secure gates, under my building, and in my parking spot. My hands were shaking so hard I couldn't undo my seat belt. I got out of the car and immediately felt nauseous. I put it down to the fact I hadn't eaten and was stressed. I needed a coffee, stat.

I went straight from the elevator to the kitchen and poured a cup of coffee, added sugar and cream. I sat at the table and took a sip of the hot liquid. It tasted sour and metallic. I spat it into the sink, threw out the contents of my cup and turned on the tap to wash it away. I made a cup of tea instead and balanced my packages and purse on my hip as I carried it back to my desk.

"That coffee in the kitchen has spoiled. Could you order some fresh coffee beans please?"

"But that was a new order. It only arrived yesterday." Ruby said.

"Is it a different brand? Maybe the cream has gone bad? It tasted awful."

"It tasted fine to me this morning. What did you have for breakfast? Did you just brush your teeth? Sometimes that makes a difference."

"I'll try it again later. Thanks." I closed my office door behind me and sat behind my desk. The woman's words rang out in my head. Could she be right? Could I be pregnant? It was time for me to take a test and know once and for all. I unlocked the bottom drawer and pulled out the pregnancy kits I had purchased a week ago in preparation. I took two kits into the private bathroom and locked the door.

❧

I stared at the kit. No doubt about it. Two kits, exactly the same results. Pregnant. Pregnant with Luc's child. Pregnant with the Devil's child. I felt frightened one minute and elated the next. I placed my hand over my stomach protectively. "Mine. Nothing else matters. You're mine, and I will manage whatever comes next."

I closed my eyes and send words of love to this tiny being inside me. I heard a tiny voice back. "I'm going crazy. Already hallucinating for sure." My pulse was hammering so much in my ears it was difficult to hear. *"Ours, this is ours and no matter what we will manage whatever comes next, my love."* . . . . I gasped. That was Luc's voice I heard in my head. That has never happened before. "Can you hear me Luc. Was that your voice I heard or am I going crazy. Is that another sign of this pregnancy? Am I losing whatever marbles I have left?"

"Yes. It seems that now we can communicate by thought. Just as Domenic and I have been able to communicate. The pregnancy has obviously made this possible."

"Where are you? Are you coming home soon?"

"I promise I will be there by your side soon. . . and Harper . . . I am delighted."

I wrapped my arms around my body and closed my eyes. Tears threatened to fall. I held onto the sound of his voice in my head for as long as I could. The knock on the door startled me and I jumped.

"Are you alright in there?" Ruby called out through the door.

"Yes, I'll be out in a minute." I tucked my hair behind my ears, wiped my eyes and straightened my dress.

I opened the door to see a very concerned looking personal assistant sitting on the edge of my desk. Ruby jumped up quickly.

"I was getting worried. I've been buzzing your desk. You have a phone call. It's the studio."

"Actually, I'm not feeling great. Can you take a message or get someone else to help them? I might go back home."

"You don't look well. Have you been crying?" Ruby asked

"I've got a stomach flu. I'll be fine."

"Do you want me to pick up Domenic and bring him back here for a couple of hours after school. You could call the school to let them know. He can use the spare computer to amuse himself. I can pick up some dinner and drop it off when I drop off Domenic."

"You know what, that would be wonderful Ruby. I'll order from Alfredo's if you want to pick it up on the way through to the house. Can you stay for dinner? Domenic and I have missed spending time with you."

"I'd like that. I've missed your little guy. And we haven't had a girls' night for a very long time."

"That's true. It will be lovely to have you."

"Great. I will be there about six o'clock."

❧

I pulled the sheet up and over the top of the soft wool blankets and tucked them around Domenic, gave Max a pat as he settled at the end of the bed, and left the bedroom with the door slightly ajar. I returned to the living room and flopped down on the couch beside Ruby. She handed me a mug of hot sweet tea. She clinked her mug against mine. "Cheers." She bit into a large chocolate chip cookie.

"Thank you so much for today. You are a lifesaver. Where's Oliver tonight?"

"He's gone out with some friends. He was quite thrilled to have a night to himself actually."

"Really. I thought you two got along famously. Richard was thrilled he had something to do with bringing you both together. When you got married, he was taking all the credit."

"Oh, we do get along. But I've been asking a lot of him lately and he wanted a night with his friends."

"Have you done more renovations to your apartment?"

"Actually, the renovation will have to wait for a while. We're pregnant? Well I'm pregnant, but Oliver did have something to do with it."

"Ruby." I was stunned. I didn't know what to say.

"You look shocked. I thought you would be happy for us."

"I *am* happy for you. I can't believe it. Congratulations."

"If you're worried about me working, I'll work as long as possible. I have someone in the office I can train to do my job while I take leave."

"No that wasn't what I was thinking."

"What then? You're still not smiling, and you look worried."

"I am having some trouble believing the coincidence."

"You're not making sense. What coincidence?"

"I'm pregnant Ruby. I just found out today."

"Now I'm the one who is confused. Richards been dead for . . ."

"No it's not Richard's. It's Luc's baby."

"Luc? Domenic's godfather? Whoa. I didn't know that you two were . . . "Ruby got up, walked a few paces and turned to face me, her hands on her hips. "This is huge. I mean I know the guy is super-hot, but I didn't think that you two would. . . you know. . . get together. Friends with benefits, huh."

"It's not friends with benefits Ruby. I love Luc and he loves me. I think I have always loved Luc even before I met Richard. The timing wasn't right back then."

"Oscar will be devastated."

"Why? Oh, don't think I didn't love Richard, because I did. But

Richard is gone now. I believe you can love more than one person in your lifetime. The time happens to be right with Luc."

"How does he feel about the pregnancy?"

Luc chose that moment to appear through the hall from the front door. "I feel ecstatic actually, Ruby. As I am sure any man would be if Harper was carrying his child." He came to me, bent down and kissed me. "I'm sorry to crash your girl's night."

"It's about time I was heading home. Nice to see you again, Luc. Thanks for dinner, see you tomorrow Harper." Ruby finished her tea, got up and placed the mug on the counter.

"Don't rush off on my accord." Luc said.

"Are you sure Ruby. You don't have to leave." I said.

"I'm feeling a bit weary actually."

"I'll see you out." Luc walked Ruby to the door.

❧

"She was a bit stunned I think." Luc sat down on the couch and put his arm around my shoulder. I snuggled into his side.

"Why did you tell her?"

"I found it strange that we are both pregnant. She is going to have to cope with me and morning sickness so she would have guessed soon anyway."

"The staff in the office are going to think there is something in the water when this gets out."

"I'm not planning on telling anyone else for the time being." I said.

"I think that's wise."

"I'm so happy you're back. I missed you so much." I twisted around, reached up, cupped Luc's cheek and kissed him. His lips parted for my tongue. A wave of longing washed through me. "Let's go to bed."

"I thought you'd never ask." Luc scooped me up in his arms and walked me through to my bedroom.

"I've been thinking perhaps it's time you moved in here with

Domenic and me. You are here most of the time now anyway. How do you think he'll take the news?"

"I think he'll be fine when he finds out he's going to be a big brother."

"I think we should tell him together."

"Definitely." Luc agreed. He sat me on the end of the bed and knelt at my feet. He removed my shoes.

"I had a very strange encounter today which frightened me. A woman started yelling at me and pointing at my stomach, announcing to everyone that I was pregnant with Satan's child."

"I'm sorry that happened to you. There are lunatics out there." Luc lifted my foot and kissed my bare ankle and began to work his way up my leg. Everywhere his lips touched my skin warmed and tingled.

"But what frightened me is that she was right, and I don't know how she knew."

"Just some psycho. Don't let it bother you." Luc had reached my knees and the hem of my dress which he slowly pushed higher.

"But it did bother me Luc."

"I have just the thing to take your mind off this morning."

His fingers hooked into the sides of my underwear, and I was captivated by his cheeky grin and the twinkle in his eye, as he drew them down towards him. He was absolutely right. I lost myself in the feel of his mouth on me, the flick of his tongue, the surge of longing to be taken by him again.

31
HARPER

No one could have prepared me for pregnancy this time around. I didn't have morning sickness. I had *all day* sickness. There were days where I could hardly get out of bed. Luc wanted to hire someone to help with the house and with Domenic. Then he decided that the house was too small, so he purchased one further up into the Hollywood Hills which was more like a mansion, than a family home. He hired Mr & Mrs Crawford, a married very British couple in their late fifties, to take care of the house, the extensive grounds, the pool and to cook for the family. There was a bluestone gatehouse which had been extensively renovated and extended into a two-bedroom home. Luc explained that Mr & Mrs Crawford had rented out their city apartment and were delighted to move onto the walled estate as part of their generous contract.

Cameron Crawford was a very dapper man, about five foot ten inches tall with salt and pepper hair and a solid physique. He was extremely clever with anything mechanical, doubled as our driver whenever he was needed, and often took Domenic to school when I was unable to get out of bed. Aimee Crawford was not a conventional beauty, but rather a tall striking woman who had presence. She wore her blonde hair in a bun which gave her a grandmotherly appearance, but she was extremely fit and with Cameron's help was able to look after the large house with ease. She had been an army nurse in her youth, which is where she met Cameron, who was also in the forces, but no one could equate her meals with army staples. She had mastered Cordon Bleu, and created beautifully presented and deliciously healthy meals, which somehow managed to tempt me even when my stomach wasn't complying. They both loved Max, and he graciously allowed them to fawn over him, and they often took him for walks when Domenic was at school. Being in the forces Cameron had worked with dogs in his overseas regiment and knew their value. I was happy that someone could exercise Max, especially when I was unable to do so.

Life took on a very different rhythm now that Luc was living with us full time. Or should I say, now that we had moved into the lifestyle to which he was accustomed. Luc came home when he was able. Domenic and I wanted for nothing. Luc had taken over the responsibility of Devil Dares and had appointed an excellent Office Manager to oversee the day to day business while I was indisposed. To be honest I wasn't sure I wanted to return to work. I didn't have the heart for the Agency since Richard had died, and as always, Luc had anticipated my needs, and taken steps to make things easier for me. I was very grateful for the company of Cameron and Aimee pottering about in the house and garden. There were times when Luc was absent for days at a time, but they were less frequent now that the pregnancy had reached the third trimester. Ruby was a few weeks ahead of me in her pregnancy and had been unwell. She had left the office to prepare for the birth, and she and Oliver had gone to stay with her mother a distance away. I missed her company and girl talk.

To my eyes I had ballooned, and I was huge and very unattractive. But my obstetrician assured me I was glowing and looked exactly how I should look for thirty-two weeks into the pregnancy. I craved the most unusual foods, which Luc managed to find for me day and night. The little girl inside me . . . yes Luc and I both knew we were having a girl . . . made her presence known. She moved about constantly, stretching and straining to mould her environment to accommodate her growing limbs.

Luc arrived home carrying several boxes piled on top of each other. I recognised the brightly decorated packaging of a children's nursery store.

"What have you brought home this time? You're spoiling this baby, and she hasn't even been born yet."

"Isn't that what all father's do? Spoil their daughters?"

"We don't want Domenic to get jealous."

"Don't worry I brought something for him too."

"What did you get him?"

"A microscope." Luc grinned as he held up a large gift wrapped in sober brown paper, obviously not a toy."What every eight-year-old child wants."

"Believe me he wants this one. They have the same one in NASA. I am combining his love of medicine and his love of Outer Space."

"Since when did he begin a love of Outer Space?"

"Since he watched Star Wars the other day."

"Isn't he a bit young . . . "

"I don't think he would agree with you."

"Christmas is not so far away, so please take it easy with all the gifts or you won't have any ideas to put under the tree."

Aimee appeared in the doorway to announce dinner was ready. Luc held out his hand and helped me to my feet. Everything took on new significance, even getting off the couch was difficult with this huge heavy watermelon attached to me. Luc put his arm around me as we walked through to the dining room.

"Thank you, Aimee. This looks wonderful." A deliciously fragrant beef casserole and bowls of vegetables were spread out on the table. Luc pulled out the chair for me to sit.

"If there is nothing else you need, I'll see you in the morning." Aimee said.

Domenic rushed into the room, with Max at his side, and took his place at the table. Max lay at his feet.

Domenic lifted the lid of the covered dish in front of him, and a big grin lit up his face. "Mac and cheese. My favourite. Thank you, Aimee."

"You're very welcome Domenic." Aimee said.

"You spoil him Aimee. You'll have some casserole too Domenic. And vegetables."

Luc passed his plate to me already loaded up with vegetables, then Domenic's plate, and I added scoops of hearty beef and gravy. My mouth was watering. I was glad to get my appetite back.

Aimee left us to eat our meal and returned to the gatehouse, no doubt sharing the same delicious dinner with Cameron. We wouldn't see her till breakfast. I had become accustomed to having household staff much quicker than I had expected. I blessed Luc every day now that I could leave the housework and the chores to someone else and concentrate on bringing this child into the world. I had never imagined I could feel so tired. I still attempted to write scripts when I could, but my heart wasn't in it. All of my strength seemed to be ebbing away the further I advanced into this pregnancy. The most disturbing part of late was the vivid sensual dreaming, and the constant pull toward them. Dreams didn't just come at night, but also through the day, when I would willingly succumb to the lure of the soft blue velvet couch in the sunny family room. Sometimes I had to be roused from these dreams to welcome my son home from school, and my body and mind struggled hard to return to the real world. My body felt drugged and sluggish. Holding onto the images, to talk to Luc about them, had become my goal. But minutes after I awoke, they drifted away like grey smoke from a smouldering fire.

Occasionally, when Luc made love to me in the early hours of the morning, I would have graphic images of bodies twisted and coupled in full sensual pleasure. Or I imagined I was in the middle of this orgy with Luc plunging into me, and everyone chanting around us.

My need for Luc began to increase with each passing day. When he had to leave us for days at a time, I was desperate for his return to my bed. I had never been this voracious in my life, had never felt so sensual or so easily turned on. Luc just had to look in my direction and smile for me to want to drag him to our bedroom.

Christmas Eve was finally here, and with that came the knowledge that as businesses closed down for the holidays, we would spend more quality time together as a family. Cameron had set up a large tree in the corner of the living room this morning, and all we had to do was decorate it before Domenic went to bed. He hadn't believed in Santa Claus for years, but he still enjoyed all the festivities, and the delicious treats that came along at this time of year. Aimee had outdone herself and made Christmas cookies, and fudge and caramel popcorn. Domenic had helped Aimee with baking and decorating a Gingerbread house and was suitably impressed with the process.

As I knelt on the floor and placed decorations on the bottom branches of the tree, a sharp pain shot through my body. I gripped my stomach and managed to hobble over to lay back on cushions on the couch. The pain had gone but a lingering sense of unease remained. Sweat popped out on my forehead. I wasn't due to deliver this baby for a few weeks yet.

Domenic arrived carrying a cardboard carton of Christmas decorations we had saved over the years. He stopped short when he saw me. Luc was behind him.

"I've found the last of your decorations tucked at the back of the hall closet. I think we have everything to decorate this tree . . . what's the matter?" Luc put down the box he was carrying and rushed to my side. "You look as white as a ghost."

"I had a pain. I'm not sure if it was a contraction. It came out of nowhere."

"What were you doing? Did you reach up too high? Did you strain something?"

Domenic came over and placed his hand on my stomach. "It isn't time yet. She's just getting ready. She's sorry she hurt you."

"What? Domenic you can communicate with her?" I asked. It was incredulous but it should not have surprised me.

"Yes. Not in words just in feelings. I feel her sorrow." Domenic said.

"Maybe we should check in with the doctor?" Luc said

"There's no need. All is as it should be." Domenic put both hands on the bulge of my stomach and closed his eyes in concentration. My skin warmed under his hands. A calmness overcame me. He removed his hands.

"I'll make you a cup of tea. With lemon and honey." Luc left the room.

"I appreciate your help with this. That pain frightened me. I sometimes forget how young you are, but I want you to know I don't want to take advantage of your gifts." I pulled Domenic in for a hug.

"I want to help if I can." Domenic said. He looked a little embarrassed by the tight squeeze.

"You'll never be too big for a hug, mister. No matter how old you get. Your intelligence might be that of a teenager, but you are still my little boy." I kissed his forehead and let him go. He smiled at me and lowered his eyes.

Luc returned with the tea, and Luc and Domenic trimmed the remainder of the tree, while I watched from the couch. I pulled the woollen blanket over my legs and plastered a smile on my face. I continued to have mild twinges, nothing serious as before, but I couldn't shake the feeling of foreboding.

❧

The dream is intense. Dark tunnels leading down into the bowels of the earth surround me. The only light is coming from the flames of lit torches dotted along the walls. I hear the low base notes of a drum beating in the distance. I am unsure which direction I should take. I know I am dreaming, but I cannot rouse myself. I am searching for Luc, but I cannot find him. Hands reach out and pull me down a long, dark tunnel which opens out into a cavern, with an altar sitting on top of a raised platform in the middle. I am dragged up the steps to the platform, lifted onto the altar and restrained. A hooded figure appears, his whole face in shadow, holding a large knife. He cuts away my nightgown from hem to ribcage and exposes my belly. The drums get louder. Shapes are moving in around me, but I cannot make out faces. Fear escalates as I realize the knife is pressing against my skin, and they want my child. They are going to cut her from my body.

Strength I did not know I had surges up inside me and I free myself from the hands holding me down. I point at the hooded figure and a flash of electricity from my fingertip sends him flying off the platform and crumpling unconscious or dead on the ground. I stand up, feet apart, my shredded night gown hanging from my chest, my stomach exposed, bulging, the baby moving inside stretching the skin to the limit. I concentrate on the power I feel surging through my body. Everyone backs away. Suddenly my water breaks, and a feeling of great pressure grips me. I have to get out of here and find Luc, before this baby is born. Each time someone approaches me, I raise my hand and they are forced back. I can see the light at the end of the tunnel, and I make my way toward it. The pressure in my stomach increases.

I wake up, drenched in sweat, and in bed alone. My waters have indeed broken and I am having contractions. I am in labor. It's too early. Where the Hell is Luc?

32

LUC

The demon called Rourke, who I had appointed to look after Hell in my absence, had let me down. Just one week, that was all I asked, one week of uninterrupted time with my family from Christmas until the New Year. And in Hell time, that is very short. Not like the Earth time of 7 days. And yet it seemed that small window was impossible, and I was called back to deal with a very difficult new guest. A pop star called Billy-Joe Rock who had been the worst role model teenagers could ever have. A pedophile enlisting fourteen and fifteen-year-old girls into his fetish fan club, then blackmailing them with explicit photographs of their dangerous practices to make sure he could continue his sordid ways. A drug addict sampling every form of man-made high you could buy, and some which were created from animal extracts that even the black market had difficulty getting their hands on. He had superior strength and a high tolerance to pain, unlike anything I'd ever witnessed in a human being. Unfortunately, his intellect was not of the same high distinction. The last bender he went on resulted in his arrival in my domain. That is what happens when you try a concoction of booze and drugs and more booze and drugs. Although he lived surrounded by hangers-on, with wealth that only a few people are lucky enough to enjoy, he died alone in his bedroom, in a pool of his own vomit.

Now, this excuse for a human being while on earth, was making existence difficult for others and making enemies, even in Hell. I gave him a small taste of my own personal touch of torture and left him wishing he had not been the cause of missing out on time with my family. Then I made my rounds of the facilities and stopped to give advice and encouragement to the workers. It took longer than I had expected, but it was worth it to see the pain and misery on many inmates' faces. After all, this was what I was sent here to do. Like it or not . . . and I was finding myself questioning my role more than ever now . . . this was my domain.

I scheduled a meeting with Rourke and we met in my Tower office. I had a three-hundred-and-sixty-degree view of my guests on the top level, from above, whether they were in their cells or in the common areas. These were the most recent inmates, who were being acclimatized to their new environment. The many lower floors housed the others chosen to be moved on, depending on their behaviour, supplication, and time spent as my guest. My demon soldiers looked after the guests and were hand-picked by me in accordance with their various talents. Lack of empathy, cruelty, ingenuity and imagination had to rate high on their applications.

"Couldn't you have handled this without dragging me back here Rourke? You have carte blanche to deal with him as you see fit." I took the chair at the head of the table.

"No matter what we do he will not bend and accept his fate here. He is the worst of the worst, and he seems to get a perverse pleasure out of all that we do to him."

I drummed my fingers on the tabletop. "I have already spent some time with him."

"The pain won't last. He laps it up. No one wants to work with him. It takes all the joy out of their job when he enjoys the pain, the flagellation, the red-hot branding irons, the boiling oil."

"And what do you expect me to do that's so different?" I asked.

"You've always managed to think outside the box. I thought you might enjoy the challenge."

"Okay. I'll think about it and check in with you when I make my rounds later. Something might come to me."

I settled back in my chair and closed my eyes to better concentrate on a punishment that would be appropriate for someone who loved to receive as well as inflict pain on others. Rourke has reached the door.

"Oh, before you go, does he still have all his appendages?"

"Yes."

"Castrate him. And remove his fingers. Then we'll talk."

A sudden sharp pain ran through my body and brought the sweat out on my forehead. I heard Harper call out to me, her pain was my pain. Something was very wrong. I left Rourke to handle Billy-Joe, and rushed to her side.

33
HARPER

NEW YEAR'S EVE 1999

It was too soon. This baby wasn't due for four weeks. But there was no denying it, this wasn't false labor. It was the real deal. My waters had broken, and I needed to get to the hospital. But the pain was so intense I could barely get dressed. The contractions were rolling over each other so fast. I managed to stuff the remaining items into a bag, then had to sit back down on the bed as another very painful contraction gripped my body, and it took minutes to get my breath back afterwards. It was late at night, but I had no choice but to call Aimee for help. She answered the phone on the third ring. I didn't have to say much, she heard in my voice that it was time. I found some items in the bathroom to pack into my bag. I flipped off the bathroom light and attempted a few steps to take my bag downstairs, another pain gripped me and I cried out. Domenic appeared at my bedroom door. He rushed to my side to put his arm around my waist, and Aimee appeared behind him.

"Oh my dear. Come sit on the bed till I check you out." Aimee pulled back the covers. "Remember your breathing."

Another contraction took hold and Aimee helped me back down onto the bed.

"Let's time these contractions. I don't think we'll make it to the hospital." She got a wet face towel from the bathroom, laid it on my brow and took my pulse.

"But we have to. I can't have my baby here." I couldn't talk, I was breathless.

"There are worse places to have a child. We have everything we need here. Domenic, go downstairs and call Cameron. Tell him we won't need the car, it's too late, but he could get some clean towels and bring my first aid kit."

Domenic disappeared. Aimee tried to make me as comfortable as possible, and I prayed that Luc would come home.

"Where's Luc? Can you contact him?" Aimee asked.

"I've tried. I hope he gets the message." Another strong contraction had me gasping for breath.

Aimee checked her watch. "These contractions are coming every 3 minutes. I'm afraid it's you and me my dear. This baby is coming tonight whether we're prepared or not. Don't worry. This is not my first time."

Domenic arrived with fresh towels and some ice chips that Cameron had given him. He sat on the bed and laid his hand on my stomach. The pain eased off a little. My darling boy was trying to help.

"It's ok Mom. She will be perfect."

He had picked up on the fact that I was worried about what she would look like. I squeezed his hand.

"I would like to have a look to see how dilated you are. Domenic, can you give us some privacy please."

Domenic left the room, and Aimee went to wash and sterilize her hands.

"You are about seven or eight centimeters dilated already and you should get to ten before you feel the urge to push. Please don't push till I let you know. Practice your breathing. Concentrate on breathing in and out deeply. Try to relax your body as you exhale."

"Luc!" I yelled out loud as another strong pain hit me. Sweat popped out on my brow and Aimee dabbed a cold compress over my face.

Luc burst through the bedroom door, with a worried look on his face. "Harper I am so sorry. Aimee how is she, is the baby alright? What's happening? Why isn't she on the way to the hospital?" Luc asked.

"There's no time. Your baby does not want to wait. She's making her way into the world. It is just a matter of whether it will be in 1999 or the year 2000."

"But that is less than thirty minutes away!" Luc said.

"Yes. Don't worry, I have delivered babies before. It is all happening just as it should."

Luc yanked off his suit jacket, threw it over a chair in the corner and rolled up his shirt sleeves.

"What can I do."

"You can help Harper to breathe through her contractions. In and out slowly. Deep breaths."

"I want to push."

"Not yet. Help her Luc. Get behind her on the bed, prop her up and take her weight on your chest. We have to make the best of what we have here." Aimee laid out the towels under me, and put some aside to wrap the baby in. She went to the bathroom to prepare and scrub her hands once more, and douse with alcohol from her first aid kit. She examined me to check my progress.

"Let's get the show on the road. You *are* fully dilated now. On the next contraction you can push. Okay."

"Are you sure everything's alright?" Luc asked. I could hear the anxiety in his voice. He was nervous. So was I.

"Everything's alright. It's just moving at lightning speed. She wants to be born tonight, no doubt about it."

With every push she made her way forward. Luc encouraged as much as he could. He held my hands while I had his in a death grip.

He wiped my sweat soaked brow between contractions. The moment she crowned I panted rapidly as I was instructed and tried not to push, lest I tear, and Aimee worked her magic turning her so that her shoulders eased out and our beautiful, perfect baby slid into her hands. She did not cry right away, but as Aimee rubbed her with a towel and wrapped her in another, she cried for a few seconds. Aimee lifted her onto my breast, and she gazed up in wonder at me and then at Luc. Aimee clamped the cord and Luc had the pleasure of cutting it. He had a grin from ear to ear.

I could not take my eyes from her face. Her perfect cupid's bow mouth, her tiny button nose, her wide-open eyes, her mop of thick black hair. Luc reached down and took her in his arms and kissed her soft chubby cheek. He had tears in his eyes, as did I.

"Hello beautiful girl." Luc said. "We've been waiting a long time to meet you."

"What are you going to call her?" Aimee asked.

"Lucia." said Luc. "It means light, and she is the light in my life. Where there was darkness now there is light."

"What a beautiful name. She is indeed a beauty. Not all babies look this good when they are born." Aimee said. She busied herself taking care of the afterbirth.

"I had no doubt she would be beautiful." Luc said as he looked at me. He leant down with Lucia in his arms and gently kissed me. My heart soared.

Domenic knocked on the door and came in to greet his sister.

"She sure is beautiful. She's a millennium baby." Domenic said, peering at her in her towel cocoon.

"Yes, she was born at one minute into the new year." Aimee said.

"Should we take her to the hospital? After all, she is early." I asked.

"She looks perfect to me. She isn't having any issues breathing. But in the morning, we can get the doctor to come and check her out. And you, of course. You were a trouper. And as this is your second baby, no stitches needed because you did very well with your breathing." Aimee said.

"Aimee I can't thank you enough." I said.

"I'll second that." Luc said.

"All in a day's work." Aimee said, packing her first aid kit and cleaning up.

"There *will* be a bonus in your account." Luc said. "And a new car. Name it. Whatever model you want."

"Oh, that's not necessary. We have a very good car. And Cameron is driving your car most of the time But, we'll take the bonus. Cameron and I want to go on a trip to the Bahamas next year."

"Done. A bonus *plus* a trip." Luc said. "I'll have my travel agent arrange it all."

"That's very generous of you."

"Think nothing of it. I'll spare no expense when it comes to my daughter. To my family." Luc placed Lucia in Domenic's arms and put his arm possessively around Domenic's shoulder. "We are a family of four now. Are we not?"

"Yes, we are a family of four now." I closed my eyes and gave thanks that everything had gone well. I had a daughter. *We* had a daughter. Lucia looked like a little angel, and she looked just like Luc. My family was complete.

❧

The euphoria of being a new Mom soon wore off. Multiple feeds, burping, washing, changing, sleeping, showering . . . and back to feeding again, filled my days. I was so very grateful for Aimee and Cameron, and I marvelled at how other women managed to cook and clean and look after multiple children without household assistance.

I was exhausted. I knew it, but no matter what I did I couldn't seem to rise above this lethargy. Of course, having a newborn took a lot out of me, but somehow, I knew there was more to this. I had been able to manage much more when I had Domenic. I had also noticed that since Lucia arrived, I could no longer communicate mentally with Luc. The closeness we had during the pregnancy, in part because I could hear him in my head, was gone. I second guessed everything he did or said.

"I've hired a night nurse." Luc announced at breakfast. He lifted his cup of coffee to his lips and looked at me over the rim.

"Why." I stopped buttering the toast on my plate.

"To help. You're exhausted."

"I don't want another person in my house. I can't turn around without bumping into Aimee or Cameron."

"It's for your own good."

"And say it . . .go on, you're thinking it. It's better for Lucia." Suddenly I had no appetite.

"I wasn't going to say that. I want you to rest. Get your strength back."

"It was an accident. I didn't mean to fall asleep holding her."

"I know that."

"I didn't drop her. She just slid down my lap a little. If you hadn't come into the room, I would've realized and pulled her up. You're looking at me as if you don't believe me."

"I'm looking at you. Not passing judgement. Just looking." He took another sip of coffee.

Lucia chose that moment to wake up for a feed. She was such a good baby, and didn't cry loudly, just loud enough so that I could hear her on the baby monitor.

"This isn't over." I said.

"I'm afraid it is. The nurse is coming tonight."

"I don't even get a say? What if I don't like her?"

"I'm doing this for you. Give her a chance. Her qualifications are impeccable."

"Why don't *you* take the night shift."

"I'm called away at a moment's notice, you know that. I can't guarantee to be here to take over. Now you're being foolish."

"I'm exhausted, I'm a bad mother, and I'm foolish . . . what else am I?"

"You're blowing this out of proportion. I'll get Aimee to bring you some tea. Go feed the baby."

"You could spend more time here. You're needed here."

"You're obviously more tired than I thought. Have you forgotten who I am? I am not some factory worker from downtown. I don't clock on and clock off. I. Am. The. Devil. I'm expected to be in Hell. I may not want to be but that is where I am supposed to be. My time on Earth is for the purpose of gathering souls. Not playing house."

Luc's voice had an edge to it that I had not previously heard.

"I see. Thank you for clearing that up for me." I got up from the table, intending to leave the room.

Luc reached out and took hold of my arm. "Look, I'm sorry I didn't mean to snap at you. I'm doing this for you, honestly, I am. I want my Harper back. The fun loving, wise cracking dare devil I fell in love with. The only way I know how to do that is to give you someone to help with Lucia. So that you can get back on your feet."

"I'm going to feed the baby." I yanked my arm out of his grasp and walked away.

"I'll see you tomorrow. I have work to do." Luc said.

I turned to reply but he had already disappeared. This was my life. Two children. No husband or partner. Just a devil who pops in and pops out of my life.

And a giant case of feeling extremely sorry for myself.

34

HARPER

MARCH 2000

It seems as though I didn't give enough credit to Luc for seeing exactly what was happening to me and trying to make it right. I had postpartum depression. Juliet, the night nurse Luc hired, had been the start of my way back. A visit to the doctor's office and medication had been the second big step. The days did not seem as long, the time I spent with Lucia did not seem as demanding. She was feeding better and growing well with supplementary night-time formula feeds.

I took the time to go through my wardrobe and selected a suitable dress to wear for dinner, applied some make-up and pinned my hair up into some semblance of a sophisticated style. Aimee had prepared coq-au-vin and had taken the children to the gatehouse for a couple of hours to allow Luc and I to have dinner alone. We hadn't been alone in the house since Lucia was born three months ago and I'd almost forgotten how to have an adult conversation. We sat across from each other at the dining room table, raised our glasses and toasted to our date night. Of course, I was drinking sparkling water.

"I need to apologise to you for the way I've been behaving. The meds the doctor prescribed are helping, and he said although it will take time, I will feel better every day. You were right, and I shouldn't have doubted you."

"No need to apologize. You're feeling better and that's all I ever wanted."

"Juliet has been a huge help. I don't know how most people do this without the help of nurses and housekeepers."

"They say it takes a village to raise a child. I'll hire a village if that is what it takes to make it easier on you."

Why did I fight this so long? I should have worked out right at the start that Luc was trying to do the right thing, instead of thinking that he doubted my capabilities as a mother. It was time to make amends. Time to show him how much I appreciated him.

"You're looking particularly handsome tonight, if I may say so." I reached over and put my hand over his.

"And you, are looking beautiful. Sleep becomes you." Luc smiled at me, turned his hand and wove his fingers through mine.

I laughed. "Never let me forget it. They say that severe sleep deprivation is the most successful means of torture."

"I would argue with that. Given what I do for a living. But it does have its merits."

Soft music filtered through the speakers in the background. A fire crackled in the fireplace in the feature wall between the dining room and the living room. The lights were low, and candles on our table cast a subtle glow over our meal. I could see a twinkle in Luc's eye, and he was smiling at me in a way he hadn't done for a while. I knew what was on his mind, and a tingle ran through my body and surprised me. The drugs were obviously working, as I had not felt like a sexual being for months.

"Would you care to dance?" Luc asked.

"Great minds think alike. I haven't been in your arms for a very long time." Luc walked around to my side of the table and offered me his hand. It brought back memories of the first time we met in the club in Monaco.

"Do you remember the night we first met. I couldn't wait to dance with you and be pressed up against you. You were a mystery to me then. A charismatic mystery I wanted to explore."

"Yes. I remember. You had the hots for me." Luc pulled me snugly against his body, and we swayed to the music.

"Delicately put." I laughed.

"My mission was to get you interested enough to follow me upstairs and gamble. There was a method in my madness."

"Why didn't you just suggest roulette to me."

"I honestly thought that you'd take a lot more convincing."

"So you used your body to convince me."

"You could say that."

"It worked. I got what I wanted, then I divorced Dean. You got what you wanted. I had a son for you to teach your devilish ways. Look at us now." I reached up and cupped his cheek. His fashionable stubble perfectly contoured his chin. "You always look so perfect. Beard cut just so. Eyebrows devilishly cavalier, skin bordering on olive. And those eyes. They change colour depending on your mood."

"What colour are they now?"

"Black. Mysterious. Inviting."

"I can hear the cogs turning in your head." Luc raised one eyebrow. "I know what you want."

"Do you?"

"Yes. A massage." Luc lowered his head and nibbled on my earlobe.

"A massage would be wonderful." Heat radiated down my neck.

"There's tension all over your body." Luc massaged my shoulders." I should take care of it. Ease out the knots." He lowered his head. His lips brushed my collar bone. A deliciously shiver ran over my skin.

"I think you're right. Yes, this is helping the tension."

Luc drew the zip of my dress down my spine, from neck to waist, and his hands wound their way inside to caress my back. He unclipped my bra, took a step back and eased the dress and bra from my shoulders. My heavy breasts tingled as they were freed from the restraints. "I love your breasts like this. Heavy and full, and with the nipples so dark, so prominent. Breasts to sustain and nurture our child. You are earth mother, look at you. So very beautiful." Luc bent his head and kissed the swell of my breast, then lathed the nipple, and drew one into his warm mouth. His tongue danced around the tip. Electric ripples of pleasure shot to my core.

"Be careful. Those are armed and dangerous."

"You don't scare me, what's a little breast milk going to do to me." Luc put his arm under my knees and lifted me effortlessly into his arms. "I think it's time I made love to you, before the children come back home, and Juliet arrives. What do you say""

"We have an hour. Take your time. Please."

35

LUC

It was time to get out of the house. I decided to take Lucia to the office to introduce her to the staff at Devil Dares. I hadn't been downtown for such a long time it felt surreal. Cameron dropped us on the sidewalk outside the office building and took off to park the car and wait in the underground parking lot.

There was a small crowd of protesters on the sidewalk and wide paved area outside the multistory building that housed Devil Dares Agency. They carried placards announcing the end of the world if we did not repent and turn to God. A tall, thin, and almost-bald man, dressed completely in black with a white clerical collar, and clutching a bible, stood on an upturned wooden crate and preached to the gathering that Satan was amongst us, and we must cast him out. A few people held up home-made banners covered in religious quotes.

I tucked Lucia against my chest inside my long charcoal coat. I drew my red shawl around my neck, covering her to shield her from the cold wind, hooked the diaper bag over my shoulder and made my way around the periphery of the crowd to the glass door of the building. Suddenly a woman began shouting and pointing at me. I turned and recognised her from the restaurant incident last year.

"There she is. The harlot of the devil. Behold, wickedness and depravity walks amongst us." Her long straggly grey hair fanned out around her face, and her black coat flapped around her legs as she ran toward me. Her ankle turned on a crack in the paving stone and she stumbled forward, landing on her knees a few feet away from me on the sidewalk. She clasped her hands together in prayer and yelled. "Oh mighty God, help us, strike down Satan's whore. Rid us of this evil." Some of the group turned and began moving in my direction. A stocky middle-aged man with red hair had reached her side and was staring at me with a malevolent expression on his face. He laid his hand on her shoulder, possessively.

I made it inside the building, and the security guard recognized me and came over to help. He stood guard at the door and locked it so that only he had the ability to allow entry. I glanced back toward the street. The woman was still praying and beseeching the heavens to help her. The group crowded around her, someone helped her to her feet. They returned to the preacher's side, dragging the uncooperative woman with them.

"I'm sorry Ma'am. I've called the local police, and they are sending someone to break up this group. They've been out there a few times this month."

"Thank you for locking the door. Please wait to let people in and don't unlock it until the police move them on."

"Yes, don't worry, I had every intention of doing so. This is the first time they have caused such a fuss though. They usually move on to another corner by themselves after half an hour or so. I can't imagine what is attracting them here at this corner."

To say this incident had spooked me was an understatement. Thank goodness Lucia had stayed asleep, peacefully unaware, tucked inside my coat. I pulled back the shawl and looked down at my little girl. Her long black eyelashes fanned out against her perfect chubby pale cheeks. Her cupid's bow mouth pouted in her sleep. I wondered what she was dreaming of. Probably her next feed and getting milk drunk. What else could a tiny baby be thinking of.

The office staff were delighted to meet Lucia. She was passed from person to person, admired and fawned over. She didn't cry, she seemed happy to add more admirers to the long list. I was able to catch up on some office information and assure myself that the Agency was managing fine without me. Business was booming. New contracts had been set up with film studio's and there was no shortage of fit, strong, handsome young men ready to sign on the dotted line and be stunt actors.

I had been tinkering with a plot idea for a new movie. I pitched the idea to Ben and Harry, a couple of our script writers, and they were very encouraging. Perhaps it was time for me to get back into writing again. It would give me an interest when Lucia was napping. I had been thinking a lot lately about returning to work downtown at the Agency. The more I thought about it, the less I wanted to do it. The idea of going to work and leaving Lucia with someone was not appealing to me. When I had Domenic, Richard took over managing the Agency, and I never had to worry if I was there or working from home. It wasn't until Domenic went to school that I went back to the Agency building to work.

But it was different now. Money wasn't an object, Luc took care of anything I needed, I just had to ask. He was aware of not going over the top to draw too much attention to our lifestyle. Although I am sure I could have asked for a Palace, and a yacht in the Mediterranean, and I would have received it. However, I did like the independence having my own business allowed me. I didn't totally depend on Luc and could manage on my own, even with two children. But I had to admit that the lifestyle I had become accustomed to with Luc was not something I could easily walk away from. I enjoyed having Cameron and Aimee to help around the house, keep me company when Luc was absent, and to make life easy for me. I still had Juliet coming in the evening, but now that Lucia was starting to sleep through the night, her contract would be terminating soon.

I didn't enjoy Luc spending so much time away from us, but as he explained, he didn't have a nine to five job. I tried not to think of what he was expected to do in a normal day. In my mind he had changed a lot since we first met. Yes, he was still the smart, self-assured, charismatic Devil he always had been and he could reduce me to a puddle of desire just by raising an eyebrow. But now he was much more. He was a father and he was protective of his family. He was giving and loving and considerate. There was nothing he would not do for Domenic and Lucia and for me, and I was very grateful.

Little did I know what this devotion was costing him.

36
LUC

There had been so many new guests arriving in Hell, the staff were complaining about unfair conditions and long hours. The suggestion box was full. Mostly telling me what a terrible example I was. Protesters had camped outside my office. I had my personal demon staff move them on. Drake was waiting for me by my door with a box of new files. It was like this every time I came down to the office to work.

"There has to be another way." I said.

"If there is, I haven't been able to work it out." Drake took a seat on the other side of the desk.

"I cannot be here all the time."

"You must admit that you've been spending a lot more time on Earth now that Lucia . . ."

"Would you do anything differently? Having a child. Watching the changes day by day. It's fascinating. I had never taken the time to examine how an infant can pick up so much information in such a short time. Their capacity for learning is amazing."

"I can't say I've taken the time. I've never been around children."

"They are teaching *me* things. Domenic is an exceptional child, although very serious. He has his heart set on being a doctor, and I have no doubt he'll achieve his dreams."

"You do sound like a proud father. To both children." Drake sat back and smiled.

"I *am* a father to both children. I hope to influence Domenic. Teach him to take over from me when he is older."

"You expect him to take over in Hell? You do realise the implications of that. The only way a human can come here to Hell is if he's deceased."

"Unlike us, humans don't live forever. He has to end up somewhere. I want it to be here."

"You said he wants to be a doctor. He's going to be doing good in the world, making a difference. I think the decision will be taken out of your hands. He'll be going up not down."

"When the time comes, I am sure I can make a case for him coming down here. The world is changing. There is evil, more than even I could've imagined, behind computer screens, lurking in the shadows, even walking the streets in broad daylight. I can't be everywhere at all times. I could do with some help from someone I can trust to follow orders. He has a lot of me in him already. I am planning on giving him more."

"I don't think that's a good idea."

"Short of cloning myself... and don't think I haven't thought about it, I can't see another way around this. I need to have more time on Earth with Harper and Lucia. He could start off with the small stuff. He doesn't have to be in Hell to do it. He can be the go between. Picking up on the cases that he'll no doubt come in contact with every day. He could be a spotter. With his intuition I imagine he could pick up on the ones that could be led into temptation."

"I'll believe it when I see for myself. No one has ever held a candle to you in luring weak humans over to our side."

"Time will tell Drake. Time will tell."

There were days like this when I doubted that I could have a normal life, without a million voices in my head. Harper had no idea what it was like to be needed everywhere at once. I had removed all the obstacles to her getting over this post-partum depression. I had provided staff, and a comfortable home for her to live in and bring up the children. I was trying to provide a safe space for them. But there were always forces at play working against me.

It had come to my notice that a few of the evil people I had taken to Hell had appeared on Earth again and begun to cause havoc. There were unknown forces at play here, and I had no idea who they were or why they had chosen this time to work against me.

The portal to move between worlds was not something that anyone could conjure up. Therefore, whoever was behind this had a certain amount of power. It was becoming obvious I was going to have to spend more time in Hell and get to the bottom of it. I was not going to be popular with Harper.

37
HARPER

JUNE 2000

The red tartan picnic blanket, bordered by plump red cushions, sat in the center of a sea of lush green grass, which was tucked in behind the east wing of the house. Lucia squirmed on my lap watching Domenic chasing Max, who was in turn chasing a yellow tennis ball. The garden bordering the lawn, brimming with flowers and greenery, enticed butterflies and bees which could be heard buzzing if you ventured near. The warm sun shone down on my little family, and I breathed in deeply, enjoying the peace and tranquillity my walled garden could provide. Cameron, who was wearing green overalls and with his shirt sleeves rolled up, was trimming some overgrown bushes and small trees around the garden wall. Even although he was doing such a physical task, he still looked like an English gentleman. I couldn't fault his ability with plants though. He had a green thumb and had brought the garden back to life. It was a beautiful oasis now and one the children and I could enjoy, away from prying eyes. We were up higher than a lot of the homes around us, at the end of a dead-end street, but that meant that we didn't have to be bothered by our neighbors or visitors coming and going, or tourists passing through. It took longer to get to downtown, but it was a small price to pay for privacy.

Aimee appeared from the house holding a tray containing fresh fruit, and a pitcher of orange juice. I asked her to sit with us for a while. She knelt on the blanket and put the tray in the middle. I could not fail to notice how much she doted on Lucia. Juliet was no longer employed for the night shift, and Aimee had taken to minding Lucia for short periods of time throughout the day, sometimes walking her around the garden in her stroller to get her to sleep, when I was trying to write. She was clearly besotted with Lucia, and Lucia was taking full advantage of this situation. She stretched out her chubby little arms to Aimee, who took her on her knee and cuddled her and kissed her warm neck. Lucia chuckled appreciatively, and smiled, showing off her dimpled cheeks and two tiny bottom teeth. Aimee held a piece of banana while Lucia happily chewed and sucked on the end. Domenic came over to join us, picked up a shiny red apple, and sat down crossed legged on the picnic blanket to join us. Max flopped down on the grass at his side, with his tongue lolling, panting and waiting for the game to begin again. I poured four cups of orange juice, handed one to Domenic, and to Aimee, and took a sip of my own.

"Cameron, come and join us. Aimee has brought us a snack, and some juice. You must be hot."

Cameron peeled off his gardening gloves and came to stand beside us. He took the cup of orange juice I held out.

"Thanks. I needed that." Cameron handed back the empty cup. "I'll keep going if you don't mind."

"Here, at least take an apple." I threw him an apple and he caught it easily with one hand and tucked it into his back pocket. He gave me the thumbs up.

"Razor sharp reflexes. Well done." I lay back on the cushion and looked up at the sky. "What a beautiful day." Aimee wiped Lucia's hands, placed her on the rug beside Domenic and stood up. "Don't go Aimee. Stay and enjoy the sunshine with us for a while."

"Thank you, but I have chores to do, and lunch to prepare and pop it in the oven. We're having quiche Lorraine with salad."

"Sounds delicious. Thanks again for the snacks." It was easy to lay back on the scattered cushions and allow someone else to arrange my food, to arrange my life. I wondered when Luc would return. Domenic picked up Lucia, kissed her cheek and placed her beside me on the blanket. He ran off with Max for another game of fetch. I tickled Lucia and delighted in her smile. "Mama loves you, baby girl."

"Mama." Lucia said.

"Oh my goodness. Say it again. Say mama again. Mama. Come on baby girl."

"Mama." Lucia said again.

I picked her up and hugged her tight. This was a big deal. Her first word. At only six months old, and it was Mama.

"What a clever girl you are. Your daddy will be so proud of you."

"What did she do?" Domenic came over, threw himself down on the rug and took another piece of fruit. He picked up a quarter of a strawberry and offered it to Lucia. She accepted it and squished it in her fingers before stuffing the remaining pieces in her mouth. Domenic got up to play with Max again. I turned to reach for a napkin to wipe Lucia's hands and face, but when I turned back, she had another piece of strawberry clutched in her hand.

"Where did you get that baby girl?"

I watched her eat the strawberry, reach out her chubby hand and another piece of strawberry lifted from the dish and floated in the air to her strawberry covered fingers. No way! My daughter could move things with her mind?

"Domenic, come over here please." I passed him the plate of fruit and asked him to take it a few steps away. "Hold up a strawberry and offer it to Lucia."

Lucia outstretched both hands, her tiny fingers wiggling in the air, and the strawberry left Domenic's palm and made its way across the garden.

"Wow, she has telekinesis. Cool." Domenic ran back and joined us again on the blanket. He popped a strawberry in his mouth.

"I'm not sure if that's a good thing or a bad thing. How are we going to stop her from just taking anything she wants? Even if it's not good for her." I tried in vain to wipe her fruit stained hands and face. More fruit appeared in the air. I pushed it back onto the plate. "Take the plate indoors please honey."

Now this was a turn of events I wasn't expecting. I wondered what else my daughter can do?

Luc returned home after dinner, when I was preparing to put Lucia to bed.

"Hello pumpkin. How's my girl?"

"I'm fine thanks . . . Oh, you didn't mean me. How silly of me to think I was your number one girl."

I smiled as Luc picked up his daughter and nuzzled her warm neck. She giggled delightedly. Still holding onto Lucia, he bent down and gave me a soft kiss on the lips.

"There's no contest. You are my number one *woman*. Lucia is my number one *girl*."

"Well your number one woman has some news for you. Lucia has either developed or discovered telekinesis. I have no idea how long she has been able to do this, but I saw it with my own eyes today. She picked up strawberries. It seems she really likes strawberries.

"Ah ha. She has some of her father's capabilities. Not just her mother's beauty."

"Oh, I think she has her father's beauty. Anyone who looks at her can see you. Those dark eyes, long thick eyelashes, full luscious lips, and able to charm anyone at a glance. A chip off the old block."

"She has her mother's sweet nature." Luc winked at me.

"You're being far too nice to me tonight. What's going on?"

"This is only a short visit. It seems that I have a big problem that I have to deal with. At work."

"Problems in Hell? That shouldn't surprise me. So, tell me what's happening."

"It's complicated."

"Isn't it always."

"There are forces trying to undermine my authority. The investigation is in progress, but it seems that every time I'm away from Hell for extended periods of time, someone is trying to take control. Evil is intensifying on earth. People are being possessed, causing a lot of damage, but it's not by me."

"It's funny you should mention that because I saw on the news that more of these "God Squad" rallies are being held around the city. They have been preaching about the Evil amongst us, about possession and casting out the devil. I see them when I drive into town, preaching on street corners. Their numbers are growing, they are spilling onto the roads, blocking traffic."

"I've been keeping an eye on them. And I agree their numbers are growing. But let's put this little one to bed and enjoy the time we have together tonight."

I tucked the blankets around my sleepy baby, watched her eyes close, and then backed out of the nursery. I was lucky that she settled down easily at night. Domenic popped his head out of his room and announced he was going to bed to read and had said goodnight to Luc. I gave him a hug, ruffled his mop of dark hair, and kissed his forehead. I returned to the living room, where Luc had lowered the lights, and music played softly in the background. He had poured two glasses of red wine. Now that I had weaned Lucia onto formula, I could have the odd glass of wine, and it was a welcomed treat to share with Luc at the end of the day. He had announced this was a short visit. I wanted to make the most of it.

I sat down beside him and accepted the glass. I took a sip,

enjoying the taste and the way the flavours lingered in my mouth. Luc took a sip of his wine and watched me over the rim. He put down his glass. Luc's fingers trailed across my shoulder, to the back of my neck, where he massaged the muscles at the base of my skull. I closed my eyes briefly. My body relaxed into the soft cushions of the couch. I turned my head and watched his eyes take on a darker hue. He cocked an eyebrow at me. It was a question he didn't need an answer to. I was always ready for his touch. He took the glass from me and placed it on the side table, cupped my cheeks in his hands, ran the pad of his thumb over my bottom lip and bent his mouth to mine. His soft kiss became more insistent and his tongue teased mine. I pulled back from his mouth.

"I don't think you're aware how much I miss this when you're gone. The simple pleasure of having you near me, sitting next to me, taking my hand, looking into your eyes. People often take for granted the time spent with a loved one, but I never do. I have a partner, a lover, a father for my children but only for a fraction of the time. And yet, I would not give that up. The minutes I spend with you far outweigh any other experiences in my life. And having the children, of course. You gave me a very special gift when you gave me Lucia. A tiny, perfect, glorious part of you. Lucia is the most precious child, charming everyone she comes into contact with. She gets that from you."

"Are you trying to tell me I'm charming?"

"You know you are. I don't have to tell you. Hence the expression 'charming devil'."

"Now who's sweet talking who tonight?"

"I mean it Luc. I miss you so very much when you're not here, but I wouldn't give this up. I wouldn't give you up."

"If there was any other way, I would do it. I'd rather be here with my family, than with the scum of the Earth."

"I'm proud of you, are you aware of that?"

"Proud?"

"Yes. You have changed a lot since I first met you. We talk more.

We share more. We laugh more. Your open up to me now. You've lightened up."

"Being around you, watching the kids growing up, has made me appreciate things. I'm eager to see what Lucia can do. The fact that she has shown abilities now, while she's so young, is exciting."

"It's exciting for you. But what's it going to mean for me? What if she can conjure something up that isn't good for her, or harms her?"

"I can't answer that. This is new territory for me too."

"I guess I'd better be prepared for anything and everything."

"Let me know when she grows a tail." Luc grinned.

"Oh my god, that's not going to happen. Is it?"

"I'm teasing you. The image you see before you is my appearance when I was an angel. This is my true form. I have no horns, I have no tail, I have no red skin. That frightening image is what was forced upon me when I was sent to Hell. It was my punishment to be marked as hideous. It was for the sole purpose of terrifying the inhabitants, and striking fear into those who were non-believers. Lucia is the child of an angel, don't worry. However, I have no way of knowing if, like me, she can change her appearance at will, when she's older."

"I'm going to have to trust that you'll be here to help me through that phase. Let's forget about it now and take the wine to enjoy in our bedroom." I stood and held out my hand. "While we can."

"Maybe I'll just turn on the TV for a while. There has to be sports on one of the channels."

"Don't dare touch that remote!"

"Come on. I'm just trying to be the normal American guy who loves his sports." Luc laughed at me. "I like it when you get worked up and feisty."

I picked up a pillow and threw it in Luc's direction, and he ducked, launched off the couch, and grabbed me around the waist. He picked me up and threw me across his shoulder.

"I could be persuaded to change my mind." Luc said.

His hand rested on my bottom. The heat from his palm scorched my skin through the fabric of my dress and underwear and shot straight to my core.

"The wine!" I reached out my hand toward the glass.

"Too late. I'll come back for it later."

"Later?"

"Much later."

38
HARPER

In the early morning light, I stirred and stretched out my hand, to find Luc's side of the bed was empty. I didn't even hear him leave. I closed my eyes and slipped back into a sound slumber until my alarm named "Lucia" announced it was breakfast time.

I slipped on my robe, fastened the tie around me, balanced Lucia on my hip and made my way down to the kitchen where Aimee was preparing breakfast. Domenic was at the kitchen table reading a book, while he ate his breakfast of toast and peanut butter. The comforting aroma of home-made bread, fresh from the hot oven, lingered in the air in the kitchen. Once Lucia was comfortable in her high-chair I busied myself with preparing her breakfast cereal. I turned around in time to see Lucia practicing her new-found skills. Pieces of banana and strawberries danced in the air and glided toward Lucia from a plate of fruit salad on the table. I quickly pushed them down onto a spare plate before Aimee turned around. Domenic had caught this display and was grinning. I raised my eyebrows at him. He shrugged his shoulders in reply. He didn't know how to stop her either.

The cereal was enough to distract Lucia for a while. I placed the plate with fruit salad on her tray and she busied herself, squashing the fruit in her fingers and attempting to eat whatever squeezed through. Domenic glanced up and smiled at his baby sister, he played peek-a-book behind his book and she giggled back at him. I drank my coffee, ate some warm bread straight from the oven, slathered with butter and honey, and watched the delighted antics of my son and baby daughter. They clearly loved each other, and that fact made me very happy. Lucia had strawberry juice all over her face, and when she giggled more juice dribbled down her chin.

"She sure loves strawberries." Amy refilled my coffee cup, filled one for herself and joined me at the table.

"I think she likes the way they squish between her fingers more than anything else."

"She is one happy baby right now."

"I'll clean up this mess and get her dressed. I have a package to pick up from the office this morning. If Cameron can come and pick us up after he takes Domenic to school, I'll take Lucia to buy some new clothes. She's growing out of everything fast."

"Leave it, I'm happy to clean her high-chair. Do you want some company? I'd love to go baby clothes shopping with you."

"Sure. Two pairs of hands are better than one when you're trying clothes on a squirming baby."

"What time do you want the car? I can let Cameron know."

"It will take me about an hour by the time I get dressed and change Lucia. I want to get in the store and out again before Lucia is ready for another nap"

"Why don't you leave Lucia here with me to finish her fruit, and you go have a shower and get dressed. I'll be happy to change her. That way we'll be quicker."

"If you're sure. That would be great."

"I'll pack a bottle in the diaper bag."

"You are a treasure Aimee. I don't know what I'd do without you."

"Go on then. Get ready."

The downtown department store was quite busy, but with a sales assistant and Aimee's help we were back on the sidewalk where Cameron dropped us, within the hour. Aimee climbed into the back seat with Lucia, and Cameron loaded our purchases into the trunk. I walked around to open the other door and noticed a man wearing dark clothes and a baseball cap staring at the car from the other side of the road. He looked oddly familiar. I had the sudden urge to get into the car and lock the door, and I racked my brain to work out why. As we drove away from the curb I glanced back, and he was still watching the car drive away. We were nearly at Devil Dares Agency building when it occurred to me where I had seen the man before. He had been outside the building the day I took Lucia to work when she was about three months old. He was standing beside that grey-haired woman who had yelled at me from the crowd. It hadn't clicked because his cap covered his red hair. No denying the malevolence in those eyes though. I shivered just thinking about it.

"If you wait here Cameron, I won't be long. Aimee I can take Lucia with me, but she looks happy here with you."

"She's fine. Do what you have to do."

"Her pacifier is in her diaper bag. I promise I will be quick."

It took me only minutes to reach my floor, pick up the package, say hello to a few staff members in the reception area, and get back in the elevator. I couldn't have been gone any longer than ten minutes. The car was not parked beside the curb, or anywhere up or down the street. I flipped open my phone and dialled Cameron's number. He didn't answer. I headed for the entrance to the parking garage, and the car appeared from around the corner. I jumped in and Cameron sped away from the sidewalk.

"I wondered where you'd gone."

"We drove around the block to keep Lucia happy." Aimee said.

"Was she upset?"

"Just a bit agitated. She settled down when we were moving."

"That's unlike her. Maybe she missed me."

"Yes, that's probably the answer." Aimee said.

Cameron turned the car off the main street and took a few back streets to get home. Aimee chatted about the clothes we had chosen for Lucia and the recipe she was going to make for lunch, and the price of groceries, but when she began to discuss the weather, I knew something wasn't right.

"Okay what's going on? Cameron, you're driving fast, and not taking the usual route. Aimee, I know you love a chat, but you haven't stopped since we left the city. If you're trying to distract me, it's not working. Why are we taking the back streets?" Cameron glanced up at Aimee through the rear-view mirror.

"Come on. Spill it. You're making me nervous."

"We're being followed." Cameron said.

"You're kidding me. Why?" I turned to look out the back window.

"I have no idea, but I think I've lost them." Cameron sped up the hill, pressed the remote for the gates at the end of the street, and glided through. The solid metal gates closed swiftly behind us. He drove around the decorative water feature in the circular driveway, pulled up beside the steps and began to unload the trunk.

Luc appeared at the front door. He took Lucia from Aimee's arms and I couldn't help but see the look that passed between them. They were keeping something from me, and I wanted to make it very clear that this wasn't going to happen again. I followed them inside.

"Can someone tell me what is going on? Luc, what are you doing here? You said you had things to attend to, that work was busy. No one is saying anything but the tension in the room is palpable."

"Calm down." Luc said.

"Don't tell me to calm down, when I know you're keeping things from me again."

"I called Luc." Aimee said. "I was worried about Lucia."

"Worried in what way?"

"There was a presence. I sensed a danger to Lucia when we were shopping today."

"A danger? To my daughter!"

"That was why we moved the car. But Cameron spotted a car following us."

"You're safe here." Luc said.

"Safe from what? From who?" I looked at both of them and fisted my hands on my hips. "Tell me."

"There's been some talk about Lucia. Some people in positions of authority don't like the fact that I have a daughter, and that she's showing signs of having powers of her own."

This comment, made in the presence of Aimee, unsettled me. And then it dawned on me. "Aimee knows who you are?" At that point Cameron appeared in the room. "And I presume Cameron knows who you are too?"

'Yes. Aimee and Cameron are both part of my world. I trusted them to look after you when I wasn't here, and to protect my family."

"Protect us from what?"

"The nether world. The people who would like to take over, and to create chaos on Earth, as if it's not bad enough already. People who've decided I've become soft since being involved with, and having a child with, a human."

"You and Cameron are not human?" I turned to Aimee.

"No."

"What are you?"

"We were human. We died in world war two. We served our time in Hell. This assignment as your security detail was a way to make amends and a promotion for us both." Aimee answered.

"So, you were never in the Army? Were never married?" I asked Cameron.

"Yes, we were in the Army, and yes we were married. We worked for an underground resistance group, but we were caught up in some . . . let's say . . . unusual behaviour. We were hired assassins. That's why we ended up in Hell." Cameron said.

"Cameron and Aimee have skills and powers I needed, and they could be here when I could not. They were not bad people. They played their part in a war. I have two of my best soldiers here with you twenty-four seven. Do you really think that I would leave you unprotected? I didn't tell you because I wanted you and Domenic and Lucia to have the most normal life possible. Knowing about Cameron and Aimee wouldn't have been helpful. You would have been nervous if I had told you . . ."

"That I have hired assassins from Hell in my house and looking after my children. Do you blame me."

"But now you've spent more than a year with both Cameron and Aimee, who have shown you nothing but kindness and care. They've done what grandparents would do, dropping off Domenic to school and looking after Lucia so that you can have time to write your movie scripts. Cameron is a wizard in the garden and Aimee is a delight in the kitchen. You *know* these people."

I looked at the two people who had been my companions for the last year or so, and saw concern etched into their faces. Their concern was not for themselves, but for me. I felt ashamed of myself for my outburst. Luc was right. I knew these two souls to be kind and always helpful. They clearly doted on the children and on Max, and their feelings were reciprocated. They say children and animals are good judges of character.

"I'm sorry Aimee and Cameron. I do know you, and I do trust you. Aimee you were there at my daughter's birth and she clearly adores you." Lucia had reached out her chubby little arms for Aimee to hold her. Once cradled in the crook of Aimee's arm, Lucia's eyelids fluttered shut.

"I'll take her up for her nap." Aimee left with Lucia, and Cameron followed them out of the room.

"You should've told me Luc. You should've trusted me with the information. But . . . I can understand what you were trying to do. And I love you for trying to give us the semblance of a normal life."

"You and Domenic and Lucia are what matter to me most on Earth, and I must protect those I love. If that means bringing in more soldiers I will."

"Tell me more about this threat. Is my daughter safe here when you're gone?"

"The grounds are protected. There are cameras everywhere and sensors around the walls. The gate cannot be opened by anyone without a special remote. If anyone manages to get through,

Cameron and Aimee are well armed to combat them and defend you."

"I guess it shouldn't surprise me. I've been the naïve one, thinking that life was normal, when in actual fact I am living with the Devil and have had his child. What could be less normal than that?"

"Believe me, I'm trying to get to the bottom of it. Someone is stirring up the masses and creating tension all over the world, and I need to find them before they manage to create another world war, and I get the blame for it. Again."

"I feel helpless, and I am the cause of this. Is there anything I can do?"

"Stay inside the house and garden walls. Don't go downtown for the moment when I am not here. I'm going to have Cameron and Aimee move into the guest suite on the ground floor for the time being. I'd feel better if they were sleeping in the house with you, and not in the gatehouse."

"What about Domenic?"

"There is no threat against him. He is not my genetic son, and no doubt they are aware he doesn't have the same powers as Lucia. He's safe to attend school. Cameron will take him and pick him up. The semester finishes in two days anyway and then he's on summer vacation."

"I don't suppose we could fly off to the South of France for a couple of months?"

"That would not be wise."

"We'll just have to hang out by the pool in the back yard and pretend we're near the ocean."

"That's my girl." Luc pulled me into his arms and kissed me softly on the lips. "Are we good?"

"Yes, I guess we're good."

"I'll be back later tonight. Try not to worry. You have everything you need within these walls."

"No more secrets please." I took a step forward, into his arms.

"No more secrets." Luc tipped up my chin and kissed me. Then he disappeared.

39
HARPER

Lucia's vocabulary was growing. She could say Mama and Dada, and Dom. She was attempting to say Aimee and Cameron, but those names were still unclear. Whenever she was in the vicinity, her toys moved around the room, and the music box often began to play. While I changed her diaper, she waved her hands in the air and a toy rabbit made of pink spotted fabric, danced on top of the dresser. She giggled happily at this show of her ability. Like any child, she was trying to make sense of the world around her, testing out how far she could go. I had become used to unusual things happening where she was concerned.

Lucia had been able to sit up by herself for a few weeks, and now showed interest in crawling. She got up onto her knees and rocked back and forth. Her progression was happening quicker than with Domenic, but that shouldn't have surprised me. We were going to have to move furniture and babyproof some edges of coffee tables for the foreseeable future. All of her teeth were coming in quickly, but apart from some sleepless nights, and red cheeks she was no trouble.

Add into this sudden growth spurt, the fact of Lucia's powers, which were being demonstrated daily, and I could see life was going to take on a different direction. The sweet tiny babe-in-arms was no more, she moved around holding onto the furniture and at this rate she would be walking on her own soon. Each day she appeared to have grown much bigger. Luc had asked me to stay within the security of the garden walls, but it was proving to be the best place where my daughter could try out her powers without fear of discovery. How would I explain a child of nine months walking and talking, with a full set of teeth, looking more like a two-year-old? How would I explain toys or fruit gliding in the air towards her outstretched hands, in public places?

The fact that Aimee and Cameron were experiencing these changes with me was really comforting. Nothing Lucia did surprised them, and they seemed prepared for all and any changes or abilities she demonstrated. We were all on high alert in case she did something to endanger herself, or others. Max followed here everywhere. He was her shadow when Domenic wasn't around. She clearly loved him, and often wrapped her chubby little arms around his neck and laid her head on his. When she slept, he dropped on the floor beside the crib, and laid his head on his paws. We left the door ajar, but any movement near her room and he raised his head. No one would get past him.

"We have to move Lucia into a bed. The crib is getting too small."

"If you call the store and order what you like, they can deliver." Luc took a sip of his morning coffee.

"And she needs more advanced toys for stimulation."

"Yes, I've noticed she has been interested in some of Domenic's things."

"You don't want me to leave the house and grounds, but we cannot stay locked behind these gates forever."

"Do you want to go into town? I'll stay here with Lucia and Domenic, and Cameron can take you to buy the things you want. Does that work for you?'

"Really? You can stay here today. In that case I'll take you up on your offer and get moving." I hugged Luc, dropped a kiss on his forehead and ran upstairs to get dressed.

I hadn't been outside the protection of the walls for such a long time I was giddy with excitement. Luc insisted Cameron drive me, but I didn't want to argue and risk him changing his mind. I had a list of things I wanted to purchase for Lucia, but also some books for Domenic, and perhaps a pretty dress for myself. I definitely wanted to pick up something for Aimee, who had been spending a lot of time with Lucia, patiently reading to her to help with her vocabulary or walking with her in the garden. Cameron would talk to her about the flowers, the birds nesting in the trees and how the bees help the garden grow. Aimee and Cameron had become the grandparents Lucia didn't have.

I told Cameron to come back in three hours. The stores weren't busy but having that many people around me after such a long time at home was strange. I was able to buy nearly everything I wanted from one store for Lucia and Domenic and arranged for delivery later that afternoon. I found a beautiful cashmere shawl for Aimee and a sweater for Cameron in a boutique, and a dress of midnight blue silk, which did wonders for my self-esteem. I was having a celebratory coffee at a café when I noticed the man with the dark clothes and red hair crossing the road heading for the cafe. My heart quickened, I didn't know what to do, but he walked by the café window, seemingly unaware I was inside. I abandoned the coffee, collected my packages and hurried to the meeting point I had arranged with Cameron.

I kept glancing behind me but could see no one following. Yet a presence, like a heavy weight pressed down on me. The flock of crows circling overhead, cast a sombre shadow, their harsh caw reverberating in my head. When I rounded the corner and spotted Cameron in the car parked by the curb relief surged through me.

"I've never been so happy to see you. Could you put your foot down and get us home as quickly as possible, please Cameron? I saw that dreadful man again, the one I saw the last time we were in town, but I don't think he saw me. He gives me the creeps. Although I was sure I was being watched all the way from the café to the car."

"Buckle up." Cameron said. "Do you want me to call Luc?"

"No just get us home please."

Cameron took the back streets again, and I had started to relax, when a black truck with a large metal grill appeared from a side street and rammed into the driver's side with such force, our car was pushed over to the side of the road and into a fence. There was no escape from that side. Two men jumped out of the back of the truck, one had a crowbar in his hand, and they wrenched the driver's crumpled door open. One man pulled Cameron out, and although he was injured and bleeding, he attempted to fight until one of them raised the crowbar and knocked him out with a blow to the head. My damaged back door was pulled open, the second man dragged me out, pinned my arms to my body and a rough burlap sack was put over my head and shoulders. It had a pungent aroma of damp earth and moldy potatoes. I was lifted off the ground, still kicking and yelling. They headed in the direction of the truck until I felt a sting in my arm and the last thing I managed to yell was "Luc". Then the world disappeared.

40

LUC

Lucia continued to surprise and delight me with her antics. She hadn't learned to control her powers, so things were happening which caught both of us off guard and made me laugh. The sun streamed down on the patio, a perfect setting for our lunch. Lucia obviously didn't want to eat the sandwich Aimee made, and dropped half the sandwich off the side of her high-chair. The sandwich broke apart and splattered on the patio floor beside Max, who thought he had been given a treat and started to eat it. Lucia had watched the food falling and when Max started to eat, she decided that it might be tasty after all. The remaining food rose from the ground and Max followed the progression trying to bite it in mid-air, which made Lucia and I laugh, and thoroughly confused Max. She reached out her fingers to Max who floated a few inches off the floor.

"No, put Max down Lucia."

"Max" said Lucia. "Max up"

"Come on, be a good girl, put Max down on the ground."

Lucia hiccupped and Max landed with a thud. He did not look impressed as all the food had disappeared.

"Where's your lunch? Bring it back Lucia."

A large bowl of fruit appeared on Lucia's tray. She looked delighted with this result.

"Where did this come from?"

Aimee appeared through the kitchen door. "Ah, there's my fruit. I wondered where it had disappeared to."

"She's more interested in fruit than a sandwich, I think." I removed a banana from the plate, peeled it for Lucia, and handed it to her. "Only one."

"I'll take this back inside." Aimee picked up the bowl.

Lucia looked disappointed but took the banana I handed to her.

Suddenly my heart began to pound faster in my chest, Harper was in trouble. I heard her call my name.

"Aimee! Watch Lucia. Don't let her out of your sight. Something's wrong with Harper."

I found the car on the back road to our house. The atmosphere around the vehicle retained the emotions. Anger, fear, adrenalin. Cameron is lying on the road by the front wheel, but there is no sign of Harper. There are tire skid marks on the road. Where are you Harper? Why can't I hear you? Your voice is always in my head. But not now, not at this moment. Why? I won't believe you're dead, because my heart is still beating. I will find you and nothing on Earth will stop me from punishing the people who have taken you. *Nothing!*

I checked to see if Cameron was still breathing and within seconds we were back inside the grounds. I laid him on a deck chair on the patio. Aimee came rushing over, with Lucia on her hip and Domenic by her side.

"Take her, I'll get my medical bag." She passed my daughter to me.

"His head wound looks pretty bad."

Cameron was beginning to come to and tried to sit up. "I'm sorry Luc. Where's Harper? Did they take her?"

"Take it easy. You're bleeding quite badly." I put Lucia down on the patio and adjusted the deck chair so that Cameron could lie back.

"I need to check if your pupils are dilated. To see if you have a concussion." Aimee said.

Domenic laid his hand on Cameron's head. "He doesn't have a concussion. His skull is rather thick. There is no bleeding on the brain. But he will have a bad headache for a while." He ran his hand over Cameron's shoulder. He has a tear in his muscle. A lot of bruising. I suggest a sling and to rest this arm for a while."

"Thank you, Domenic." Aimee said. "You're going to make a fine doctor one day." Aimee pressed a sterile gauze pad onto the wound on Cameron's forehead. "Hold this pad here Domenic, while I clean the blood from his face."

"Can you tell me anything about what happened? I gather there was one vehicle which rammed the car. How many attacked you? Did they say anything?"

"A black truck with a metal ram bar came out of a side-street, rammed us and forced us over the road. They must have been waiting. One man was driving. Two men jumped out of the back, forced the car door open and we fought but I don't know if there were others as I was hit with something pretty solid."

"Was there anything about them you recognized? Were they from our world?"

"No. I'm pretty sure they're not. They had no powers and they came at me with nothing more than their fists and a crowbar. I had no chance to use any of mine before I was knocked out. It was over in minutes."

I heard the sound of wings flapping and looked up to see a flock of black crows circling above the garden. Max raced onto the lawn and started barking up at the birds. They swooped down, trying to peck at him.

It was then I turned around and saw Lucia tottering across the lawn in the other direction toward a huge black crow which had obviously landed on the grass while we were occupied. Her little hands were out in front of her as if she was reaching out to touch the bird. Max turned direction and ran at full speed toward Lucia. The crow took flight, grabbing her by the shoulders and lifting her off the ground. It instantly disappeared through the veil to the underworld before my eyes.

"No!" I yelled, and everyone turned around, but she had gone. I moved through the Veil between worlds as quickly as I could, but she had disappeared, and there are so many tunnels and directions I had no idea which way they had gone. The crow had obviously cloaked her in his dark magic, I couldn't hear her. Someone was obviously using pretty amazing powers to stop me from finding my daughter.

Fury bubbled up through every fiber of my being, shaking the space around me, causing the walls of the tunnels to crumble. I had to control this anger, not destroy the tunnels, or I would never find her.

And then I heard Harper's voice in my head. Good. Now I had something to go on. Just keep thinking of me Harper. I'm coming for you.

Harper first. Then Lucia.

❧

The dwelling was hidden from the road, surrounded by a thick band of trees on one side, and a steep drop to the canyon below on the other side. The black truck Cameron had described was parked outside. I located Harper in the basement, laying on a single bed pushed up against the brick wall. Her hands and feet were bound with rope, and a cloth blindfold covered her eyes. The look of relief when I removed her blindfold, constricted my heart. How could I tell her now that our daughter was missing in the underworld?

"Thank God you came, I was hoping you would hear me. Is Cameron alright? He was knocked out."

"There was a long period when I couldn't hear you."

"They injected me with something. I passed out."

"Come on get up. We have to go." I removed the rope ties. Harper stood up but was unsteady on her feet.

The basement door burst open and a man of advanced years with grey wiry hair, dressed in black and with a clergyman's white starched collar, stood in the doorway clutching a bible and large wooden crucifix in one hand and a glass bottle of clear liquid in the other. Behind him on the stairs stood two tall and heavy-set younger men dressed similarly in black.

"We have you now Satan, vile instrument of evil. Destroyer of all things pure and wholesome. You fell into our trap. In the name of Jesus, the authority of the Bible, and the power of his Gospel, be gone!" The clergyman took a step forward. "This holy water will destroy you, remove you from this Earth never to return. God will send you back to Hell where you belong. You have corrupted this woman. She is evil just as you are, she has brought a child into this world, and now she must also pay the price!" He lifted his arm to throw the liquid.

I raised my hand and paused time, and the liquid froze mid-air. I picked Harper up, took her outside and set her down outside the building near the road.

"Wait here for me, I will only be a few minutes." It pained me to leave her when she was shaky on her feet and anxious, but it had to be done.

I returned to the room, unfroze time, and returned the liquid to the bottle. My human form changed and I allowed him to see the Devil he saw in all his nightmares. His eyes widened and he took a step back.

"Stupid man. I have no time for your games. You laid hands on the woman I love. You shall rot in Hell, but first I will give you a taste of what's in store for all of you."

I blew a breath over the three of them and their clothes burst into flames, their skin bubbled, and their flesh melted. I left the room, watched the flames ignite the building, picked up Harper, wrapped my wings around her and returned back to our home.

Aimee, Domenic and Cameron rushed in to join us in the living room.

"Thank goodness you are alright. Do you need any medical attention? Or just a stiff drink?" Aimee asked.

"I'm fine. Shaken up, and scared, but not hurt."

"Thankfully."

"Where's Lucia. Is she asleep?"

"I have something to tell you, but I want you to keep calm."

"Now I'm not calm. What is it?"

"Lucia has been taken to the underworld. Minutes before I heard you call to me."

"What! *My baby is where*? Get her back Luc. You are the Lord of the Underworld. Get. Her. Back."

"Cameron and Aimee, stay inside the house and look after Harper and Domenic. Don't go outside. Don't let anyone inside."

I passed through the veil and went straight to my office where I gathered all of my trusted demon soldiers. A search party was sent out with clear instructions to notify me if they found something but not to act. With every passing moment my fury grew. Then quite clearly, I heard Lucia say "Dada".

In an alcove, in the furthest chamber, in the deepest cavern, I found them. A group of demons who were obviously foolish in their belief that they would be given protection by Cayden, a demon who had caused me trouble in the past. I had been informed Cayden had been stirring up the masses to revolt against a leader who they decided had gone soft. My crime was falling in love with a human and having a child. And it had come to this. A challenge to my leadership in the worst possible way, by taking someone I love hostage.

As I entered the cavern, the walls shook, the floor vibrated, the flames of the lit torches on the walls flared with the sheer magnitude of my fury. Although I tried to restrain myself as much as possible because ahead of me, on a stone altar, sat my beautiful baby daughter Lucia. Frightening her was not ideal, but she would see me now as the Devil, and there was no way around that. The demons wearing hooded robes backed away from me and my trusted soldiers, and I could see by their expressions they were suddenly unsure of the part they played in this atrocious act. Using a baby to bring me here, to force a battle of wills between myself and Cayden, was not the smartest of ideas.

Lucia showed no fear and raised her arms to wrap them around my neck when I picked her up. I hugged her and whispered words into her ear that no human would understand, but she did. I wasted no time questioning these back-stabbing fools. That would come later when Lucia was safely in her mother's arms. I instructed my soldiers to make sure everyone stayed exactly where they were, returned to my human guise and passed through the Veil to my home.

Harper saw us appear in the hallway and burst into tears.

"Mama." Lucia said, reaching out for Harper who took her and hugged her tight.

"Is she alright, was she hurt?" Harper dashed away the tears and checked Lucia's face for signs of trauma. Lucia had the same happy expression she always had. Moving from Earth to the underworld had not phased her. As her father I was proud of her.

"She's fine. They only took her no doubt, to force me to pay attention to their demands."

"I don't understand. What could they achieve by taking Lucia?"

"I'm going to find out. Take care of her. I have to go back."

"Can't you stay for a little while. This day has been so hard on all of us."

"That is why I must go back, to make sure this never happens again." I kissed Lucia on the forehead.

"I'm worried for you. For all of us." Harper laid her hand on my arm.

"Domenic, I need you to be the strong man of the house and help your mother to stay calm."

Domenic came over and placed his hand on Harper's shoulder. I saw the worried look on her face soften slightly. I took a last look at my family, and Cameron and Aimee who were like members of our family and passed through the Veil to make these usurpers pay the price for their actions.

"You took my daughter! *My. Daughter*. You caused the woman I love to be fearful for her child! Do you have any idea how angry I am?" As my voice rose and bellowed, my body expanded, and I became twice, then three times my normal size. I had reverted to my Devil, Lord of the Underworld appearance. My head almost touched the roof of the cavern. I dwarfed the other demons, who had moved away and were backed up against the walls. Fury fed the bright red flames which licked and danced along the surface of my skin. The walls shook and as rocks and debris broke loose, fell and hit the ground, plumes of dust rose from the dry compacted surface. Cracks appeared and steam broke through the fissures from the bowels of the Earth.

"Where is the demon who has dared to challenge my leadership? Where is the degenerate scum who sent you to kidnap my daughter?"

A demon I had dealings with before named Apollo took a step forward. "My Lord, we intended no harm against your child. We brought her here for safety. We saw what happened with the crow. I stepped in and brought her through the Veil to protect her."

"*You* brought her through the Veil. That action could have killed her. No human can survive that. You had no way of knowing if she could survive."

"I took the chance. She is your daughter after all. It was that or have her taken by the crow to a cult of Bible preaching fanatics intent on proving she is evil incarnate. You saw her, she was not afraid, she was not harmed. We are not your enemy. We are working with you to oppose Cayden. He has sent demons to earth to follow you and your human family, to gather information."

"And how do you know this?"

"I was nearby in a chamber when I heard them plotting."

"Why didn't you inform me, or Rourke, my second in charge, about the threat."

"We were trying to determine if it was true. We are in a very precarious position if we oppose Cayden and he finds out. We were going to make the familiar talk. The black crow. We captured him."

"Where is he?"

A demon brought a steel cage and gave it to Apollo. "I've clipped his wings. Without flight he cannot produce magic and leave here."

I opened the cage door and tipped the crow onto the ground.

"Return to your human appearance." I yelled at the bird. "Now!"

He morphed into a man, obviously in pain. His arms hung loosely at his sides. He bowed his head.

"Who is your master? To whom do you report."

He said nothing. I blew a breath of liquid flame aimed at his feet. His pants caught alight. He rolled around on the ground until he put the flames out.

"Answer me. What is his name?"

"Pastor Hunter."

"And when you took my daughter where were you taking her?"

"I was told to bring her to the Pastor's farm up near Bronson Canyon."

"Apollo make sure this pitiful being remains locked up and cannot leave."

"Yes my Lord."

"Stay away from Cayden, until I work out what is going on."

❧

The farm in Bronson Canyon appeared to be like any other property in the area, with buildings a distance from the main road. The winding private access road led to a large farmhouse, with equipment and machinery buildings off to one side and a huge barn in the rear of the property. Multiple cars, utilities and trucks were parked in a cleared paddock beside the farmhouse.

Raised voices coming from the barn drew me there first. I stood inside the door at the back of the barn, invisible to those around me. This building was used as their church. Wooden benches were set up in orderly fashion, facing the far end. A middle-aged man, with a clerical collar, stood on the raised platform at the other end preached their gospel to the congregation.

"The sins of the fathers will be brought to light in the actions of the child. That is why we must rid ourselves of this evil. We must purge the evil living amongst us. Cast out the devil worshipers living in Hollywood right now. They could be our neighbors. They could be walking next to us on a busy street. It's up to all of you to call them out. See them for what they are. They turn our heads away from God and his glory, to live a life of debauchery and depravity. It has come to my attention that there has been a child of the devil born in this very area. We need to put a stop to this. And we will. I am expecting a visitor very soon to bring me proof of this atrocious act." He raised his arms to the heavens. "Lift your voices and praise the Lord."

The organ in the corner started playing a hymn. The pastor led the song and the congregation joined it. A man stood up from the front bench and walked between the rows of people, holding out a wooden collection plate for offerings. He was a stocky middle-aged man dressed in dark clothes, with a sallow complexion, and fiery red hair. He paused when he approached the back of the congregation and looked in my direction. He could see me, and without a doubt I could see that he wasn't human at all, but a demon in human form. Or a human that has been possessed by a demon. His shock in seeing me here immobilized him. I froze time, picked him up and took him outside to question.

"You're . . .you're . . ." He stumbled back against the tree trunk.

"The Devil. My Lord. Your worst nightmare. Take your pick." I took a step forward, close enough that he felt my breath on his face. "What is your name?"

"Rupert."

"Tell me Rupert, what you are gathering for today. It's not Sunday."

"I don't know."

"You're lying. Tell me" I grabbed his jaw and forced him to look me in the eye. He was struggling between the knowledge that I would destroy him whether he gave me what I wanted or not, but he had no choice but to be truthful.

"Pastor Hunter called an emergency meeting because I told him the woman was in town without the child. It was our chance to take the woman. Our chance to get to the child at home."

"Unfortunately for them, I was here. The thugs who took Harper are no longer of this world. What part do you play in this?"

"I was sent to find out where she lived."

"So you reported back to the Pastor and he sent his goons to kidnap Harper. Then what was supposed to happen?"

"Joe was supposed to bring the child back here."

"And what were these upstanding people going to do with her?"

"The pastor thinks he is going to perform an exorcism. But Cayden will make sure she is destroyed."

"So Cayden is using these idiots to do the dirty work for him?"

"Yes. He's not strong enough to come to earth yet. He needs to syphon the power from Lucia. Cayden wants an army of followers more powerful than you. Take away your leadership. He wants to rule Hell. We are here to make an example by sacrificing your child."

"What good will it do to sacrifice Lucia?"

"She's your daughter. He thinks she will have as much power as you when she grows up. Cayden knows that together you will be indestructible. He wants to get rid of her now. While you are soft and behaving more like a human every day. He knows she is your weakness. You are losing your following in Hell."

"I hate to tell you Rupert, but Lucia is not coming here today. This congregation is going to be disappointed."

"What are you going to do?"

"I'm not sure. But whatever I do it has to make a difference."

"No. I mean what are you going to do to me?"

"You have served Cayden and caused my family misery. I think you deserve to be punished, don't you?" I clapped my hands together once and he burst into flames, quickly turned into ash, crumpled and fluttered to the ground. I stepped over the small pile of gray flakes, intent on finding out what Preacher Hunter could tell me.

I took on my human appearance, marched into the crowd, up to the front of the congregation and sat on the front bench. All eyes swivelled as I walked by. Pastor Hunter did not stop his sermon but looked questioningly in my direction. I read the multitude of thoughts in his mind. Apart from wondering who I was, he was wondering where his men were and why they hadn't brought Harper to him. He was wondering why Joe his "familiar" had not brought the child to him so he could exorcise her of her demons. I had to stop myself from laughing out loud at the audacity if this man, standing up in front of his followers, preaching about God and all his wonderful bounty, and explaining that I'm the evil one and responsible for every bad thing that ever happened in this world. His congregation needed to see what this man was really capable of. I raised my hand to ask a question.

"Yes, can I help you."

"What was the purpose of the meeting today? You said you were expecting a visitor." I locked eyes with the Pastor, making him unable to look away and unable to tell anything but the truth.

"I'm expecting a woman to be brought to me. She has succumbed to Satan and I have been told she has had a child. I'm going to make an example of them both." Pastor Hunter's face was red in an effort to stop the truth of his words from escaping.

"What are you planning on doing?"

"I'm planning on exorcising her and the child."

"I've seen some of those exorcisms. They can get violent. What if you hurt the woman or the child?"

"I don't care. As long as I get my point across and I'm seen as the good guy protecting all these God-fearing folks from evil. As long as the money keeps rolling in and I can buy my farm equipment and my fancy cars. As long as I can continue to have sex with as many of the young woman in my congregation, like Poppy over there, and Emily over in the back sitting beside her impotent husband, and Annie sitting down the front with her Mother pretending she's a virgin. And my wife doesn't find out." His face had now turned purple as he desperately tried to stop the flow. He slapped his hand over his mouth, but it was too late. His congregation had heard him, loud and clear. The whispered voices were buzzing around me.

"So, you're willing to potentially hurt a woman and a child, by casting out the Devil, to raise your profile. All the while you are as bad as the so-called evil people you condemn. You are a lascivious womanizer by all accounts. Preying on the woman in your congregation who come to you for guidance. You don't sound like a God-fearing preacher to me. What are your qualifications?" I forced his hands away from his face and down to his sides. His eyes became wider, his lips pursed, and his cheeks puffed out with the effort to stop the words from spilling out, but it became impossible.

"I got my license from the internet. It's my license to print money. These fools in this congregation are happy to give me their money if I pretend to care for them and their spiritual needs." He was shaking his head in disbelief at the truth spewing from his lips. He tried to wrench his eyes from mine, but he was wasting his time. I had him locked in my sights and he wasn't going anywhere.

The whispers had become angry raised voices now, and people were standing up around me. I froze him on the spot, and I turned to watch the action. The women he had singled out were busy trying to deny or explain to their families. A young woman was out of her seat chasing after a man leaving the barn, who I presumed was her husband. One young woman was sobbing as her mother berated her. She must have been Annie, the self-proclaimed virgin. A middle-aged woman came flying down the aisle between the benches and launched herself at Pastor Hunter, scratching his face and pounding his chest with her fists. I released him from his frozen state. I presumed this was the wife. He tried to hold her at arms-length to reason with her, but she wasn't listening, she was screaming at him. From what I could gather the farm belonged to her parents, and she wanted him off her property by sundown.

I stood to leave. My work here was done. He would be coming to me soon in Hell. I let the human torturers have their way with him for now.

41
HARPER

I couldn't sit down, and I couldn't stay still. I walked around and around the garden. The minutes turned into an hour and then two hours and Luc hadn't returned. I paced the patio and kept checking the baby monitor, but Lucia was asleep in her crib, and had not moved. Aimee appeared at the door, and I could see by the worried expression on her face she was as concerned as I was.

"I've made some tea. Would you like some? Can I bring you something to eat?"

"Thank you, Aimee. Tea will be fine thanks."

"I'll bring it out here. Cameron has gone down to the gatehouse and he's taken Domenic. Your delivery has arrived, and he's not allowing anyone in the gates."

"That's a good idea. Luc said to let no one in."

Aimee returned with a tray and 2 mugs of tea. We sat on the patio to drink it.

"Can I ask you something?" Aimee handed me a cup.

"Sure."

"Did you know who Luc was when you got involved with him?"

"Yes, I did."

"And you weren't afraid?"

"Afraid of Luc? No."

"Afraid of what could happen."

"I fell in love with Luc over a long period of time. He showed me another side of his personality. Everyone thinks of him as this terrible entity. I think of him as a partner, a lover, a dedicated father. And my best friend. He has the ability to be good. It was not his choice to be evil. That was something forced upon him. If there are forces out there that want to cause us harm, I trust that he can deal with them."

"I know he has a good side. Cameron and I are witness to that. He placed us here to look after your family, but I also think he did that for us. We proved ourselves to him in Hell. We never had children. The War made that impossible. Spending time here with you and helping with the children has been wonderful. For me and for Cameron. He talks about the children often. He loves to teach them about nature. I try to answer Domenic's questions about medicine when I can. He's a very clever young man."

"The children adore you both. I can see it in the way they look at you, the way they interact with you. We've been blessed to have you. I'm sorry you didn't have children of your own."

"We've been given a second chance, here with you. I'm grateful."

"Domenic and Lucia don't have grandparents. You have filled that gap in their lives."

I saw the tears glisten in Aimee's eyes. She didn't speak, just nodded, and busied herself picking up toys from the floor and returning them to the wicker toy basket.

Lucia woke up. We could see her on the baby monitor, moving in the crib, and Aimee went upstairs to attend to her. Cameron appeared from around the side of the house pushing a wheelbarrow full of boxes, with a single bed mattress stacked on top. Domenic strode alongside him, carrying a toolbox.

"You can take that up to her room if you like. She's awake. Do you need a hand putting it together?"

"I can help." Domenic said.

"Looks like you're all sorted. Oh Cameron, what are we going to do about the car?"

"I arranged for the car to be picked up and assessed. They will repair it if they can, or replace it. I've salvaged your personal items from the trunk and they're in the living room."

"You're on top of it all."

"I have to do something to keep occupied. I'm just as worried as you and Aimee."

"Lets' get her bed set up. That should keep us busy for a while. I'm sure Luc will be back soon."

I said the words, but I had no faith in them. This was something Luc had to do alone, but every one of us in this house was sending him positive thoughts.

I only hope he can hear us.

❧

I woke up with a start on the couch, fully clothed, and totally exhausted after the day full of drama. Luc stood over me, prepared to cover me with a blanket.

"What time is it?"

"Ridiculous o'clock. I'm sorry, I didn't want to wake you."

"It's okay. I should've gone to bed, but I was waiting, hoping you would come home." I rubbed my eyes and sat up straighter. I patted the couch beside me. "You don't look tired at all, but you look worried. Are you okay?"

"I've had better days." Luc sat down beside me and took my hand in his.

"Tell me what's happening Luc. My intuition tells me that this is not the end of the trouble. It's as if my world is breaking apart, and I don't know how to stop it."

Luc sighed, closed his eyes, and rested his head on the back of the couch. The seconds ticked by, and I had no doubt Luc was struggling with information he did not want to talk about. His thumb stroked the back of my hand. He sat up and turned toward me.

"There's a power struggle going on in Hell. A demon named Cayden with a large following wants to take over, because he believes

I have become soft, spending more time on Earth than I need to and now fathering a child with a human. He is a particularly vicious Demon who would wreak havoc on Earth given the chance. He sees no good in anyone and would corrupt society even more if he had his way."

"What are you going to do?"

"I *have* to stop him. Since the beginning of time I've been seen as the bad guy, the ultimate evil, the entity that no one wants to have in their lives. I've been shunned, I've been loathed, I've been despised and blamed for doing unmentionable things. I have sought out the deprived and degenerate human beings, encouraging them to be corrupt, and making deals with them in return for their souls. And I am not trying to pretend that didn't happen. But I *have* witnessed another side of life, I've witnessed what I can do when I'm helping someone. I have made a positive difference and I'm hungry for more."

"You don't have to convince me. I know you have it in you to be a force for good."

"But don't you see. I can't be that force for good. I am the Devil. I am Satan and I belong in Hell, not living the dream in the Hollywood Hills. I was chosen to do a job and I cannot change that. There is only one person who can change. He would have seen everything that has happened, and if he wanted to stop this situation from going any further, he would have. BUT I also know that and if he wanted to give me another chance to be the Angel I once was, I would know about it by now."

"So, because you have fathered a child, you are seen as soft. What were they going to do with Lucia? What were they going to do with my baby, Luc? Don't sugar coat it, tell me?"

"They were going to exorcise her!"

"What! Call the devil to leave her body? She's not possessed. But that would not have achieved anything. Would it?"

"I honestly don't know. It may have hurt her. She is flesh of my flesh after all. She has powers. I don't know how many she will have when she is fully grown but she shows signs of potential for powers equal to mine."

"And now I'm more afraid than ever."

"I will do everything within my power to protect her. To protect you and Domenic. And that is why I will have to go back to Hell."

"What do you mean? Go back to Hell. You go back often."

"I have to stay in Hell, Harper. Not play happy families with you here, on Earth."

"You're leaving me?"

"I have no choice."

"There has to be another way. Find another way Luc."

This was the moment I had been dreading. The words I did not want to hear. It had come to this and Luc had to choose. To keep us safe he could not be a part of our daily lives. Tears ran unchecked down my cheeks. There was no point in begging him to stay. He was doing this for us, and it was hard enough for him without me making it more difficult. He knew what I was thinking, I could not hide those facts from him. But he would also be able to tell how much I loved him and how much I wanted him to stay.

"If there was any other way, you know I would take it."

"Lucia." I broke down with a sob.

"She's with me always, as I am with her in her head. We will talk often. I will guide her as best I can, from a distance. You will be a wonderful mother and will give her all the love she needs. For now."

"Maybe one day things will be different, and you can come back."

"Maybe."

There was no conviction in Luc's voice. We both knew that wishing for this was just that. A wish. A hope that in the future things could be different. He held me then, and I let the tears flow.

42
LUC

Cayden is standing on the large stone podium at the far end of the Great Hall, addressing the crowd of his supporters below him. He has a powerful physique and is a commanding presence in his buckskin trousers and ankle length cape made out of animal pelts. His grey hair is pulled back off his angular face, secured with a leather strap at the base of his skull, and woven into a long braid which hangs down over his left shoulder. His muscled chest is smooth and oiled, the skin has a golden hue due to the constant searing temperature in Hell. He would be classed as handsome if he lived on Earth. Cayden has been in Hell for eons, nearly as long as I have, but his body has stayed at age thirty-seven, the same age as when he arrived,

As I walked, the crowd of demons parted before me, and made a passageway to the podium. I climbed up the rough stone steps to face my enemy. The crowd fell silent waiting to hear what I would say. He braced himself as I approached, expecting a blow.

"It seems Cayden, that you are under the illusion that you are an ideal replacement for me in Hell."

"There is no one more fitting than me. I have been here nearly as long as you have. I have a great deal of power, and I have loyal followers."

"You are also under the impression that Hell needs another ruler. But I didn't get the memo. On whose authority did you make this decision?"

"It's obvious you don't want to be down here with us. You spend so much time on Earth pretending to be human, pretending we don't exist. You've grown weak with all your interaction with humans, you're not even trying to create chaos on Earth anymore. We expect a full-time ruler, not a part time imposter who shows no respect for the position. I am the best demon for the job."

"You're getting a little ahead of yourself."

"What do you mean."

"There is no opening for the job. There never was a "job" to begin with. My Leadership in Hell is under no threat. Someone far greater than you or I decided that Hell was my domain a long time ago, and he has not given me any instructions to change that. Heavens knows I would like someone to step into my shoes and give me a little break now and again. But, and it is a big but. There would be no expectation for me to hand over my crown."

"Look around you. All of these demons are prepared to follow me. They are loyal to my cause."

"These demons? Is that right? You want to follow Cayden to wreak havoc on Earth?" I addressed the crowd.

The demons below us shuffled nervously, nodded their heads, talked amongst themselves, and raised their fists high in solidarity. Their mumbling became louder, gathering momentum.

"There might be five hundred or so demons in this space. Would you say that was right?" I asked.

"Maybe six hundred."

"And at the back there you see some of my loyal demon army, and others are guarding the inmates, and controlling the underworld. Thousands of loyal demons at my command."

I walked around him, noting he had no weapons on his person, and returned to stand a few feet away.

"Okay show me what you've got. Give it your best shot." I removed my jacket and bared my chest. I favor leather clothing in Hell.

He raised his hand, conjured up a bolt of lightning and threw it at me. It bounced off my chest. He tried this time with a fireball, I blew it away. He lifted his hands to the heavens and acid rain began to fall above me. It fell to the ground all around me, sizzling on the stone, but did not touch my skin. He waved his arms. Shackles made of iron appeared on my wrists, but I shook them off.

"Enough! You cannot hurt me, you cannot imprison me. I'm tired of these games. You sent demons to Earth to hurt those I love. I'm going to show your followers what I do to traitors."

I snapped my fingers and chains appeared on the ground and snaked quickly up his body from his ankles to his throat, imprisoning his hands by his sides. He struggled but could not get free.

"Your so-called power is nothing compared to mine. I cannot imagine why you ever thought you could take over." I raised my hand and he lifted ten feet off the ground. A snap of my fingers and a large vat of acid appeared below him. I lowered him into the liquid. His cries echoed around the walls. Within seconds he was no more. I snapped my fingers and the vat disappeared. I turned to his followers.

"Now what am I going to do with all of you?"

The demons turned and began to move toward the exits, but my loyal followers blocked their path.

"There is no place in Hell for anyone I cannot trust to be one hundred percent behind me." I raised my arm in the air and lowered it in one quick fluid motion. Anyone in the room who had the slightest intention in their mind of following Cayden became frozen to the spot. I blew a breath of fire over the Great Hall. The traitors turned to ashes and fell to the floor. The Great Hall was empty in an instant.

I addressed my loyal demon soldiers stationed at the exits.

"Enough fun for one day. I'm sure you've seen enough to make sure my leadership is never questioned again. Spread the word. Now, time to get back to work."

The mood was more somber than usual. News of what had happened travelled fast. No one looked at or addressed me for the rest of the day. Which was just as well because I was in no mood to talk to anyone, no mood to interact with anyone. I dropped in to see Harper and my family but stayed in the shadow world. It was obvious that Harper was suffering.

I had an idea to help her. It was drastic, but I couldn't watch her suffering.

43
LUC

It had been a month since I had seen Harper. I was appalled at how much weight she had lost, at the dark circles under her eyes, at the look of utter defeat in the way she carried herself through the day.

I waited until she had tucked the children into bed and made her way to her own bedroom, until she was turning off the light, before I approached her.

"Oh Luc. Luc. I've missed you so." She threw her arms around my neck and clung on tight.

"My love, where are you disappearing to? You've become so thin."

"Who has an appetite, when their heart is breaking?"

"You have to eat. Please tell me you will try. You have to look after yourself, for the children."

"The children are fine. I have Cameron and Aimee to help, and they are a Godsend. Oh, sorry."

I took her hand and led her to the bed.

"Come sit with me. I only have a short time tonight."

"Please stay for a little while." Harper kissed me. It was a kiss full of sadness.

"Okay, only for a little while. I have work to do on Earth tonight. Then I must get back to Hell."

"Make love to me. Please Luc. I miss you so." One single tear ran down her cheek, and that was the straw that broke the camel's back.

I pulled her into my embrace and kissed Harper with all the pent-up longing I had also been harboring. We separated but within seconds we were naked and once again in each other's arms. Lust coursed through my body. The only place I wanted to be was deep inside her, riding wave after wave of pure desire. That thought pushed me to rush our coupling, there was no foreplay, no tender words to entice or encourage, no easing into it, just pure unadulterated passion. I knew I wasn't being gentle, but I couldn't help the need that had welled up inside me. My heart was beating so fast I was sure it was going to explode within my chest. This was where I wanted to be. With my love, with the woman who made me want to be a better . . . man? Hang on. This was so wrong, because I will never be a man, will I? I will always be a ghost, a shadow, an imitation of a human being. And I will never be enough because I can never be here all the time. These crazy thoughts made me drive into Harper harder and faster, and then suddenly I remembered what happened the last time I fully let myself go. Lucia was conceived.

Harper dug her nails into my skin. I edged her to the brink and held her to my chest when she called my name. I allowed her to reach her peak, but I held back. I could not let it happen again. I could not be that cruel.

❧

I tucked Harper into the curve of my body and held her while she went happily to sleep. She looked so beautiful, so peaceful, with her blonde hair framing her face and fanning out on the white pillowcase. I know what I have to do but I need a few minutes to watch her sleeping before I have to leave her.

I dressed quickly and took a gold locket from my pocket, opened it and put it on the bedside table. It had a picture of Harper and Lucia on the day she was born. I smiled as I looked at it, because it was my favorite photograph of them both. I bent over Harper, took her face in my hands and gently kissed her lips. Her eyes stayed closed and she sleepily kissed me back. I made sure she stayed in a deep sleep. I pressed my fingertips to her temples for a few seconds and then I eased away from her. As I pulled my hands back a fine red mist followed my fingers. I directed this mist into the locket, then closed it and sealed it with fire. I clasped the locket around her neck. I placed my fingertips on her temples once more. This time a blue mist swirled in the air around her head.

When Harper awakes the only memory of the last couple of years will be of losing Richard. She will believe that both children are Richard's offspring, and she is bringing them up alone. She will constantly wear the heart shaped necklace she believes Richard gave her.

Removing all romantic memories of us is the kindest thing I can do for her. The only way I can truly demonstrate I love her with all my heart.

THE END.

EPILOGUE

LUC

I've removed all of Harper's romantic memories of us as a couple, from the first night we were together, the night we conceived Lucia. I've imprisoned these memories in the locket, and no one will be able to open it or return those memories to Harper, except me. Instead I've implanted the memory of Richard as the father of both children, that she had just become pregnant with Lucia the day before Richard died, and she had been alone since his death. Lucia appears older so she won't question it. I will provide another birth certificate. She has kept pretty much to herself since she got pregnant, and only Ruby and Oliver know about us. I will make sure they have no memories either.

I had already discussed my plan with Cameron and Aimee Crawford. They would stay and look after the family, just as they had been doing. Their time with the family was infinite, as demons never age, but Harper and Domenic and Lucia will grow older. It will be good for them to have Cameron and Aimee who will support and protect them when I'm not around. If Harper has difficulties with blanks in her memory, the mention of the recent car accident, and possible head injury will be a perfect excuse.

I spoke to my children telepathically as I had always done.

Domenic was very understanding, but I did not expect any less from him. He is wise beyond his years. Lucia was not as easy. But I have asked her to be patient and told her I will guide her as her Godfather, just as I do with Domenic. I won't be around as much, but when I am on Earth and visiting them, I have explained she must not call me Dada. She must also not use her powers around Harper. Domenic will help her to keep them a secret.

This is the only thing I can do to protect my family. I cannot have another uprising. I must spend most of my time in Hell, and it would be cruel to see Harper suffering because of my absence. I will have to return to pop in now and again, to be the Godfather I once was for Domenic and now for Lucia.

ABOUT THE AUTHOR

Savannah Blaize lives in Melbourne, Australia, after emigrating from Scotland many years ago. She enjoys writing fiction of all genres, in which the reader can step inside and visualise the world she creates. A member of the Romance Writers of Australia, the Melbourne Romance Writers Guild, and Sisters In Crime, she is passionate about writing a good contemporary story and engaging with readers.

Deal With The Devil is Savannah's third published novel. Her first novel From Paris To Forever was published in 2017. Her second novel The Class Reunion was published in 2018.

ALSO BY SAVANNAH BLAIZE

From Paris To Forever

The Class Reunion

Savannah's Short Stories published in Anthologies:

Baby Did A Bad Bad Thing

Knight In Shining Combat Boots

If the Shoe Fits

A Tartan Christmas

Lightning Source UK Ltd.
Milton Keynes UK
UKHW022023130522
402975UK00006B/1081

9 780648 467533